The Secret of Matterdale Hall

MARIANNE RATCLIFFE

First published in 2022 by Bellows Press

A CIP Catalogue of this book is available from
the British Library

ISBN: 978 1 739 71010 1

Cover design by
Candescent

Typeset by
Typo•glyphix
www.typoglyphix.co.uk

Printed and bound in England

To my wife, Sharon

1

New Beginnings

U ntil shortly before her eighteenth birthday, Susan
Mottram lived an idyllic existence, loved by her parents
and adored by her younger sister. A clergyman's
daughter, she lacked for nothing that could give her pleasure or
extend her active mind. Her parents' sole regret was that they
had no son—no future protector for Susan and Florence in the
distant eventuality of Reverend Mottram's decease. In lieu of a
male heir, Reverend Mottram took pains to educate his daughters
as he would a son. He taught them Latin and Greek and
employed masters for modern languages. He was an amateur
natural philosopher and the girls were barely out of pinafores
before they were familiar with the common and Latin names of
every plant and creature that made its home in the lush countryside that surrounded the parsonage. Artistic sensibilities were
actively encouraged. When Susan showed an early aptitude for
music, a pianoforte was installed in the front parlour. Books

would arrive, fresh from the printers, and their pages never stayed uncut for long. The young Miss Mottrams developed a marked preference for gothic romances, in which they were generously indulged by their ever-loving parents, with only a few gentle warnings that such stories should not be taken as models for life.

The capricious fates abhor contentment and two months before Susan's eighteenth birthday Reverend Mottram took ill. What the apothecary initially diagnosed as a mild fever turned putrid and within a shockingly brief time he was dead. The grief of his wife and daughters can be imagined, yet Reverend Mottram's death was not the only grievous blow, for he left behind substantial debts. The same generous nature that could deny his daughters nothing had been equally evident in his dealings with his parishioners—thus had he exceeded his income. Although his wife was a woman of good understanding, she had trusted her husband completely in the management of their affairs. It was a great shock when his family discovered that, not only had they lost the dearest of fathers and husbands, but they must quit their beloved home and scrape a living on the tiny annuity due to a clergyman's widow. Everything of value was sold; the pianoforte was swiftly followed by most of the furniture and all the books so lovingly collected in Reverend Mottram's library.

When they took up residence in their new home, a poky little cottage with only two bedrooms and a single parlour, the younger Miss Mottram flung herself into the room she must now share with her sister and sobbed heartily. Susan was made of hardier material. Battening down her grief, she spared no effort in arranging the disposal of what could be sold and negotiating with the numerous tradespeople with whom her father had run up debts. Yet she was eager to do more. One evening, as she sat with her mother in their tiny parlour, Susan expressed her determination to improve their situation by finding paid employment.

'For,' she said, 'I am fortunate enough to have a good education and excellent health. Why should I not put them to good use?'

'Oh, do not think of leaving us, Susan,' pleaded her mother, her pale, slender fingers plucking at her black collar. 'What would I do without you?'

'No worse than at present. Here is another letter from Mr Willis, saying we shall have no more coal until our account is settled. And I do not know how we shall pay the butcher unless I sell my cashmere shawl.'

'You must not think of it! It was your last gift from your dear papa. You will soon have nothing but rags to wear. I am still in anguish about your pretty gowns.'

'What need have I now for gowns? Dearest Mama, much as it would pain me to part from you and Florence, I could not bear to watch you shivering by an empty grate, half-starved because we haven't money for meat. And dear old Harriet, staying with us even though we cannot pay her. I will not abuse such loyalty.'

'But what would you do?'

'I might teach. Or become a governess, supposing I could persuade anyone to entrust their child to someone so lacking in experience.'

'Alas, we have no friends of influence who might recommend you for such a position. And as for being a teacher, it is too dreadful to contemplate.'

'I do not think it would be so bad. You know how much I enjoyed explaining things to Florence when she could not follow Papa's teachings.'

'Your dear sister has such a pliable disposition. In a school, who knows what class of girl you might be faced with?'

'Papa saw good in everyone, no matter their parentage, and I shall endeavour to do the same. Any girl will surely be grateful to learn, when our sex has been denied the opportunity for so long.'

'But what will people say? Even in our reduced circumstances, you are still considered a gentlewoman and may yet make a good marriage. As a lowly schoolteacher, you will be a nobody.'

Susan raised an eyebrow.

'Dear Mama, if we are to rely on marriage to make our fortunes then we must look to Florence. She is ten times prettier than I am, and with her disposition being so pliable she is infinitely more suited to being someone's wife.'

'Susan, this is no matter for jest. You are by no means unattractive. You have lovely green eyes and, although you are not as tall or graceful as Florence, your figure is not displeasing. Mr Weston was quite delighted with you last summer. You might be engaged already if only you had shown him a little encouragement.'

'His delight has diminished notably since we became penniless. I fear this approach will not suit, Mama. Without beauty, height or fortune, I cannot expect a queue of suitors.'

And if I do marry, Susan added silently to herself, *I hope it will be for love.*

'You are not without admirers. Mr Potts of Ten-Acre Farm has hinted he would make an offer, were you not in mourning.'

4

'With three wives already buried, he is certainly not fastidious,' Susan admitted. 'But a farmer's wife—are we really brought so low?'

'At least we would not starve. Last week he told me he hoped you would soon be smiling again, for you have lovely teeth.'

'A fine compliment. Were I a horse, I would be delighted to receive it. Alas, it is not one I can return, for Mr Potts has more gaps between his gums than offspring.'

'To be sure, if Mr Potts was as diligent at farming as in the begetting of children, he would be a rich man,' her mother said with a sigh.

'Setting aside the manifold attractions of Mr Potts, I would prefer to rely on my own efforts than to throw myself upon the mercy of a man who, once we are married, must shackle me to his own fortunes with no power to save myself should he prove unworthy.'

Susan's mother gave her a sharp look.

'I hope this is not a slight against your father?'

Susan coloured and pressed her hand to her mother's. 'I couldn't have wished for a kinder, dearer papa. Don't I owe it to him to put the education he gave me to some purpose?'

'I do not think he would approve. Who knows what sort of persons you will meet, or what manner of temptations will be cast in your way?'

'You are in danger of making the prospect more attractive, rather than less,' Susan said with a smile.

'Won't you at least wait a little longer before you make such a fateful decision? You have not had time to grieve.'

Susan threw her arms around her mother's neck and rested her forehead against her shoulder.

'Dear Mama, I shall carry my grief with me, but it shall not prevent me doing all in my power to make you and Florence as comfortable as possible.'

Mrs Mottram knew her daughter well enough to apprehend that further protest would be in vain. Susan lost no time in looking for positions advertised in regional and national newspapers. After several disheartening rejections, she received a letter from a Mrs Claybourn of Matterdale Hall, North Yorkshire, informing her that, due to unfortunate circumstances, they had immediate need for a new teacher, adding Miss Mottram's application would be looked on favourably if she were to present herself at Matterdale Hall within the week.

'Unfortunate circumstances!' exclaimed Susan's mother. 'I do not like the sound of that.'

'I must pack at once.'

'Susan, I beg you will reconsider. You are such an innocent, trusting girl, I cannot bear to think of you alone and friendless in such a strange country.'

'Mama, you talk as if I am venturing to some foreign land with mysterious customs, but I go only to Yorkshire. And I shall not be alone. Mrs Claybourn seems a kind, motherly sort of person. See here, in her letter, how she advises me to pack woollen stockings and shawls, that I might not catch a chill. And one of her daughters is also a teacher. I am sure we shall become great friends.'

'I wish it may be so, my dear. But, as a paid employee, you are unlikely to be treated as well as you expect. Certainly not as well as you deserve.'

'Nonsense. We have always treated Harriet quite as part of the family, though she is a servant.'

'Not everyone is like us,' her mother said sombrely. Susan was too occupied with thinking of what she must pack to take notice. Although sad to be leaving her mother and sister, she was filled with a rising sense of excitement. Her favourite novels had taught her that a young lady setting out on a journey in interesting circumstances was bound to meet with adventure. She was eager to discover what the future might bring.

2

Matterdale Hall

Susan stood before the doors of Matterdale Hall, her last sixpence disappearing with the young man who had carried her trunk from the nearest village. Two miles across the open moor in cold, mizzling rain—the poor lad had earned his money. She wondered who would choose to build a schoolhouse in so remote a location, with only a dirt-trodden track connecting it to civilisation. And who, with such interesting surroundings, would build something so lamentably practical? Lacking any embellishment, Matterdale Hall was a plain, two-storied building, constructed of local grit limestone. It was situated at the base of a bowl-like depression as though embarrassed by its own mediocrity. Three intersecting wings formed a rigid T-shape, and the slate roof was adorned with nothing but functional iron guttering. The only colour was provided by a ring of glistening moss, which crept round the base of the house like grass-stains on the hem of a petticoat, and patches of untrimmed ivy that obscured some of the ground floor windows.

'What a disappointment!' Susan said aloud as she approached a plain oak door, leached to a pale grey by exposure to the elements. She pulled hard on the bell, but there was no answering chime from within. The whole place seemed strangely quiet. When nobody came, she raised her fist and rapped firmly on the door. It was opened at last by a young girl who wore a dirty apron over a plain dress. She could be no older than ten.

'Good heavens, are servants so young in Yorkshire?' Susan exclaimed.

'I'm not a servant.'

The girl indicated by a flick of her head that Susan might enter. 'You the new teacher?'

Susan admitted that she was. 'And, pray, what is your name?'

'Tabitha. You're late.' Tabitha closed the door and headed across a square hallway before Susan could protest that she could not help it if the country coach were behind schedule. She hurried to catch up with the child.

'No running in the hallway, Miss.'

'I beg you would slow down,' Susan implored, after stubbing her toe on the uneven flagging. The creeping ivy blocked much of the light from the windows and the hallway floor was lost in shadow. Heedless of her plea, Tabitha hastened past a square, spiral staircase whose broad wooden treads were worn down in the middle. Beyond it, an empty doorframe led into a dingy corridor. Windows the size of small portraits ran at head height down the wall to her left, curtained with fly-spotted cobwebs. Opposite them, doors were spaced at regular intervals. Grit scratched the soles of Susan's boots as she followed Tabitha down the corridor. The lack of cleanliness dismayed her. Were all schools so dirty? And did they all smell like damp cloth? Tabitha tapped on the first door down and made to disappear.

'Could someone bring in my trunk?' Susan called after her.

'You could ask old Mr Clegg,' the girl said, without stopping, 'but it'd be quicker t'fetch it yourself.'

'I am not expected to carry my own trunk, surely?'

'Mrs Claybourn says folk should fend for themselves.'

Left alone in front of the closed door, Susan took a steadying breath and turned the iron doorknob. She entered a dim parlour. Despite the fading light, no lamps or candles had yet been lit. A feeble fire spluttered in the back corner of a hearth designed for something more generous, yet even such a gentle heat was welcome after Susan's damp walk. The furnishings were plain and much worn. A chaise longue with faded pink upholstery had been placed as close to the fire as possible without being set alight and was occupied by a reclining young woman with thick eyebrows and cheeks slathered with rouge. An older woman sat beside one of two casement windows, mending a pair of trousers by what little daylight remained, her needle flying in and out of the torn seam with remarkable speed. A gentleman with cheeks the shade of ripening cherries turned at Susan's entrance. His figure resembled an upright frog, with slender legs and feet splayed outwards, a bright mustard waistcoat thrust boldly through the lapels of his frock coat as if to show off its owner's rotundity instead of disguising it. Susan couldn't help but smile at such a peculiar sight.

'Aha, Miss Mottram!' the man said, beaming as he ushered her into the room. He seemed unable to contain his bonhomie, which exploded out of him at regular intervals in the form of a deep chuckle. 'Here is a happy countenance—it cheers me despite the weather. You had a good journey, I hope, heh-heh? I am Dr Claybourn. Delighted to make your acquaintance, my dear. I believe my wife has been your correspondent.'

The older woman paused her sewing to examine Susan over the top of a pair of half-moon spectacles. Her pale blue eyes darted about Susan's person, taking in her rain-soaked bonnet and muddy boots.

'She looks barely out of school herself, Henry,' she said, frowning. 'And she's late. I cannot abide tardiness.' The young woman on the chaise longue lifted her head a few inches so she might glance at Susan. A strong scent of rosewater failed to disguise an odour not unlike mouldy cheese.

'Why, she's tiny,' the young woman said languidly. 'Miss Smythson was much taller. Even Miss Jones was not so short, and you sent her away before she had taken off her bonnet.'

'You did not mention a lack of height in your application, Miss Mottram,' said Mrs Claybourn. 'That was remiss of you. I trust you are in robust health? Miss Jones arrived with a red nose and a damp handkerchief. I rescinded my offer of employment at once. I have no time for shirkers.'

'I'm sure Miss Mottram is no such thing, heh-heh!' her husband protested. 'Such bright eyes and rosy cheeks.' With three pairs of eyes fixed on her, Susan felt like a museum exhibit being inspected for its authenticity. She had her long walk to thank for any rosiness of cheek and for the first time was grateful for the poverty that had prevented her hiring a trap. She could not afford to share the fate of poor, sniffling Miss Jones. Swiftly, she untied her bonnet, resisting the urge to raise herself up on her toes. She had always been short and saw no sense in pretending otherwise.

'The girls will never respect her,' sighed the young woman, reverting to her prone position. 'We should have advertised for a master. Men are always better at these things, aren't they, Papa?'

'It is true the female brain is more prone to neurasthenic disorders. But as to teaching, I am not aware of any proven differences in capability.'

'Helena, you forget that young men are vastly expensive,' said Mrs Claybourn, yanking her thread taut. 'And Marion has no trouble keeping her class quiet.'

'Marion would frighten a savage into submission.'

'Your sister is tall, which is a definite advantage.'

Alarmed at the prospect of being turned away, Susan injected her voice with what she hoped was authority. Mama and Florence were depending on her, to say nothing of how she would make it home without a penny in her purse.

'As I indicated in my letter, ma'am, I was schooled at home by my late father. I have Latin, Greek and a good understanding of Italian and French.'

'What a splendid thing, my dear,' said Dr Claybourn, looking at his wife. 'And very good for the school's reputation, I dare say.'

Mrs Claybourn snipped her thread with a pair of scissors and set aside the trousers, taking up a shirt with a frayed collar in the same movement. 'Tell me, how do you intend to discipline your pupils, Miss Mottram?'

'I believe good behaviour will follow naturally if my pupils are engaged and enthusiastic in their lessons.'

Dr Claybourn grasped Susan's hand and raised it to his lips.

'A highly original notion! I am delighted to welcome a fellow pioneer to Matterdale Hall.'

13

'You think our girls wish to learn?' Mrs Claybourn's pale eyes glimmered above her half-moon glasses. 'This is too much naivety. They come to us because they are unwanted at home, or their parents are too miserly to employ a governess. Henry, tell Miss Mottram about that mute creature who was sent to us last spring.'

'Mary Martin.' Dr Claybourn shook his head, although his smile remained on his lips. 'Clearly witless. Unable even to speak. Fortunate not to be locked away.'

Susan was surprised to hear them speak with such dismissiveness about one of their pupils.

'A disgrace to her family,' added his wife, attacking the frayed collar with military speed and precision. 'They begged us to take her off their hands. I wish you luck finding any enthusiasm there.'

'If she does not speak then she is unlikely to cause any disturbance, at least,' Susan remarked with an attempt at a smile. Mrs Claybourn took her words in all seriousness.

'That is indeed a blessing. Girls can be so unruly.'

'It seems tranquil enough now.' Indeed, it was so quiet that Susan was beginning to wonder if the school had any pupils at all.

'The girls are at supper.'

'So early?' Susan was surprised. It could be no later than five o'clock.

'An early supper, followed by two hours of handwriting and straight to bed. That's my prescription for an orderly school.'

'Two hours!' Susan exclaimed in undisguised dismay. This was not her idea of learning. 'My father would never—'

'I will not be questioned regarding my methods,' snapped Mrs Claybourn. 'Unless you wish to share the fate of your predecessor?'

'We had to let Miss Smythson go,' added Dr Claybourn with a regretful sigh.

'Poor Miss Smythson did not deserve such a fate.' Helena's languid tones rose from the chaise longue as if the furniture itself was speaking. 'She wore such pretty dresses.'

'She caused too much trouble,' Mrs Claybourn insisted. 'Which reminds me – Miss Mottram, you will ensure the girls stay away from my husband's infirmary.'

'You have an infirmary? That must be a great comfort to the parents.'

'It is not for the girls!' the chaise longue cried piteously. 'They must not go near it.'

'I am no common physician,' explained Dr Claybourn. His chest expanded with such pride the buttons on his waistcoat were in danger of pinging from their settings. 'I am an alienist—I specialise in diseases of the mind. Helena is my greatest triumph. When she was young, she suffered from fits. I cured her with a novel method and my paper outlining my discovery was very well received. You are surprised, perhaps, to hear of my philo-sophical pursuits? Like many, you mistake me for a mere man of fashion, heh-heh?'

'Never,' said Susan, eyeing his waistcoat, whose gilded buttons did nothing to soften its assault on her eyes.

'My infirmary is strictly out of bounds. I am afraid there are some within who could be dangerous.'

'And the air—do not forget the air,' added his wife. 'You are aware of miasma, Miss Mottram? The risk of contagion? We cannot have our girls turning lunatic. Or our teachers.'

'Good heavens, is that possible?' Susan asked in alarm.

'Tell Miss Mottram about those factory girls that all went

mad together,' said his wife. 'That proves the possibility of infection.'

'Ah, the Lancashire cotton mill case,' said her husband sagely. 'A fascinating instance of mass hysteria. Dr St. Clare was justly celebrated for his cure. What would I give for us to have such an interesting case here?'

'I should hope not!' exclaimed his wife. 'If Matterdale Hall were to be the scene of such infamy, it would be the ruination of us all. I will not tolerate any hint of scandal. Miss Mottram, I trust you have no dark secrets?'

'None at all, ma'am. The nearest our quiet little village came to scandal was when Mrs Milton's gardener misheard her instructions for creating a topiary ship (her husband being nautical) and instead rendered a ewe and ram out of her privet, the latter with such anatomical accuracy as to cause a vast deal of amusement.'

'I will have none of that here,' insisted Mrs Claybourn.

'Amusement?' Susan queried innocently.

'Disobedience,' clarified Mrs Claybourn. 'I expect my orders to be obeyed to the letter. Although I cannot abide giggling among the girls. You will discourage it.'

'But surely, there are some things so ridiculous, one cannot help but be diverted?' Susan said, her gaze attracted once more to Dr Claybourn's waistcoat.

'I understand you are musical,' Mrs Claybourn remarked, clearly in no mood to entertain further discussion on the topic of merriment. 'We have a pianoforte in the second parlour. We had thought Marion might have been our instructor but, alas, she has no ear for music.'

'I'm sure I would play very well if I didn't suffer so much from cramp in my fingers,' murmured the chaise longue.

'Your inability to sit up straight would seem the larger problem,' said her mother. 'The piano may need tuning—I expect you will attend to that, Miss Mottram.'

Susan was again surprised and admitted she was not so qualified. Dr Claybourn shook his head apologetically.

'My wife is so active and practical, she entertains vastly unreasonable expectations of us mere mortals.'

'I work hard and make no apologies for expecting the same of my employees. You must be prepared to earn your keep, Miss Mottram.'

'I am not afraid,' Susan declared stoutly. Dr Claybourn squeezed his hands together.

'Excellent, excellent. My dear, I think Miss Mottram will do very well.'

Susan's breast swelled with relief. She was not, after all, to be sent away.

'You are always too quick to approve, Henry,' said Mrs Claybourn. 'Let us see how Miss Mottram acquits herself before we pass judgement.'

'But how thoughtless of us.' Dr Claybourn patted his paunch complacently. 'You must be fatigued after your journey. I beg you will take some refreshment.'

'That is very kind,' said Susan gratefully, for she had been travelling since before dawn and had taken no breakfast. She removed her cloak and looked for somewhere she might deposit it and her bonnet before taking a seat, but there was no servant to hand them to. Mrs Claybourn rose and ushered her to the door, her sewing still in her hands.

'Hurry along to the kitchen and ask Mrs Clegg to find you some scraps. In future, you'll eat with the girls.'

'Am I not to take meals with the family?' Susan asked, still clutching her cloak and bonnet.

'You are staff, Miss Mottram, not a guest. Tabitha will show you to the kitchens.' She rang the bell. 'Tabitha makes herself useful. I wish more of our pupils would follow her example. You will encourage any such promising inclinations in your charges.'

The young girl with the dirty apron reappeared. Dr Claybourn followed Susan into the hallway.

'I beg you will make allowances for our strange ways,' he said in a low voice. 'My wife is exacting, but if you keep to the rules, all will be well, heh-heh.'

In Which Susan Learns
What it is to be a Teacher

The next day, the Claybourns' eldest daughter, Marion, showed Susan to her classroom, situated at the far end of the west wing. Marion was tall and narrow-hipped, her figure imprisoned in a starched black dress. She wore her hair pinned back with such severity it tugged the skin at the edge of her face into ridges. She made no move to take Susan's hand when they were introduced, but rather stared at her with a strange look that Susan found extremely discomfiting. Marion explained, in clipped tones, that there were two classes of senior girls, taught by Mrs Claybourn and herself, and that Susan would be required to teach the juniors.

Susan's class contained fifteen girls, aged six to twelve years old, who froze in their seats as Marion stalked between the pairs of desks with the manner of a cat after a flock of birds, a cane gripped tightly in her white hand. One of the girls made the mistake of sniffling. Marion stopped dead and tapped the unfortunate pupil's desk with the tip of the cane. The girl, who was very young, slowly placed her hands on the desk, fists clenched. Marion rested the tip of the cane on the knuckle of the left hand, and the girl unfurled her fist. Susan gasped as the cane down with a sharp smack. The girl yanked away her injured hand, a tear running down her cheek.

'No sniffling!' Marion handed the cane to Susan. 'That is Mary Martin, a sullen child who refuses to learn. You must keep them cowed if you are to please my mother. If you cannot, she will find another.' She turned to the class. 'Miss Mottram is your new teacher. Attend her well.'

Susan waited until Marion's heavy footsteps had faded and the clang of another door indicated she was safely within her own classroom. Fifteen pairs of eyes looked at her, waiting for her to speak. Susan flexed the cane thoughtfully and each girl flinched. With brisk resolve, she lifted her knee and snapped the cane across her thigh, before throwing the fragments into a nearby drawer.

'I will trust you all to give me your attention and your best work without recourse to such encouragements.' She reached through her skirts to her pocket, retrieved a kerchief and knelt down beside Mary, who was clutching her wounded hand to her chest. Gently, Susan took up her tiny hand and dabbed at the knuckles, where flecks of blood had begun to seep through the scoured flesh.

'Wipe your tears, Mary. You need not fear me.' But Mary looked at her blankly, showing no sign that she understood.

'No use speaking to Mary,' said a girl whose blonde hair was darkened at the roots with grease. 'She ain't got no wits.'

Susan turned to her.

'What is your name?'

'Gwendoline, Miss.'

'Well, Gwendoline, we do not say "ain't". Neither is it kind to say someone hasn't got wits. I'm sure it's not true, is it Mary?' Mary might have been a statue for all the heed she paid her teacher.

Susan returned to the front of the class and asked each girl their name and bade them write their alphabet on their slates. She was shocked to discover that less than half were able to complete even that simple task. Throughout the morning, Mary stared blankly at her desk, never even reaching for her piece of chalk.

In the days that followed, Susan's attempts to encourage interest and enthusiasm among her students were met with poor return. Mary remained silent and unhappy, despite Susan paying her particular attention. She wrote the alphabet on her slate for her to copy, guiding Mary's hand to demonstrate what was required, for the little girl did not seem to understand her instructions. In response to much gentle prompting, Mary began to trace out the letters on her own, but Susan was not convinced that she understood the purpose of the task. The other girls had to be coaxed into doing any work. Susan was dismayed by the general absence of even the most basic of accomplishments. Only Anne Fordyce, a pale girl of about ten, could read with any fluency. When Susan asked who had taught her, she whispered, with the reluctance of a thief admitting his crime, that one of her brothers had tutored her in his holidays.

Other tasks besides teaching fell to Susan. She was to ensure the girls went to bed at the allotted hour, as well as rousing them at dawn. The girls slept in first-floor dormitories filled with narrow bunks, and Susan was assigned a tiny chamber immediately adjacent to the stairwell. The room was so small that she had to slide her trunk beneath her bed, or risk tripping over it on the way to the door. Besides the narrow bed, it contained nothing but a washstand with a chipped bowl and a rust-spotted mirror. On first arriving, Susan had looked in vain for a wardrobe. Mrs Claybourn had pointed to pair of rusty hooks behind the door, upon which dresses may be hung, and advised Susan that her own trunk would serve perfectly well as a repository for the remainder of her clothes. A small window overlooked the yard, admitting more draughts than light. Although there was a fireplace, it was never lit and Susan began to understand Mrs Claybourn's insistence on woollen stockings.

'You can keep an eye on the dormitories from here,' Mrs Claybourn explained in satisfaction. 'I like to plan everything for the greatest convenience.'

'So I see,' said Susan, noting that the family rooms were at the end of the north wing, as distant from the dormitories as the layout of Matterdale Hall allowed. The Claybourns would not be disturbed by any noise the girls made in the night. It was certainly convenient for them. Susan was less fortunate. Several of the girls cried themselves to sleep, and others would wake in the night, screaming from some nightmare. Susan, who was suffering with homesickness herself, could not disregard such distress, and would rise to offer a quiet word of comfort and reassurance, and it was rare for her to enjoy a full night's sleep. She felt a burst of sympathy for her predecessor, the unfortunate Miss Smythson. The level of drudgery required of her post dismayed her, but not as much as the lack of interest among her pupils. Such a contrast to the happy days she had spent with Florence, learning Latin and Greek with her dear Papa. Perhaps Mrs Claybourn had been right to call her naïve. Yet Susan would not believe the girls did not wish to learn. The fault must lie with her. She would do better. What was it that Alexander the Great had said? *'Nothing is impossible to him who will try.'*

4

An Unexpected Encounter

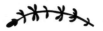

Susan woke at the beginning of her second week and looked out of her chamber window to see the moors bathed in pink and gold by the rising sun. She resolved to take her class on a nature walk. Bad weather had prevented her going out onto the moors on her first half day and she was eager to seize such an unexpected opportunity to escape the dark corridors of Matterdale Hall. And she was sure the girls could not fail to be enthused by such an undertaking.

'I'm not sure it would be wise,' Mrs Claybourn remarked when Susan broached the subject. 'We cannot have them getting chills. Tinctures are so expensive.'

'It makes me ill just to think of it,' said Helena, from her usual position on the chaise longue. 'To venture outside in such cold weather. I'm sure I would rather stay by the fire.'

'I'm sure you would,' said Marion sourly.

'I will encourage the girls to wrap up warmly,' Susan said.

'A teacher does not encourage. She insists.' Mrs Claybourn began to clean her half-moon spectacles with a small rag.

'It would be a grievous mistake,' insisted Marion. 'Once their animal spirits are raised, the girls will be impossible to tame.'

'Surely we invite more trouble by keeping our pupils cooped up like prisoners?' said Susan. 'It cannot be healthy to repress nature.'

Marion gave Susan a pinched look.

'It has taken centuries to harness man's baser instincts and become civilised. You would prefer atavism?'

'I think it unlikely a walk on the moors will result in the ruin of civilisation,' Susan returned with a smile.

'Miss Smythson would have agreed,' remarked the chaise longue. 'She was a very active sort of person, was she not, Papa?'

Dr Claybourn was, at that moment, entering the parlour sporting a tartan waistcoat of vivid crimson threads, crossed with even brighter greens.

'What is this about a walk on the moors?' he asked.

Susan explained her plan.

'Aha! You share my interest in the natural sciences. I wish there were more like you. Even though my research into defects of memory will bring great benefit to mankind, I cannot find a patron. If only—'

'Henry, Miss Mottram is too busy to humour you by listening to your theories.'

'On the contrary, I would be delighted to hear more,' Susan began politely, but Dr Claybourn held up his hands. 'My apologies. My scientific fervour does, on occasion, get the better of me. My wife does right to chastise me. As for this nature walk of yours, I do not see any harm in it. Exercise is known to improve health, heh-heh.'

Marion turned to the chaise longue.

'Did you hear that, Helena? Perhaps you should join Miss Mottram's excursion.'

'Marion, you know your sister is delicate,' said Dr Claybourn. 'We cannot risk a relapse.'

'How can you consider my sister cured when she is of no practical use?'

'You are only jealous because my case was written up in the Transactions,' protested the chaise longue. 'Whereas your condition of being a miserable old spinster remains incurable.'

'Girls, girls, you know I do not like this bickering,' Dr Claybourn said mildly. The chaise longue issued a languid sigh and Marion pressed her lips together and said no more. Once Susan had assured Mrs Claybourn that the walk would entail no expense there were no further objections.

Susan requisitioned an armful of empty jars from the housekeeper, Mrs Clegg, an aged woman with grey hair that grew so wild that she resembled a dandelion gone to seed. Susan felt for her. Although her equally aged husband tended the gardens and hothouses, it fell to Mrs Clegg to serve the family as well as feeding nearly fifty girls, with only occasional help from Tabitha. Susan thanked Mrs Clegg and exhorted her class to repress their excitement until they were out of earshot of the school. They passed Dr Claybourn's infirmary, a rect-angular yellow brick building set against the low dry-stone wall that bordered the grounds. A row of arches along its length suggested it had originally been built to stable horses, but they were now bricked up, giving it a blank, featureless appearance.

Wary of Mrs Claybourn's injunction, Susan instructed the girls not to approach. Her warning proved unnecessary. The brooding silence which hung about the infirmary seemed to infect the girls and they all held their breath as they went past. Remembering Mrs Claybourn's warning about miasma, Susan found herself doing the same. Mary Martin was so fearful she attached herself to Susan's skirts until they reached an iron gate in the boundary wall. Mr Clegg was digging up the peaty soil close to the wall. Like his wife, he resembled a dandelion, albeit one that had suffered under strong wind, for he was bent double by rheumatism and retained not a single hair on his barren pate. He was so concentrated on his task that he did not raise his head to acknowledge Susan's friendly greeting.

Once beyond the school grounds, the girls' spirits lifted. The ground was soft and spongy underfoot and Susan led her class in a brisk walk, relishing the fresh air and the exercise. The bell heathers were past their best, but the tiny purple flowers of the common *Calluna vulgaris* still brightened the landscape, and the gusts of winds were filled with their perfume. How her papa would have loved this! She resolved to pick an armful on her return. A vase of scented heather would do much to liven up her little chamber. In lower-lying areas, fruiting asphodel grew around muddy puddles, adding splashes of marmalade orange to the purple carpet. A flock of plovers weaved overhead, their wings black against the pale grey clouds. A blustery wind tugged at Susan's skirts, but the air was warm and with the sun occasionally breaking through the layer of cloud it was not unpleasant.

Susan instructed her pupils on the different species of plants and animals. The girls were particularly delighted by the butterflies. It had been a warm summer and second broods had been common so there were still plenty about. With Susan's help the girls identified Speckled Woods and Painted Ladies fluttering gaily above the heather. She handed out jars and some of the girls began collecting. Others, led by Gwendoline, started a game of 'it'. Susan asked them to stop and take heed of the lesson, but they seemed determined not to hear her. Seeing the pleasure on their faces as they chased each other, Susan relented and resolved to let them play. A part of her was envious of their unrestrained delight, recalling her own childhood games with Florence. She blinked away the memories, but her heart remained heavy as they proceeded towards an outcrop that jutted up from the moorland, providing the only high point for miles. Eager to make use of such a promising vantage point, Susan found a narrow path winding up the side of the sheer rock face and led her class upwards.

As her ragged party of giggling girls broached the top of the escarpment, they came unexpectedly upon two women, seated upon a tartan blanket. The nearest was slender and neatly attired, her African heritage revealed by the colour of her skin, its rich brown tones forming a pleasing contrast with her ivory day dress. She was of similar age to Susan but her dress was cut in an old style, the skirts narrower and less cumbersome than the current fashion. At their sudden appearance, she started up in alarm, her skirt fluttering behind her. Susan's feet rooted her to the ground. The young woman's eyes were as dark as the peat of the moors. She wore no bonnet, her black hair falling in coiled tresses around her face and down her back. The natural grace of her bearing recalled Diana's nymphs, or even the goddess herself, disturbed in her bower. Her lips parted and a heart-breaking moan emerged.

'I'm… I'm sorry,' Susan stuttered, finding her voice at last. Gwendoline pointed towards the young woman.

'She's all dirty,' she said with a snigger.

'She needs a bath!' exclaimed Agnes, another of Susan's students.

The young woman's eyes flicked from one girl to the other, fear shimmering up from their umber depths. With another muffled cry, she turned and fled, dropping the large book she was holding. It landed heavily on its spine and fell open, its pale leaves whipped into a frenzy by the gusting wind.

'Wait!' Susan darted forward to rescue the book. A small beagle limped towards her, yapping furiously. The young woman's companion, an older lady, gathered up the blanket and clicked her fingers at the dog.

'Come away, Eppy!' she commanded crossly. The little dog obeyed instantly, running off with a lopsided gait. The woman scowled at Susan before turning to follow her young companion.

'Wait, please—your book!' Susan held out the discarded item but the young lady and her companion paid no heed, intent on hurrying away as fast as they could.

'What an odd-looking creature,' Gwendoline said. 'What can she have been doing here?'

Some distance beyond the escarpment, a black lake spilled like an inkblot on the landscape. A clump of woodland extended from the far side and within it something glinted in the sunlight. Susan shaded her eyes and discerned a steeply sloping roof with a tall spire behind. The two women were heading towards it, the younger easily outstripping her companion as she ran, one hand lifting her skirts to give her booted feet more room.

'It's the witch from the big house!' cried Agnes. 'I bet she was collecting frogs and snails for her potions. What's in the book, Miss? Is it spells? May I look?'

'You may not.' Susan clutched the book firmly to her chest. 'You should be ashamed of such discourteous behaviour.'

'But Miss…'

'But nothing. We must return to Matterdale Hall, since you have proven unable to behave with propriety.'

Gwendoline and Agnes continued to protest, but Susan remained firm, regretting that she had not been stricter before. Had the girls not been overexcited by their games, they might not have behaved so dreadfully. Only Mary did not obey her exhortation. The little girl remained crouched down in the heather, oblivious to all around her. Susan touched her on the shoulder and pointed towards the school. The little girl jumped up and obediently joined the line of girls that formed behind Susan. It was a shame, Susan thought, for it had been the first time she had seen the girls in such lively spirits, but she could not let such shameful behaviour go unpunished. They returned to the classroom and spent the remainder of the afternoon pressing flowers and mounting their specimens. Only then did Susan realise, with regret, that in her rush to get the girls back to Matterdale Hall she had forgotten to pick any heathers.

'Look, Miss!' cried Gwendoline as Anne gave a scream. The girls had formed a circle around Mary. Susan edged between them. Mary's hands were cupped around something.

'Let me see,' Susan said, gently opening Mary's hands. Inside, trembling, was a tiny grey field mouse. Mary ran her forefinger tentatively along its back.

'Did you find it on the moor?' Susan asked.

Mary, as usual, did not respond. The mouse rubbed its face between its front paws, eliciting sighs of admiration from the girls.

'Gwendoline, please run to the kitchens and ask Mrs Clegg for a crust of bread and a basket with a lid,' Susan instructed. The mouse hopped out of Mary's hands and onto the floor. Anne let out another scream.

'It will bite me!' she cried, jumping up onto the nearest chair.

'There's no need to be afraid,' said Susan calmly. Her father's living had been in a rural parish and mice had been frequent visitors to the vicarage. Gwendoline returned with the requested items. Susan broke off some breadcrumbs and laid them in a line on the floor, leading towards the basket, into which she placed the remainder of the bread. The class watched in rapt attention as the little mouse scavenged the crumbs and then hopped into the basket. Susan placed the lid on top and then gave it to Mary.

'It shall be yours to care for.'

Mary snatched the basket and hugged it to her chest, staring up at Susan with a mixture of fear and hope. Susan nodded encouragingly. 'You can keep it. You must feed it every day.' Yet, as Mary carried the basket to her desk as gingerly as if it were made of china, Susan did not know whether she understood.

5

A Little
Kitchen Gossip

The girls took their meals in a draughty chamber situated between the Claybourns' parlour and the kitchen. The walls and floor were bare stone, despite which Mrs Claybourn insisted on grandly referring to it as the refectory. Crude wooden benches were placed at even cruder tables and the girls crammed in next to each other, shoulders and elbows digging into their neighbours. A small trestle table at the top of the room was set aside for the supervising teacher, another role that fell to Susan. That evening, Mrs Clegg wheeled in a large pot of gently steaming porridge. The tiny wheels of her trolley snagged against a raised flagstone. Susan rushed to help her. The instant they had lifted the trolley through the door, the girls surrounded them, grasping for the metal bowls stacked unevenly around the porridge pot.

'One at a time!' pleaded a flustered Mrs Clegg. 'I only got one pair of hands.'

'Girls, please show some manners,' Susan implored. 'We are not at a fish market!' It took several further remonstrations before the girls formed an orderly queue.

'Lordy, ain't I gone and left the sugar in the kitchen?' Mrs Clegg pressed her palms to her forehead. 'I'd forget my own name if it weren't Hephzibah, which took such pains to learn.' She seemed too distressed by her mistake to take any remedial action and so Susan offered to fetch the sugar herself. She returned to find the girls swarming once more around the trolley like bees round a hive. She felt she could not abandon Mrs Clegg and assisted her by spooning out sugar as fast as the housekeeper could ladle the now lukewarm porridge into the metal bowls.

'You're a sight too generous with that sugar, Miss,' said Mrs Clegg forlornly. 'Mrs Claybourn will have it out my wages if that don't last the whole week.'

Susan, to the obvious disappointment of the next girl in line, shook most of the sugar from her spoon before depositing what little was left on top of her portion of porridge. Poor Mrs Clegg departed with her trolley, hunched over as though she carried an invisible sack of coals on her back, her feet scraping along the floor as if she could not summon the effort required to pick them up.

After supper, it was time for the girls to fetch their copybooks. They must be supervised during their evening study period, yet another task allotted to the junior teacher. Having settled them down, Susan was free at last to examine the book that had been left on the moor by the young lady. It was heavy and bound in crimson suede. She brushed her fingertips against the soft material before opening the book. Excepting a few blank pages, it was filled with sketches in pencil or charcoal of flowers or moorland scenes, as well as some fine watercolours. One drawing of a bee dipping into a thistle flower had been rendered in such exquisite detail it seemed as if the insect might fly off the page at any moment. Another page held a red grouse, whose white-rimmed eye regarded Susan with the complacent air so typical of that species. Each illustration was labelled in a neat, elegant hand. Enchanted by the vivid and engaging images, Susan was eager to know more about the young woman who had created them.

The girls from the middle class began to whisper. The whispers turned to giggles and then laughter. They began to nudge some of the younger girls, making them blot their copybooks. Susan asked sternly for silence but, after a short hush, the tittering and nudging began again. She quickly identified the ringleader, a button-nosed girl from Marion's class called Isabella Brownloe, and she directed Isabella to bring forward her copybook. To her surprise, Isabella was happy to oblige, skipping towards Susan with a laughing glance at her schoolfellows.

Tonight the girls were copying a biblical quotation. The text at the top of the book was from Proverbs: '*The wicked flee when no man pursueth: but the righteous are bold as a lion.*' Isabella, to the great amusement of her classmates, had copied it out in a sprawling hand, replacing 'bold' with 'bald' and removing all reference to lions.

'Mr Clegg may find such a verse inspiring,' Susan said, maintaining a dry tone despite her inward amusement, 'but I doubt Mrs Claybourn would agree.' She tore out the offending page. 'Try again and take greater care to keep within the lines.'

Isabella smirked and returned to her bench. However, she continued to whisper and nudge her companions. Susan soon found her voice growing hoarse with unattended reprimands and was relieved when it was time to send the girls off to bed. That task completed, Susan made up a couple of posies with heather she had collected just before supper, it being the first opportunity to do so since the ill-fated nature walk. She took one to the kitchen. Tabitha was scrubbing the pots from the family supper and Mrs Clegg was dragging a damp cloth slowly across a flour-covered table, leaving doughy streaks behind. Susan offered her the posy.

'I brought you this, to thank you for letting us take the jars.'

Mrs Clegg stopped what she was doing and let out a weary sigh.

'It's kind of you, but I'll need a vase and the Missus don't keep any.'

Susan found a glazed jug, filled it with water, arranged the stalks of heather within and placed it on the windowsill.

'There!' she said with satisfaction. 'Don't they smell lovely?'

'You should give your heathers to Miss Helena.' Tabitha wrinkled her nose. 'She don't like the trouble of washing.'

'Hush now, Tabby. Miss Mottram is used to polite society. She won't want to listen to your gossip.'

'Polite society is nothing *but* gossip,' said Susan, pulling up a plain wooden chair. 'Who is rich, who is marrying who, who got caught kissing a servant girl by the side of the church. If not for gossip, we would be reduced to dreary talk about the weather.'

'The weather?' said Tabitha in disbelief. 'But all it does here is rain.'

'Exactly so, Tabitha. To be avoided at all costs.'

'So, it's gossip you've come for, is it?' Mrs Clegg asked, nodding as if Susan had confirmed her worst suspicions. Susan held up her hands in surrender.

'You have found me out. I am eager to know who owns the big house across the moor. The one by the lake.'

'That's Heathersage Manor. You should stay away,' Mrs Clegg said morosely.

'A witch lives there,' added Tabitha.

'Don't pay no heed to Tabby here. She talks a deal of nonsense.'

'Then why warn me to stay away?'

Mrs Clegg sat down with a heavy sigh.

'Mr Sutcliffe don't take kindly to visitors. He took his shotgun to William Berslow just for taking a shortcut across his land. Mind you, the Berslows always have game in their larder, if you know what I mean. Why you asking?'

Susan related what had happened, her cheeks flaming as she recalled the behaviour of Gwendoline and Agnes.

'That's Mr Sutcliffe's daughter,' said Mrs Clegg. 'A half-breed.'

'A witch,' Tabitha insisted. Susan threw her a look of stern disapproval and Tabitha swiftly returned to washing the pots. *I must try that look on Isabella*, Susan thought.

'They say she's simple in the head,' said Mrs Clegg. 'Sins of the father, an' all. No wonder he keeps her hidden away.'

'He locks her up?' Susan exclaimed in horror.

'I don't say that exactly. But they invite no company and they never go to church, 'cept Yuletide and Easter. Last year, the young miss slighted Mrs Claybourn. Didn't even offer to look at her when the missus went to say hello. Although if the lass is simple, she mayn't know what she was doing.'

Susan thought of the book of drawings and the expressive gaze of their creator. She was certain Miss Sutcliffe was anything but simple. Yet she had seemed very afraid. She longed to know more, but neither Mrs Clegg nor Tabitha could tell her anything else, although Tabitha continued to insist that Miss Sutcliffe was a witch.

'When the wind is in the right direction you can smell her foul potions,' she said, wrinkling her nose. 'I can smell them right now.'

It was true that a faint, unpleasant odour hung in the air.

''Tis only rat droppings, right here in this house,' returned Mrs Clegg. 'I'll have my Jack put down traps.'

The door from the corridor opened, bringing a cold draught into the warm kitchen. A man entered, wearing a tatty pea-green frock-coat over working clothes. The coat's hourglass shape betrayed its age. Where once there had been three buttons, only the middle one remained. Its wearer might have been considered handsome had his features not been marred by crooked front teeth. Mrs Clegg shook her head.

'Dickie, you shouldn't be in the main house. You ain't left your post, I hope?'

'Let me by, Ma. That madhouse is cold enough to freeze porridge.' He pushed past her to open his coat in front of the stove, stealing its warmth from the other occupants of the kitchen.

'You know the master don't like you calling it that. An' you should get a proper coat, 'stead of that tatty cast-off.'

'A gent needs his frock coat.' Her son squared his shoulders, the action straining the stitching of his coat seams. He turned his head to cast a sharp eye over Susan. 'Who's this then?'

'It's the new teacher.'

He stepped towards Susan and grasped her hand, though she had not offered it, clicking his scuffed heels together in such an affected manner she wondered if he were mocking her.

'Richard Clegg, Esquire. Pleased to make yer 'quaintance.'

'My boy,' said Mrs Clegg wearily. 'Brought into this world to be a worry to me and his pa.'

'She's small, ain't she, Ma? Like a little sparrer chick that's fell into a nest of crows.'

'I do not believe size has any bearing on my ability to perform my duties,' said Susan stiffly, retrieving her hand.

'I speak as I sees, Miss Sparrer. Such a little thing, you'll soon be out of your depth in a place like this.' Something must have shown in Susan's face, for he laughed. 'Already floundering are we, little sparrer?'

Susan's courage rose under his scorn.

'If I am beyond my depth, I shall learn to swim,' she said stoutly.

'You don't look like you've the strength for it. Anyone weak in mind or body don't last long here.' He flexed his right arm, bunching his fist so the muscles bulged beneath his coat. 'Feel that! Like iron, is that.'

Susan looked to Mrs Clegg, disturbed by her son's declaration. 'Miss Smythson. Why did the Claybourns let her go?' It was not just curiosity that made her ask. She had no wish to share her predecessor's fate.

'I reckon Dr Claybourn was sweet on her,' said Tabitha, wiping her hands on her pinafore. 'I saw her once, sneaking into that infirmary. Maybe that's why Mrs Claybourn got rid of her.'

'To be sure, she was a flirt,' said Mrs Clegg. 'Always had her followers, hanging about the place. But there ain't no husband more devoted than Dr Claybourn. Oh Dickie, those ain't for you!' she protested as her son plucked an apple from a nearby basket.

'The old hay-bag won't miss one little apple.' Richard bit into the apple and masticated the hunk of white flesh without feeling the need to close his mouth. Susan wondered how women were supposed to find men attractive when they behaved in such an uncouth manner.

'Missus knows how many we have, to the very last one. Do you want me to be dismissed? And if the master finds you not at your post, you'll be out on your ear, an' all. And who else is going to employ you, after you-know-what?'

Richard curled his fist around the lapel of his coat.

'Don't fret so. Old Claybourn knows my value. An' if he don't, I'll remind him what *I* know.'

Susan was shocked by such open disrespect. Even her father, who had been nothing but kind to the servants, would not have accepted such insolence. Richard took a last bite from the apple and threw the core into the stove.

'Well, Miss Sparrer, I shall get back to work. The likes of you and me must do as we are bid.'

Susan didn't like the insinuation that they were the same. She was a teacher, not a servant.

'Oh-ho! You'll have to hide your feelings better than that, Miss, if you're to keep Mrs Claybourn's favour,' Richard remarked with a knowing smirk.

Susan felt her cheeks redden. Her father always said he could read the thoughts on her face as easily as the headlines of his newspaper. She didn't like to think that a man like Richard Clegg could do the same.

'You're no better'n me, Miss Sparrer,' he continued. 'One of our ladies was a teacher, like you, afore she came to the madhouse.'

'I would not work in that place for all the tea in China,' said Mrs Clegg. 'The other day I was in such a hurry to get eggs from the coop, I went too close to the wall. When I got back, I'd clean forgot what I was going to cook. I must have breathed some of that bad air.'

'It's the ghosts that frighten me,' said Tabitha. 'Them poor little girls that died there, haunting the place with their wailing and crying.'

'Poor little things. The master was inconsolable,' said Mrs Clegg. 'Even the missus was upset.'

'She never likes to lose a paying customer, that's true,' said Richard, flicking a lump of moist apple flesh from his shoulder with a fingernail.

'I heard they was bad girls,' Tabitha whispered. 'They died because of their sins.'

'Nonsense,' declaimed Mrs Claybourn from the doorway, causing the occupants of the kitchen to start in surprise. Any ghosts that might inhabit Matterdale Hall could take lessons from its mistress, for Mrs Claybourn evidently possessed the ability to appear from thin air.

'It was the typhus, plain and simple.' Mrs Claybourn's pale eyes darted about the kitchen and came to rest on the barrel of apples. 'Such things happen in any school. They were given a

Christian burial in Hustanton church. No reason for them to be haunting us.'

'No, mum. Sorry, mum,' mumbled Mrs Clegg.

'Richard, I hope it was not your footstep I heard in my corridor a few minutes since?'

The smirk dropped from Richard's face, although Susan thought she caught a flash of resentment as he bowed his head.

'No mum,' he muttered.

'I am sure my husband does not pay you to warm yourself in my kitchen.'

He dipped his head and exited swiftly via the back door, which led into the yard.

'Miss Mottram, I hope you are not keeping my housekeeper from her duties?'

Susan bit back an instinctive 'No mum,' that had formed on her lips. She would not behave like a servant, even if Mrs Claybourn treated her like one.

'I brought Mrs Clegg a posy,' she said. 'I know she is kept too busy to pick flowers herself.'

'I detest flowers. They provide no nourishment and wither away in a few days, making a mess with their dead petals. Mrs Clegg, I came to tell you we shall not need any more coal tonight. Miss Helena went to bed an hour since, and it is only for her sake that I permit such indulgence when it is not yet winter. But I see that you prefer to gossip with my junior teacher than attend to your duties.'

Susan rose. 'I beg you will not blame Mrs Clegg. It was my fault entirely.'

She retired to her chamber, her mind returning to the house she'd glimpsed from the top of the escarpment. Her sympathy for Miss Sutcliffe had only been heightened by what Tabitha and Mrs Clegg had told her. From what she had witnessed, there was nothing about Miss Sutcliffe to fear or censure. Yet the unfortunate young woman was spoken of scathingly, and shunned by all. What a lonely existence it must be. Susan, herself suffering under the pangs of homesickness, felt a strong fellowship with the young lady, and longed to know more about her.

6

Susan Pays a Visit

Susan resolved to return the sketchbook to its owner. Such a precious object was certain to be missed. The idea of meeting the formidable Mr Sutcliffe or the surly older woman who had attended his daughter on the moors was unsettling, but she felt responsible for the incident that had caused the book to be lost and would not rest easy until it had been returned. And her curiosity regarding the book's owner remained strong. In moments snatched from her duties she had perused the book several times, lost in admiration of the beautiful pictures and often recalling the expressive brown eyes of their creator.

That weekend the weather was fine and as soon as she was released for her half day, Susan set off on her errand. At the top of the escarpment, she paused for breath. To the southwest was the school, its T-shape outline clear against the purple heather, with the oblong infirmary in the foreground. The madhouse, as

Richard had called it. Further afield, the stone-tiled roofs of Hustanton cut sharp slashes across the landscape. When she had alighted from the country coach, she had been too weary to notice more than a few well-kept cottages. She resolved to visit on her next half-day. To the northwest the black lake provided her bearing. The far side of the escarpment sloped gently towards a bracken-smothered beck that bubbled cheerfully across her path. A series of flat stones formed a crossing. Susan hopped from one to the other and followed a narrow path, her skirts brushing against knee-high heather until the path widened as it approached the lake.

Up close, the water was not, in fact, black, but stained tea-leaf brown by the surrounding peat. Thirsty after her walk, Susan crouched down and cupped her hand to drink the cool water. A pair of snipe, unaware of her presence, bobbed their straight, sword-like beaks up and down near the shoreline. She dried her hands on her skirts, rising carefully so as not to disturb the birds. The woodland that grew on the far side of the lake was an uneven mix of oak and ash, broken up by pale slashes of silver birch. Rowans with their red berries added dots of colour. She circled the lake, her boots crunching on a gravelled path, and a sprawling building of age-blackened limestone loomed out of the greenery. Gothic in style, stuffed with decorative stonework, a church-like tower at the rear was topped by a dramatic spire that pointed heavenwards in supplication. Susan exclaimed with delight. *This* was a building to stimulate the imagination! The sort of building where skeletons might be buried under floorboards and where locked cabinets contained obscure parchments, writ with unnatural histories. As she watched, a shadow flitted across one of the mullioned windows of the tower and her heart fluttered. Was someone watching her? The shadow did not return and she wondered if it had just been a trick of the light.

As she drew closer, a row of arched windows with curved lintels seemed to frown at her, and she wondered at her own temerity. Suppose Mr Sutcliffe was prowling the grounds with his shotgun and mistook her for a poacher? The shrubs that bordered the lake might provide her some cover, but she decided that creeping among them would make her seem more like a criminal, rather than less. Openness and honesty must be her best policy. She stepped out boldly onto the rutted track that ran from the house towards Hustanton, her heart beating fast and strong.

Nobody accosted her as she passed through a wrought iron gateway and into the grounds. Mature shrubs were dotted about manicured lawns, in pleasing contrast with the brooding house whose gargoyles screamed silently at her from every corner. A vaulted entrance sheltered a vast oak door with decorative iron hinges that spread across it like tangled thorns. Only the distant honking of geese broke the silence. The heavy iron knocker was cast in the shape of a coiled dragon. She lifted it, and let it drop. It clanged heavily. Nobody responded. She tried again, with no answer. Did no-one expect visitors in these parts?

Convinced of the virtue of her errand, Susan walked round the side of the house in search of the servants' entrance and came upon another immaculate lawn with a walled orchard at the rear. Some distance away, the young lady from the escarpment and her companion appeared locked in a furious argument, both gesticulating wildly with their hands. Such was the violence of their movements, Susan grew concerned for Miss Sutcliffe's safety. The small beagle was running in rings around them, its nose ploughing through the grass. Raising its head, it saw Susan and began to bark. The older woman spun round and made a firm gesture towards her companion. Miss Sutcliffe retreated hurriedly. Disturbed by what she had witnessed and eager to make her purpose understood, Susan stepped towards them. The older woman strode to intercept her, eyebrows knitted.

'My name is Susan Mottram. I'm a teacher at Matterdale Hall,' Susan began.

'One who cannot control her pupils, as I recall.'

Susan flushed.

'I apologise if they upset the young lady.'

'Miss Sutcliffe was exceedingly distressed by those girls. Pointing and laughing as though they were at a circus.'

'They have been reprimanded,' Susan assured her, raising up on tiptoes to peer over the woman's shoulder. 'Might I address your mistress? I wish to offer my regrets directly.'

'Miss Sutcliffe is not my mistress. I am her companion,' the woman snapped. Susan, however, refused to be intimidated.

'You appeared to be threatening her,' she said. 'Tell me the truth—you are really her gaoler.'

The woman laughed. A harsh, cold laugh that chilled Susan's bones.

'I see nothing amusing about holding a young lady prisoner against her will.'

'Have you walked all this way to bring such slanderous accusations?'

Susan took the sketchbook from beneath her arm.

'I came to return this. If you might allow me to give it to Miss Sutcliffe?' She attempted to step towards the young lady. The woman barred her way and wrenched the book from Susan's grasp.

'I will return it myself. You may leave.'

'I will leave when I hear from Miss Sutcliffe's own lips that she is well and happy,' Susan returned, astounded at her own forwardness. The air filled with honking as a flock of geese came in to land on the lake, their webbed feet sending up plumes of spray as they skidded across the surface.

'From her own lips?' The woman hesitated. Somewhere, a door slammed so hard that the geese aborted their landing, flapping their wings in a flurry of panic as they rose and circled away. A well-dressed man of middle years strode across the lawn towards them. From his angry countenance it could only be Mr Sutcliffe.

'Will none of you leave us in peace?' he cried. 'Why must everyone be poking about my business?' He looked anxiously towards his daughter, who remained at a distance, staring at Susan in a mute plea. Trembling only a little, Susan turned to him.

'I came to return Miss Sutcliffe's sketchbook and to enquire after her,' she said. 'I was afraid we alarmed her the other day.'

'Alarmed?' His scowl deepened. 'How so?'

'We were accosted by a rabble of schoolgirls, under the care of this… this girl who can barely be out of school herself,' interjected his daughter's companion. 'They called Miss Cassandra dirty—'

'Can this be true?'

'Some of the girls were thoughtless,' Susan admitted, her cheeks burning with shame under his disapproving gaze, 'and I am most anxious to apologise to Miss Sutcliffe for any distress she may have suffered.'

Mr Sutcliffe's neck suffused with blood.

'My daughter does not receive visitors. I would thank you to leave.'

Alarmed by his passionate aspect, Susan took a step backwards, stumbling as the heel of her boot caught against the root of a shrub. Mr Sutcliffe lunged towards her as she fell and she barely evaded his grasp, her heart fluttering against her ribs as she fled. Only after gaining some distance did she dare glance over her shoulder. Mr Sutcliffe continued to stare, but did not pursue her. Susan retreated towards the lake, her heart still thumping wildly. Such a stern occupant of such a formidable house! How his poor daughter must suffer, with such a parent, and such a companion.

7

Dr Claybourn Calls on Mr Sutcliffe

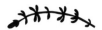

Concerned for Miss Sutcliffe, Susan sought advice from the Claybourns, openly confessing all that had occurred, not withholding the parts that reflected badly on her. They proved reluctant to interfere although each for different reasons.

'This all might have been avoided, if you had been able to control your class,' said Mrs Claybourn severely.

'Mr Sutcliffe is entitled to his privacy,' said Dr Claybourn. 'A man should dictate what happens in his own house. It does no good to meddle. He is a man of much influence locally and I would not wish to offend him. Of course, the incident on the escarpment was unfortunate, heh-heh.'

'If you remember, Papa, I advised against the excursion,' said Marion. 'Miss Mottram has shown poor judgement. We should let her go.'

'That poor girl,' offered the chaise longue, inhabited as usual by Helena. 'She must be lonely, trapped in that dreadful house. Excepting poor health, loneliness must be the very worst thing in the world.'

'I pity anyone who lives in a situation lacking warmth and friendship,' said Susan, with some feeling. The chaise longue issued a weary sigh.

'I have often wondered if I should call upon her. But the walk is beyond my strength.'

Marion snorted. 'Everything is beyond your strength, sister, save eating and sleeping.'

'You must not think of calling on that girl,' Mrs Claybourn snapped. 'Not after she slighted me last Easter. She cannot possibly think she is better than me, not with who her mother was.'

'I believe she is unhappy,' Susan exclaimed. 'Cannot we help her? Might we ask the local constable to intervene?'

'We shall do no such thing,' Mrs Claybourn said firmly. 'If we fetched a constable every time somebody was unhappy, we would need a thousand of them.'

Susan continued to plead her case to the one person she thought might help.

'Dr Claybourn—I cannot believe a physician such as yourself could stand by while an innocent young lady may be suffering.'

'Innocent? Pah!' snorted Mrs Claybourn, but Dr Claybourn scratched his head.

'Upon consideration, perhaps I *should* pay Mr Sutcliffe a visit,' he began.

'No good can come of it, Henry,' insisted his wife.

'But he is rich, my dear. You yourself said I should seek out a patron for my infirmary. This, ahem, unfortunate misunderstanding may provide an unlooked-for opportunity to broach the subject.'

'He will hardly look favourably on the man who accuses him of locking up his daughter.'

'Oh, it must be approached delicately, to be sure. One cannot be too careful with gentlemen of uncertain temper, heh-heh! But I believe I shall attempt it. I am sure there is a reasonable explanation. At the very least, we may put Miss Mottram's mind at rest.'

'Oh, thank you!' Susan cried gratefully.

The very next day Dr Claybourn set off for Heathersage Manor. He was no horseman, and the Claybourns did not keep a carriage, so he left on foot. Just a few hours later, Susan heard the main door open and slam shut. Bursting with curiosity, she could not resist rushing out of her classroom. Dr Claybourn was in the hallway, just returned. His usually ruddy cheeks had darkened to a deep purple and his lips were pressed together as he tore off his gloves and flung them into his hat. Mrs Claybourn emerged from her own classroom.

'What happened?' Susan asked eagerly. 'Miss Sutcliffe, did you speak with her?'

'I did not.'

'Did Mr Sutcliffe agree to be your patron?' asked his wife.

'He did not.'

'I told you it would do no good.'

'So you did. You were right, as you always are, my dear. I had hoped that a man of means might wish to do good in the world. I was mistaken. He absolutely refused to fund my research. And most impolitely, too.'

'And Miss Sutcliffe?' Susan asked.

'I saw the young lady. She appeared quite well, although extraordinarily reserved. I do not recall her speaking a word to me the whole time. Mr Sutcliffe insisted that it was nobody's business how he ran his household, and I couldn't help but agree with him. That was my own opinion, if you recollect.'

His usual affability had disappeared, and Susan feared that she may have lost the only friend she had at Matterdale Hall. Yet her concern for Miss Sutcliffe made her press the matter.

'But, Miss Sutcliffe—cannot we help her?'

'The young lady did not even deign to answer my greeting. I would advise you not waste your sympathy on such a person.'

'A proud, ignorant creature!' said Mrs Claybourn, with evident satisfaction. 'Miss Mottram, please return to your class. Let us hear no more on this matter.'

8

In which Susan Receives a Lesson in Discipline

D r Claybourn aside, Susan was beginning to suspect that the Claybourns may not be altogether agreeable. It was a disloyal thought and Susan baulked at it, for in general she liked to think the best of people. However, there was little to admire in the way Helena rarely stirred from the chaise longue, her only topic of conversation the listing of her many ailments. Marion, in whom Susan had hoped to find an ally, had rebuffed all Susan's attempts to draw her into conversation. Whenever they met in the corridor, Marion hurried swiftly by, as if conversing with her fellow teacher were a mortal sin. If only Mrs Claybourn shared her eldest daughter's reticence, Susan might have been happier, but her employer was all too often on hand with a reprimand. 'I beg you would encourage your pupils not to press so hard on the slates. It wears down the chalk at an unacceptable rate,' she would say. Or, 'If you must permit your girls to read our books, pray ensure they do not crease the pages.' Without warning, she would appear in Susan's class-room to observe her lessons or turn up in the refectory at mealtimes and admonish Mrs Clegg for being over-generous with her portions. She was forever complaining about how Susan and her pupils contrived to cost her money. Susan's sug-gestion that the girls be provided with hot water each morning to encourage much-needed improvements in cleanliness had been met with especial scorn.

'You have no idea how expensive coal is, Miss Mottram,' she said. 'Above a pound per ton, and extra for delivery. Tabitha tells me you requested two jugs of hot water this morning for your personal use. Two!'

Susan was eager to explain such apparent profligacy.

'One of the girls had an accident. I used the water to wash down the bed.'

'Which girl?'

Had Susan noticed the dangerous glint in Mrs Claybourn's pale eyes, she might have hesitated to reveal the culprit, but her own generous heart never thought to blame Mary and it did not cross her mind that anyone would not be sympathetic to the little girl. Like many assumptions she had made since arriving at Matterdale Hall, this proved erroneous.

'It was poor Mary Martin. I feel very much for her. How hard it must be to live in a world she does not understand.'

'You punished her, of course?'

'Punished her? For something she could not help?' Susan did not hide her astonishment.

'Damaging school property is a serious matter.'

'I am sure Mary did not mean to do it.' Susan's heart plunged as she realised, too late, that she had inadvertently placed Mary in danger. 'I believe kindness is more likely to prevent a recurrence.'

'I did not ask what you believe. You have many foolish notions, Miss Mottram. Discipline is all. You will use your cane on that girl or leave my employ.'

Susan felt quite ill as she called her pupils into the afternoon lesson. Her eyes were often drawn to Mary, sitting silently at her desk, oblivious to the fate that awaited her. So small and frail. Who could think of punishing such a troubled child? Susan was convinced such a step was cruel and would do nothing to cure Mary's bedwetting. Yet she could not afford to lose her position—Mama and Florence were depending on her. As the girls were copying a list of countries and their capital cities onto their slates, she eased open the drawer that held her broken cane. One fragment was longer than the other. Still long enough to beat a child. She closed the drawer, her throat dry. For once, time moved all too swiftly and the hands of the clock soon showed it to be time for supper. She dismissed her class, keeping Mary behind. The girl looked up at her quizzically. Susan was shorter than most women, yet Mary barely reached her waist.

'I'm so sorry,' Susan whispered, her hand shaking as she reached for the drawer. Mary's eyes widened a fraction and her lip trembled. Her expression was fearful, but also hurt, and at that moment Susan knew she could not obey Mrs Claybourn's injunction. She sent Mary away with a gesture. Mrs Claybourn found her slumped over her desk, her head in her hands.

'It is done?'

Everything in Susan's nature yearned to confess, but another spirit seemed to take hold of her at that moment and spoke with her voice.

'Yes,' she whispered, unable to look at her employer.

'Next time, you will be swifter in dispensing justice.'

Susan's heart sank to its lowest ebb. She could almost hear her father's voice, reading the scriptures. *Thou shalt not bear false witness.* She had saved Mary from a beating and remained in a position to support her family. But at what cost to her soul?

For the next few days, heavy rains and grey skies mirrored Susan's mood. The single spark of hope amidst the gloom came in the form of Mary Martin's pet mouse. It had become a firm favourite with the class and the tiny creature was taken out and admired each morning, never wanting for scraps of food. Mary carried it everywhere with her and even started to take it to bed, as Susan discovered when she roused the girls early one morning and saw the basket next to Mary's bunk. She was about to insist that the mouse remain in the schoolroom at night when Mary held up her blanket with a timid smile. The blanket and the bed were dry. Susan could not pretend to know what went on inside Mary's mind but it was clear that her little friend was a comfort. For once, Susan was glad that supervising the dormitories fell under her purview. She permitted the little basket to remain in the dormitory at night.

On Friday evening, as the girls were practising their handwriting, Marion entered the refectory. The general hum stilled instantly.

'You have received a letter, Miss Mottram.'

'Surely it is too late for the postman?'

'It was brought by a servant, direct from Heathersage Manor,' said Marion disapprovingly. 'It appears to be a lady's hand.'

Susan placed the letter in her pocket. Although surprised to receive correspondence from such an unexpected quarter, she had no desire to share its contents with Marion. After a perfunctory glance at some copybooks, her fellow teacher departed. The instant she left, Isabella Brownloe rose and approached boldly.

'Aren't you going to see who it's from, Miss?'

'My letters are no concern of yours. Please return to your work.'

Isabella sidled up to her.

'Oh, go on, Miss. Perhaps you have an admirer. Although if it's a love letter you should know that Mrs Claybourn doesn't approve of hangers-on. She was always telling Miss Smythson off about hers.'

'I very much doubt it being a love letter.'

'You won't know 'til you read it,' insisted Isabella, leaning towards her. Before Susan realised what she was about, Isabella had slipped her hand into her pocket and borne away the letter in triumph.

'Isabella Brownloe!' she cried, jumping to her feet. 'That letter is my property. I insist you return it at once.' But Isabella paid her no heed, dancing around the room with the letter held triumphantly above her head. A few of her acolytes began to laugh and clap. Susan bit her lip and debated what to do. To chase Isabella round the room would be ignominious, to say the least. It would mean her losing any last shred of dignity and she doubted she would catch the girl anyway. As she hesitated, Isabella sprang up onto one of the tables and the girls cheered.

The door crashed open and Marion reappeared. The cheers subsided in an instant.

'What is this commotion? You, girl—get down from that table at once!'

But Isabella, inflamed by her success, had lost all sense of self-preservation.

'You're only jealous,' she cried. 'Miss Mottram has a love letter and nobody ever sent you one.'

'Impertinent child!' Marion strode towards Isabella. The girl froze and Marion tore the letter from her grasp.

'Miss Mottram, you will hand me your cane.'

Susan admitted she did not have a cane about her. Marion stared at her in disbelief.

'No wonder the girls are turned heathen. Even Miss Smythson, who had many faults, knew how to maintain discipline.'

She stalked out of the room and a terrible hush descended. Isabella shifted from one foot to the other, plucking nervously at a curl of hair on her freckled forehead. Marion returned with a cane.

'Is there not another way? I am sure Isabella is sorry,' Susan pleaded.

'You know the rules. Didn't you apply the cane to Mary Martin?'

'I… I could not,' Susan admitted.

'Then you do not belong here.'

Marion seized Isabella by her upper arm.

'Bend!'

Before Susan could make any further protest, Marion began to thrash her captive, her long arm rising high with each stroke.

She seemed almost in a trance, her face blank and emotionless. The room had grown so silent that each swish of the cane seemed unnaturally loud. Five swift blows were given, each followed by a strangled whimper, before the culprit was released. Isabella retreated, head down, to her allotted position. Her neighbours sprang apart so that she might lower herself gingerly onto the bench. She pressed her elbows against the rough wooden table and hid her face behind clenched fists. Marion addressed the room.

'You will attend your tasks quietly or face the same punishment.'

She returned the letter to Susan with a stiff nod and departed. The girls returned quietly to their copybooks. Susan retired to her seat and shielded her eyes with her hands so that the girls might not see her tears dropping onto the little trestle table. She wept for poor Isabella and the cruelty of her punishment, but also from shame that her own incompetence had been the cause. She had failed, and as soon as Marion informed her mother of Susan's perfidy she was bound to be dismissed. She had barely recovered herself when the time came to send the girls to bed. She forced herself to go to the family parlour to make her usual report, unable to look at Marion, although she felt the tall woman's attention fixed upon her.

'I understand there was an incident, heh-heh,' said Dr Claybourn, sympathetically.

'Poor Miss Mottram,' said Helena. 'It comes of being so small.'

'It comes from not punishing Mary Martin immediately,' said Mrs Claybourn. 'By delaying your duty, the girls sensed your weakness.'

Susan glanced at Marion in confusion. Why had Marion not given her away? Her fellow teacher's features remained inscrutable. Mrs Claybourn launched into a lecture regarding the need for a firm hand. Susan listened, knowing she could never do what Mrs Claybourn commanded. She was forced to acknowledge the truth. She had been ill-prepared for this responsibility. Alexander the Great may have believed that nothing was impossible, but he had clearly never been a teacher at a girls' boarding school. The girls showed no inclination to learn and she could not make them behave. It could not be long before she suffered the same fate as Miss Smythson.

9

Susan Reads a Letter

Susan slept poorly that night, waking before dawn. On rising, she caught a glimpse of her face in the mirror, her eyes red from weeping, and her cheeks puffy. She looked positively ill. If Mrs Claybourn were to observe her in this state she was sure to be dismissed at once and so she repaired to the kitchen in search of hot water, so she might restore her appearance to something resembling good health. She found Mrs Clegg eyeing the stove in bleary-eyed confusion, the hair on the side of her head squashed flat as though she had just that instant risen from her bed. There was no sign of any pots.

'Do you need help?' Susan asked. Mrs Clegg gazed at her with such bewilderment that Susan was forced to repeat the question. For a brief moment, Susan wondered if the housekeeper had been walking too close to the infirmary, imbibing its dangerous emanations. However, on reflection, she surmised it more likely that Mrs Clegg was merely forgetful, like many of her advanced years.

'Well, that's kind of you, Miss. I barely slept a wink. This damp weather is cruel on my old body. I feel as if some savage has speared me with a roasting fork and set me against his fire. I haven't even filled the pots. It'd be a mercy if you threw some coals into the stove. Oh, but you'll dirty your dress.'

'I'll do it,' said Tabitha, arriving at that moment. 'You trying to do me out of my apple pie, Miss?'

'Why don't you fill the pots, Tabitha?' Susan suggested, for Mrs Clegg was still rooted to the spot. 'I shall get the coals. I promise I won't expect anything in return.'

She wrapped a linen apron around her waist to protect the russet dress she was wearing. It was past her official period of mourning, but she had not yet felt any inclination to wear anything gayer. In any case, there had been no call for dressing up at Matterdale Hall. The Claybourns did not appear to entertain and, even if they did, Susan was unlikely to be invited to join the party. She emptied the coal scuttle into the stove.

'Coal bunker's in the corner.' Mrs Clegg nodded towards a sloping hatch. 'Take care you don't fall in, for I'm sure we'd never fish you out, for all that you're such a tiny little thing.'

The hatch opened above a vast pile of coal. Susan reached in and scooped a bucketful from the top without much trouble. The scuttle replenished, she helped Tabitha to fill the pots and kettles. The activity revived Susan's spirits. It pleased her to feel useful, even performing such a menial task. The door to the yard opened and Richard came in. He was carrying an empty bowl which he slung into the washtub.

'I got bigger portions in prison,' he declared.

'Dickie!' exclaimed his mother, with a sideways look at Susan. 'That ain't anything to boast about.'

64

He placed his hands in the pockets of his trousers, thrusting back the sides of his tatty green coat with an air of studied nonchalance.

'I've no time for your you-know-whats and you-know-wheres. Folks can take me as they find me. Miss Sparrer's been hauling coal, I see. We ain't none of us above a fall from grace.'

'You are not ashamed of your misdeeds?' Susan remarked in surprise, wiping her sooty hands on her apron. She had no desire to make conversation with Richard but curiosity got the better of her. 'What was your offence?'

'What d'you suppose, Miss?' he asked with a leer. 'What kind of villain d'you think I am? A thoroughly bad one, I bet.'

Susan could not believe it. He actually seemed proud of being a criminal!

'Since you are still a young man, your sentence cannot have been long. Your crime must not have been a heinous one,' she observed.

He seemed disappointed by her calm deduction.

'It weren't even a crime, by my reckoning. Some folks took exception to my opinions, that's all.'

'I wasn't aware having an opinion was a criminal offence,' Susan said doubtfully.

'I had a drop of ale and a couple of fellows didn't like being told the truth about themselves. There was a bit of a scuffle. I've seen plenty of gentlemen with Malmsey noses in a worse state after a bottle of fine port, but they don't get put away, do they? When I'm as rich as a duke, I shall say what I like and nobody will care.' Richard leaned towards her and twitched his nostrils, as if scenting for prey. 'You been crying, Miss?'

'You shouldn't ask the poor girl such a thing,' said his mother.

'I speak as I find. Miss Sparrer won't mind telling me the truth, I'm sure. Being so moral an' all.'

Susan removed her apron. The pots were only just beginning to steam and she could not bear to remain in the same room as Richard whilst waiting for them to boil.

'I tried to warn you, Miss Sparrer,' said Richard, as she was halfway out of the door. 'Them girls can sniff out weakness quicker than a jailbird.'

Susan fled to her chamber, his laughter echoing behind her. She paced up and down, wondering how long she should wait before venturing back down to get her hot water. Only then did she remember the letter that Marion had brought her. In her distress at Isabella's beating, she had quite forgotten it. She retrieved it from her pocket. To think she had overlooked something that might shed light on Miss Sutcliffe's circumstances, or perhaps even be a plea for help. She tore it open. It was short and written in a neat hand.

To Miss Mottram, teacher, Matterdale Hall

I have debated at some length the propriety of writing to you when we are not acquainted, but Mrs Grainger apprised me of your conversation and I felt it my duty to her and to the dearest of fathers to disabuse you of the remarkable misapprehensions you have formed concerning my circumstances. Please be assured I am no prisoner. I am well looked after and as beloved as any daughter could be. Mrs Grainger informs me that you believe Heathersage Manor to be some place of confinement, risen from the pages of a sensational novel. While I have often enjoyed such

books myself, in mistaking them for life you do my father and companion
a grave disservice. I am sure your concerns arise from a gentle heart, but
I have good reasons for preferring seclusion to society. To explain requires
a confidence and my reluctance to give it to a stranger must excuse the
delay in sending you this letter. However, Dr Claybourn's visit made it
clear I can put off this difficult task no longer, lest my father's reputation,
which suffers much already on my behalf, be further besmirched. I will
lay out my history and trust to the honesty I perceived in your
countenance to keep my secrets close.

That I am of mixed heritage is well known and no shame to myself or
to my father. He loved my mother dearly and I know they made each other
very happy. She died when I was still very young. Since then, I have known
nothing but love from him, as well as the devoted attention of Mrs
Grainger, the companion and protector he provided from my earliest
youth. However, I am profoundly deaf. My earliest years were a swirl of
confusion. My dear papa thought me lacking in sense when I was merely
struggling to understand the world around me. My playmates and even
some of our own servants made fun of me, laughing and pulling faces.
They thought I could not understand their cruelty, but they were wrong. I
understood well enough, and ever since have been wary of strangers. Once
the source of my difficulties was established, I was taught to make myself
understood by writing and by sign language. What you imagined to be an
argument between myself and Mrs Grainger was no more than a
conversation. My father can be formidable in his defence of me, but it
arises only out of concern for my welfare. They both know I prefer to

remain at home, free from misunderstandings and safe from the contempt of the public gaze.

I thank you most sincerely for taking the trouble to return my sketchbook. However, I hope you will make no further applications to the house, either in person or by proxy. My father keeps a shotgun for killing rats and for the discouragement of poachers, and while I am certain he would never deliberately harm anyone, his eyesight is not what it was. I would not wish any accident to befall you or your friends.

Yours etc,

Miss Cassandra Sutcliffe, Heathersage Manor.

Susan's first reaction to the letter was one of disbelief. Something so stiff and formal could only have been written by Mr Sutcliffe himself, to allay suspicion. Or that woman, Mrs Grainger. The threat at the end was clear. She determined to show it at once to Dr Claybourn, as confirming all her suspicions, and beg him to act on behalf of poor, imprisoned Miss Sutcliffe. But before taking such a step, she read the letter again and became less certain of her ground. To be sure, deafness would explain the gesticulation. And past teasing was a perfectly rational explanation for Miss Sutcliffe's avoidance of society as well as her horror at the behaviour of Gwendoline and the girls. That Susan had enjoyed certain types of novels, she could not deny. The works of Mr Richardson and Mrs Radcliffe had been within her father's library, and recent works such as Mr Bell's *Tenant of Wildfell Hall* had been read and re-read with great enjoyment by all the Mottram family. Had she let her imagination run away with her?

Cast in the light of protector to a beloved daughter, Mr Sutcliffe's actions took on a different cast. She recalled Tabitha's accusations of witchcraft, a belief shared by the other girls. Would not a protective father do all in his power to keep his daughter safe from such slander? A third perusal convinced her of the truth of the matter. Miss Sutcliffe was her correspondent. Indeed, the handwriting, identical to the annotations in the sketchbooks, should have convinced her at once of its authenticity. She was forced to review her own conduct and found it lacking. Her inexperience of the world had left her deceived by appearances and had led into wild speculation. Small wonder the letter was stiff and formal—she deserved nothing better. Any lingering hopes of a friendship developing between her and Miss Sutcliffe had surely vanished. And yet Miss Sutcliffe, despite Susan's outrageous suspicions, had been charitable enough to assign her an honest countenance and a kind heart, as well as honouring her with a precious confidence. Susan put away the letter, dismayed at her own conduct and pained by the hurt she had caused an innocent young woman who already suffered misfortunes enough.

It was with little appetite and no anticipation of any satisfaction that Susan approached the new day. The spirits of the girls in her class seemed as depressed as her own. Heads were bowed, all save Mary, who watched her with her usual, open-mouthed blankness. On impulse, Susan decided that today she would be a little less formal. Perhaps the girls would respond better to warmth and kindness. She began with a lesson of oral French, explaining basic phrases and asking the girls to repeat them. Everyone except Mary took part, and Susan provided praise and encouragement whenever it was warranted. The girls began to show signs of enjoying themselves. The delicate Anne Fordyce, usually the shyest of her pupils, proved to have an excellent ear and soon outstripped the others.

'Excellent, Anne,' she said brightly, after Anne had recited a phrase perfectly. Unused to praise, Anne squirmed in her seat and knocked her slate with her elbow, sending it crashing to the floor. She started up in alarm.

'Oh dear!' she cried in distress. But Susan's attention was fixed on Mary Martin. The noise of the slate hitting the floor had made everyone else jump, but Mary hadn't even flinched. Susan walked between the desks until she was standing behind Mary. She turned and clapped her hands together. Mary didn't move. *How had she not realised it before?*

'What are you doing, Miss?' asked Gwendoline.

'I believe Mary may be deaf. That's why she doesn't respond when I speak.' She crouched in front of Mary until the little girl turned her eyes towards her. A small crease appeared between her delicate eyebrows.

'Mary, do you understand? Can you hear me?'

Mary looked at her blankly. Susan took up her slate and wrote 'MARY', and then pointed towards the girl, who looked back in confusion.

Susan scrubbed out the letters and thought for a moment. She drew a picture of a mouse. She was no great artist and the thickness of the chalk did not help her. The mouse was sadly deformed, with a nose far longer than it should be and whiskers as thick as its tail, but Mary's eyes widened in recognition. She bent sideways to the basket that was, as always, by her feet. She picked it up and offered it to Susan with a questioning look.

'Yes.' Susan nodded with an encouraging smile. 'Well done.' She patted Mary on the back of her hand and Mary offered a shy smile in return. It was a beginning. A tearful Anne retrieved her slate, which was cracked down the middle.

'Mrs Claybourn don't like breakages,' said Gwendoline. 'She'll send Miss Marion to teach Anne a lesson.'

Anne's lower lip began to tremble. 'M-must we tell her?'

'We must, for how else will we get you a new slate?' said Susan. 'Do not fret. I will speak to Mrs Claybourn about it myself and tell her it was an accident.'

'Better find out your thickest skirt, Anne,' Gwendoline said sagely. 'And put on all your petticoats.'

That evening, to Susan's surprise, Mrs Claybourn asked if she would take a glass of Madeira with the family before retiring. Susan took a seat next to the chaise longue and sipped at her glass, enjoying the warmth of the wine across her tongue as much as the heat from the fire. Mrs Claybourn wasted no time in coming to the point.

'Marion tells me you received a letter from Heathersage Manor. Since I cannot believe the daughter is literate, I suppose it must be from Mr Sutcliffe?'

'Does he mention a subscription?' asked Dr Claybourn hopefully. 'For my infirmary?'

Susan was shocked at such an impertinent attack on her privacy. She responded as politely as she could, informing her interlocutors that the letter was indeed from Miss Sutcliffe, perfectly intelligible and written in a fine hand. Mrs Claybourn pursed her lips.

'I own I am surprised. What did she say?'

'Ma'am, you cannot expect me to reveal the contents of a private correspondence?'

'Heh-heh,' chuckled Dr Claybourn. 'Miss Mottram is quite right. Her letters are her own business.'

'Henry, would you wish me to advise you on the care of your patients?'

'I would not, heh-heh,' her husband chuckled, as if the idea amused him greatly.

'Then I beg you would leave the management of my staff to me.'

'Of course, my angel, quite right.' He looked at Susan apologetically. 'I am forgetting *"Vir sapit qui pauca loquitur".' It is a wise man who speaks little.*

'And yet words cost nothing,' Susan returned with a smile, 'so I would have thought you to be on safe ground.'

'No such thing in Matterdale Hall, heh-heh!' returned Dr Claybourn cheerfully.

'I only thought Miss Sutcliffe might have mentioned me— perhaps to make some apology for her previous behaviour,' said Mrs Claybourn. Susan was happy to inform Mrs Claybourn that the letter bore nothing pertaining to her at all.

'I wonder at the propriety of such a correspondence,' remarked Marion, perched so stiffly on the front of her seat that a full hand's breadth could be seen between her rigid back and that of the chair. 'Miss Mottram is young and inexperienced. We would not want her led astray.'

Susan bridled at the implication she was a weak-willed simpleton.

'I am confident I am in no danger,' she said.

'Marion makes a good point,' said Mrs Claybourn. 'I feel in a position of guardianship, with you being so far from your mother. We would not wish you to become unwittingly entangled in an inappropriate acquaintance. Perhaps I might peruse the letter, to ensure everything is as it should be?'

'I thank you for your kindness, ma'am, but you must allow me to make my own judgements on the matter.'

'Your judgements?' Mrs Claybourn exclaimed. 'You are too young to be wise in such things.'

Susan coloured for, after her recent errors, she felt there was some justification in her employer's assertion. Yet she held her ground.

'If I am old enough to be entrusted with the care of fifteen girls, I believe I might be permitted to decide with whom I may correspond.'

'My dear,' Dr Claybourn interjected with another little chuckle, 'I believe we must importune Miss Mottram no further on the subject.'

Encouraged by his support, Susan broached the subject of the slate.

'Which girl was responsible?' Mrs Claybourn asked sharply. Susan was about to explain when she recalled what had happened with Mary.

'It was an accident, for which I take full responsibility,' she said carefully.

Mrs Claybourn examined her over the top of her half-moon glasses.

'If you take responsibility, then you must be prepared to bear the cost.'

Susan readily acquiesced to the deduction of a few shillings from her quarterly wages and took her leave before she could be questioned more closely about the culprit.

10

A Lost Kitten

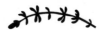

Having identified Mary's condition, Susan's first thought was to seek guidance from Heathersage Manor. Miss Sutcliffe's drawings were proof of what might be achieved by a deaf girl, if given help and encouragement. Yet she hesitated. Miss Sutcliffe's letter had made it clear she did not wish to further an acquaintance so badly begun, and Susan dared not contemplate visiting again uninvited. On her next half-day holiday, she wrapped her shawl around her shoulders and escaped onto the moors, soft underfoot after a week of steady rain. She made for the escarpment, with half a hope of finding Miss Sutcliffe and her companion there. If they were to meet by chance, there could be no impropriety, and she could raise the subject of Mary's deafness. She had barely made it beyond the grounds when she came upon an elderly woman, crouched so low among the heather that Susan did not see her until she was upon her. The woman, who wore a shapeless calico smock and a woollen cap, started up at Susan's approach, her cheeks blotched purple from the cold.

'Have you seen my cat?' she asked distractedly. Her voice was considerably more genteel than her appearance.

'I have seen nothing, but I will help you look,' Susan offered, for the woman appeared exceedingly distressed. 'How came your cat to be out here?'

The woman clutched Susan's hand. She wore neither shawl nor coat, and her fingers were as cold as freshly drawn water. 'We must find her! She's so pretty, my dear little kitty-cat. Such a shame what happened to that poor dear girl. If only she could speak and tell us what is wrong.'

'Why, you talk of her almost as if she were a person!'

'Of course she's a person!' the woman snapped. Susan was forced to conclude that the woman was not completely sensible. The woman blinked rapidly. 'Where's Mama? She said if I was good, we could go to the village dance together, but I can't remember if I've been good or bad. Do you know?'

She tugged fretfully at her cap. Judging by the deep lines on her face, her mother was almost certainly no longer living. If she was by some miracle alive, she must surely be too old for dancing.

'I fear you are unwell.' Susan removed her own shawl and placed it around the old woman's shoulders. It was cashmere, a present from her father on her seventeenth birthday. The woman stroked the dense weave with delight.

'So soft,' she said, tears glistening in her eyes. 'Have you seen Mama?'

From her confused and rambling phrases, Susan deduced that the woman must be one of Dr Claybourn's patients. She eased the woman gently back towards the infirmary.

'How about we get you a nice cup of hot tea?' she suggested. 'Or some broth?'

The woman stopped short.

'Where are you taking me?' she asked suspiciously.

'There's nothing to fear, I assure you.'

But the woman began to pound furiously at Susan with her fists, and Susan was forced to stop. Yet the woman did not flee, instead chewing on her lip and looking about her in confusion. Susan attempted once more to calm her.

'My name is Susan. What is yours?'

'Amelia. It's always been my name. Poor kitty, they changed her name. I had a red dress for my birthday. Can I play with Bessie when we get home?'

'Of course you may,' said Susan soothingly.

'I'm cold,' said Amelia with a shiver.

'Let us get you into the warm.' This time Amelia made no protest as Susan led her back to Matterdale Hall, and the small door that lay at the end of the infirmary, farthest from the main hall. Usually it was closed, but now it stood ajar.

'Hello?' Susan asked hesitantly. There was no answer. When Amelia darted inside, Susan felt she could not leave her. Cautious of the possibility of an infectious miasma, she took a deep breath and pinched her nose between her fingers before entering. The door opened into a large chamber with a vaulted ceiling that disappeared into the shadows. With the windows bricked up, it was gloomy, a pair of oil lamps in sconces high on one of the walls providing the only light. A beech wood cabinet sat against one wall, with a large porcelain bowl and an enamelled jug on top. A small stonemason's hammer lay beside them. In the middle of the otherwise empty chamber was a metal-framed chair with a high back and leather straps. Beside it was a shrouded object, about the same height as a small child, although one with an abnormally large head.

'What is that?' Susan asked, without breathing inwards. She felt drawn towards the object, which appeared more human as she neared.

Amelia tugged at her skirts. 'Horrid thing. Leave it alone. We shall have tea.'

But Susan's curiosity demanded satisfaction. She reached for the hem of cloth with her free hand but before she could unveil whatever was hidden beneath, an iron hand grabbed her wrist. The shock was enough for Susan to draw in a lungful of air through her mouth. The air felt so thick she almost choked on it.

'Don't you know that curiosity killed the cat?' said Richard, for it was he who had hold of her wrist.

'I found Amelia, wandering the moor,' Susan said, recovering herself enough to pull away from his grasp. She was gasping from the shock, as if she had run a race. If the air was truly filled with insanity, it had now contaminated every last inch of her lungs.

'Don't know how the old puss got out. I swear I locked the door behind me,' Richard muttered. A loud thumping from somewhere in the building made Susan jump.

'What is that?'

'Poor kitty,' said Amelia, scratching at her forearm.

'Nowt to concern yourself with, Miss,' said Richard. The thudding increased in volume and frequency, as if a horse were galloping on soft turf. It was coming from the end of a narrow corridor.

'Someone is in trouble!' Susan lifted her skirts and ran down the dim corridor, past open doors that led into windowless cells, faintly illuminated by pinpricks of light entering via airbricks. At the very end of the corridor was a closed door. It shook from the force of the blows coming from within.

'You don't want to go in there, Miss,' said Richard. Susan turned to him.

'You keep your patients locked up? Is this a place of healing, or a prison?'

'Trust me, this ain't nothing like prison,' Richard said bitterly.

Dr Claybourn appeared, breathless and florid.

'My... dear... Miss Mottram, a...thousand...apologies. I hope you are not...ah...hurt?'

He took out a green silk handkerchief and dabbed at his forehead.

'Miss Sparrer wants to join our merry band,' said Richard, with a leer.

'I want no such thing,' Susan protested. 'Dr Claybourn, is this how you treat your patients?'

'It is for Maria's own protection. We use the padded cell only as a last resort, heh-heh,'

'Are you not concerned for her wellbeing?' asked Susan, as the pounding intensified.

'I assure you, Maria is quite safe. If you feel strong enough to bear witness, I will show you.'

'The missus won't like it,' said Richard.

'The infirmary is my domain,' Dr Claybourn insisted. 'Miss Mottram has an inquiring mind. I wish to prove to her that I do not ill-treat my patients. Hand me the keys.'

'Yessir!' said Richard, as swiftly and sharply as if he were a soldier on parade. Almost too swiftly, Susan thought. He brought forth a large brass key from the pocket of his frock coat. Dr Claybourn took it from him.

'Please take care. Maria is a most fascinating case, but she can be a little, ah, fractious. If I find a cure, Sir Charles Locock himself will be first in line to shake my hand. I might be elevated myself, for such a discovery. Sir Henry Claybourn has a fine ring to it, heh-heh!'

The door opened with a harsh grating sound.

'Richard, did not I tell you how important it is to keep these hinges greased?'

'Yessir!' Richard made a mocking salute behind his employer's head. The doorway was so low that even Susan had to bow her head to get through and Richard and Dr Claybourn were forced to bend almost double. The room was just high enough for the men to stand, although Richard's hair brushed against the ceiling. Before them stood a young woman. Her hair was shorn so short it was difficult to know what colour it had been. Chestnut perhaps, or auburn. Her arms were secured in front of her body by a plain leather straitjacket. Her dress was darkened with dirt, obscuring a faint paisley-pattern beneath. She might have been pretty, if not for the rage that suffused her face.

'How are you today, Maria?' Dr Claybourn asked brightly. The woman shook her head like a puppy worrying a toy and mumbled incoherently.

'What's wrong with her?'

'She has forgotten how to speak, alas.'

'Boats, crabs and lemons,' shouted Maria, the words exploding out of her as if propelled by a set of bellows. Susan stepped back, bewildered by this nonsensical outburst.

'Why is she kept like this?'

'Mops and bracelets!' Maria jerked so furiously against her bonds that her shoulder crashed against the wall, which was covered in padded leather. Dr Claybourn touched the cushioning with obvious pride.

'Horse-hair. We spare no expense to ensure our guests do not hurt themselves.'

Maria issued another string of nonsense, wriggling in vain against her bindings.

'Now, Maria. This will do you no good. You must master yourself before we can release you.'

Maria hissed at him. Her eyes narrowed as they landed on Susan. She looked her up and down. When her glance reached Susan's hands, her nostrils flared.

'Cobwebs!' she cried in obvious distress.

'What is it?' Susan held out her palms to show Maria they were empty, embarrassed to note that her cuffs were white with powdered chalk. Even though she brushed them every night, they never seemed to stay clean. Maria wriggled furiously and shouted a heap of disconnected words, including some that Susan suspected might be obscenities

'I was afraid of this,' said Dr Claybourn. 'We are distressing her. We had better leave.'

Maria jerked violently towards Susan, who flinched back in alarm. Richard stepped forward to restrain Maria and Dr Claybourn propelled Susan swiftly from the padded cell.

'I'm sorry you had to witness that,' said Dr Claybourn, as Richard locked the door. 'Her inability to communicate frustrates her, with unfortunate consequences. Richard, make up a sedative, will you?'

'I… I should leave,' said Susan, desperate to leave such a dismal place. Maria's plight had shocked and appalled her. A sharp ache pinched the bridge of her nose and her lungs burned. She hurried back towards the chamber.

'Won't you come to tea?' asked Amelia, from the doorway of one of the small chambers, but Susan hurried past, in urgent need of fresh air. From another chamber, a skeletal figure appeared. She was so gaunt her shaved head appeared almost skull-like. Amelia called out to her.

'Sarah, we're having tea. Won't you join us?'

The skeletal woman shuddered and disappeared back into her cell. Susan continued on, through the high chamber, bursting out into cold, clear air. It was so bright after the dimness of the windowless, airless infirmary, she had to close her eyes or go blind.

'That woman—Sarah.' she gasped in horror. 'Is she starved?'

'Do not mistake what you have seen,' said Dr Claybourn. 'Sarah has a severe neurasthenic disorder that gives her a terrible fear of food. It's her own choice not to eat. We do what we can, feeding by tube when her condition is at its worst.'

'How many patients have you?'

'Just four. Those that you have seen, and poor Mr Brinish, who is another case of senile decay, like poor Amelia. I hope you are not distressed. My own enthusiasm for the subject is so great, I feel certain that others will wish to share it, but I see that you are too delicate for such sights. Forgive me.'

Susan took another steadying breath. She could not deny the experience had shaken her.

'Poor Maria. Can anything be done?'

'I will try. She has no money herself, poor thing. My wife… my wife would have me get rid of her, but I am determined to find a cure, whatever the expense.'

'I honour you,' said Susan, shivering. She had forgotten to retrieve her shawl from Amelia, but could not countenance going back for it. 'To have forgot how to speak—how dreadful.'

'Let me get you some tea,' Dr Claybourn insisted, leading her gently back to the main house.

In the kitchen, there was no sign of Mrs Clegg. One of the bells was jangling furiously. The tinny sound intensified the ache behind Susan's eyes and she sank into a chair and pressed her palm to her forehead. Mrs Claybourn entered.

'What has occurred?' she snapped. 'Miss Mottram, you are not unwell, I hope?'

'Ah, my dear,' said Dr Claybourn, licking his lips. 'We have had a small incident. One of my patients absconded, but all is well now. Miss Mottram returned her.'

'Which patient?'

'Amelia. The old lady,' said Dr Claybourn promptly.

'You permitted Miss Mottram to enter the infirmary?'

His wife pressed her lips together so tightly, they went white.

'I found Amelia out on the moors,' Susan explained, regretting the opprobrium being directed towards the blameless Dr Claybourn. 'She was very cold, so I felt it best to return her to the infirmary as soon as possible.'

'Was Miss Mottram exposed to any of your other patients?'

'She met them all except Mr Brinish,' her husband admitted.

'Maria?' Mrs Claybourn gave him a thunderous look. 'I understand she can be temperamental.'

'I wished to show Miss Mottram we had nothing to hide.'

'Well, I hope there will be no unfortunate consequences. Miss Mottram's health is not to be trifled with.'

'Thank you, ma'am,' said Susan gratefully.

'And we must think of the privacy of your patients. I hope, Miss Mottram, we may rely on your discretion?'

'Of course.'

'Won't you take some tea and cake?' suggested Dr Claybourn solicitously, looking around for Mrs Clegg. Susan declined his offer. She was still too unnerved to think of eating. Tendrils of fear sprouted within her breast. Suppose she had been infected with Sarah's affliction. Or Maria's? The idea made her shudder. The bell continued to jangle, which did little to help with the pain in her head. At last it stopped. A few moments later the door from the corridor opened to admit Marion and Helena.

'We have been calling for tea this half hour!' Helena protested.

'Why is Miss Mottram here on her half-day?' asked Marion, glaring at Susan.

'She was discovered in the infirmary.' Mrs Claybourn sniffed her disapproval.

Marion fingered the back of her head as if searching for a loose pin, although, as usual, her hair was secured so severely it might have been encased in wax. 'Let us give the place its true designation. An asylum, plain and simple. Miss Mottram, I hope you did not inhale?'

'It seemed preferable to suffocation,' Susan said weakly.

'I am hopeful no harm was done,' said Dr Claybourn. 'We were inside for a short time only, and Miss Mottram's cheerful disposition is a certain guard against disorders of the mind.'

'In that case, we should be more concerned for Marion,' Helena remarked.

'Nevertheless, even a small dose could be dangerous to one so diminutive,' Marion insisted, ignoring her sister's jibe. 'We should send Miss Mottram home. If she be afflicted, her people may seek recompense.'

It was not the first time Marion had suggested Susan should be let go. Susan wondered why her fellow teacher was so eager to be rid of her.

'I am quite well,' she insisted, concerned that Marion's argument was exactly the kind to find favour with Mrs Claybourn.

'We must be watchful,' said Dr Claybourn. 'There must be no further exposure. And Miss Mottram, let me know if you grow forgetful or distracted. Or if you have any dark or unnatural thoughts. We must guard against the slightest hint of paranoia.'

'And never enter that place again,' said his wife. Susan, her head throbbing, was happy to promise never to set foot inside the infirmary again, if it could possibly be helped.

11

A Gift of Books

Susan was relieved to find her appetite quickly restored and that there was no sign of her forgetting how to speak, even if the exact date of the Battle of Bosworth temporarily escaped her during a lesson on the Wars of the Roses. For days it did nothing but rain. Damp seeped into the stones of the school and the walls began to give off an unpleasant odour. Whenever Susan saw Tabitha, the girl would jerk her head in the direction of Heathersage Manor and whisper of witches and potions. Mrs Claybourn said it must be rats, and stalked the corridors, knocking on wooden panels and pressing her nose against the stone as if she might sniff them out herself. She was trailed by Mr Clegg, shoulders hunched by rheumatism, his bony arms laden with rat traps as he struggled to keep up with Mrs Claybourn's brisk pace. When this approach proved only modestly successful, Mrs Claybourn obtained a scrawny black cat with little white disks beneath each eye, that reminded Susan of the half-moon glasses worn by its new owner. It had a vicious temper. When Susan tried to make friends, it curved its back and hissed at her. From then on, she left it well alone.

Since it would be another week before Susan was again at liberty, she decided that, if she were to help Mary, she must apply to Miss Sutcliffe in writing. Once this resolution had been made, her letter was soon written.

Dear Miss Sutcliffe,

I hope you will excuse my writing to you. Be assured, I have no intention of repeating those mistaken assertions for which you so rightly reprimanded me. I blush to think of my foolishness and can only beg forgiveness and hope you will forget my baseless accusations as swiftly as I wish to myself.

I will come at once to the point of my application. There is a little girl in my class who has been of much concern to me. She has yet to speak a word in my hearing and seems to live apart from the world. Indeed, until recently, she has shown little desire to engage with it at all. I was informed by my employer that she was a girl of limited understanding. Although I never believed this to be true, I had no suspicion of the true state of things until I received your letter. Your own experience suggested to me a possible cause for Mary's conduct: that, like you, she is deaf. As I am ill-qualified to help her, I wonder if I might prevail upon you to visit Matterdale Hall, that myself and Mary might benefit from your guidance? I believe her lot will be greatly improved if she could learn to communicate. Nothing but an earnest admiration for your accomplishments and a hope that you might share my desire to further Mary's happiness would bring me to make this request. From what you were so generous to confide in your letter, I understand this would entail significant sacrifice on your part, one that I have no right to ask of you. Yet if you could see Mary and how much she has to share with the world, I believe you would wish to help.

Yours, most respectfully,

Susan Mottram

The letter was sent by the penny post and Susan awaited a reply with impatience. When days passed with no response, Susan was surprised by the intensity of her disappointment. Although Miss Sutcliffe had no obligation to respond, she had felt certain that the young lady had a sympathetic nature. Had she been wrong? She had almost given up expecting a reply when a large parcel arrived as the girls were at luncheon, hand-delivered by a servant.

'I see it is from Heathersage,' Marion remarked stiffly. 'You should be wary of gifts from such a source.'

The parcel contained two large books. Susan opened the first to reveal pages and pages of line-drawings of hands and fingers in various attitudes. Beneath each drawing was typed the associated word or letters. The pictures and writing were large, perfectly suitable for a child. As Susan opened the second book, which proved a duplicate of the first, a note slipped from between its leaves, penned in a neat hand that Susan recognised.

Dear Miss Mottram,

Please accept the loan of these two books from my father's collection. I have sent two so that you might learn alongside Mary, for a child cannot communicate in isolation. I regret I do not have the courage to visit Mary in person, but I hope these books will help her, as they did me.

Yours most sincerely,

Cassandra Sutcliffe

Susan felt a jolt of regret that Miss Sutcliffe would not be visiting the school. However, she quickly dismissed her disappointment as unworthy. It had been generous of Miss Sutcliffe to send the books, and it would be unfair to wish her into a situation she must find distressing.

'What have you there?' Marion asked.

'Miss Sutcliffe has sent these books to help poor Mary Martin.'

'What made you apply to such a person?'

Susan would not betray Miss Sutcliffe's confidence, no matter how much Marion glared at her.

'I understand Mr Sutcliffe keeps a good library.'

'How would someone so new to our neighbourhood know anything about the state of Mr Sutcliffe's library?'

Susan coloured. She was unused to deception and it seemed she wasn't very good at it.

'I'm surprised you are not better acquainted with the Sutcliffes,' she returned, rather than answer Marion's question, 'you being such close neighbours.'

'You are aware of the rumours concerning the daughter?'

'You cannot believe such nonsense?'

'Sorcery must be in her blood. How else could her mother, a complete blackamoor, induce an Englishman to marry her?'

'If Miss Sutcliffe's mother were half as handsome as she, there would be no mystery.'

'It seems you are quite under the young lady's spell,' Marion said with an odd expression.

'She does not deserve to be reviled purely for the colour of her skin. I make no apologies for wishing to know her better. I have so few acquaintances in these parts.'

'You do not make much of our poor company, I see,' said Marion. 'I hope you may come to appreciate it, in due course.'

She attempted a smile. From the strange contortion of her lips, Marion was as little practised in smiling as Susan was at deception. At that moment Mrs Claybourn appeared in the doorway, an open pocket-watch in her hand.

'Marion, Miss Mottram, why are the girls not back in the classroom? I have been waiting for my students these past five minutes.'

12

A Gift of Apples

The arrival of Miss Sutcliffe's books sent the junior class into a flurry of excitement. Susan was happy to encourage anything that hinted at enthusiasm and permitted the girls to examine them. However, the girls' zeal soon waned as they realised that study and application were required to learn this strange new language. Only Anne Fordyce showed any inclination to continue. Mary pored over her copy, the patch of skin between her pale eyebrows dimpling in concentration as she ran her forefinger across the pictures. Yet her progress was slow. Interpreting many of the signs required an ability to read and Mary's education had been so neglected that she was illiterate. Susan started with objects that she could point out to Mary, using the illustrations in the book to form the signs. Some, like 'house' or 'bird' were quite intuitive, but others were harder to memorise. Susan spent the evenings practising with Mary while the other girls were at their writing, learning alongside her pupil.

She even gave up her half days so that they might continue their lessons, her spirits lifting as she felt, at last, as if she were doing some good.

Perhaps someone else appreciated her efforts, for one evening, as she went into the refectory, she found a bowl with four ripe apples waiting for her upon her trestle table. There was no note or explanation, but there could be no mistaking they were meant for her.

'Mrs Clegg, did you leave me those apples?' Susan asked, as she helped serve up mutton stew, struggling to discern any meat amongst the lumps of turnip and carrot peelings.

'Apples is for the family only, except what I set aside for Tabby,' said Mrs Clegg, hefting her ladle as if it were filled with lead instead of a watery concoction of vegetables that may have briefly shared a pot with some mutton bones. 'Mebbee they're from Heathersage Manor, like them books?'

Susan's heart leapt. Could they be a gift from the intriguing Miss Sutcliffe? Perhaps an overture of friendship after all? The idea warmed her, for she had felt so friendless and alone since leaving Mama and Florence. And the generous gifts of the language books proved that Miss Sutcliffe had a kind heart. Mrs Claybourn materialised in the doorway.

'Where did you get those apples?' she asked.

'They were left as a gift,' Susan explained quickly, before Mrs Claybourn could mistake her for a thief. 'I wondered if they were from you? Or Dr Claybourn, perhaps?'

'What a ridiculous notion!'

'Yes, quite,' said Susan.

'Why on earth would we do such a thing, when you are paid a perfectly good wage?'

'There can be no rational reason for such a step, indeed,' Susan agreed.

'Even supposing I were satisfied with your performance, which I am not, for the girls are making too much noise. We can hear them from the parlour. If you cannot meet my expectations as a junior teacher, I will employ someone who does.'

Susan wished to remark that any person who could meet Mrs Claybourn's expectations must be in possession of an extra set of arms or the ability to split herself in two. Remembering her mother and Florence, she held her tongue.

After supper and overseeing the girls with their copybooks, Susan took her apples to her chamber. She came across Richard Clegg on the first-floor landing, his hands in his pockets. She wasn't certain, but she thought he had emerged from the passage that led to the family chambers.

'How come you to be here?' she exclaimed, unsettled by his sudden proximity.

'What you got there?' he grinned, nodding at the apples. His eyes glinted in the light of her candle. For a horrid moment, she wondered if they might be from him.

'They were a gift,' she said stiffly. 'I do not know who from. I would return them if I could. Secrecy in the giving of gifts is most improper.'

'If I gave you a gift, it'd be sweeter than a bowl of apples.'

'Such as comfits, or candy?' Susan asked with a puzzled frown.

'That ain't what I meant.' He grinned as if his words had a secret meaning that Susan did not understand. 'Sorry to break yer heart, but it weren't me.'

'I will endeavour to overcome my disappointment,' returned Susan drily.

He fingered the lapel of his pea-green coat.

'Your person is pleasing enough, but you've no money. I intend to be a gentleman. Young lady or widder, I'm not particular, as long as they're rich. Purse your lips, will you? You don't like plain speaking?'

'I admire few things more than frankness, but no woman of sense would welcome the attentions of an acknowledged fortune hunter.'

'Yet I bet that if someone had left you a hundred pound instead of them apples, you'd not be looking to give it back.'

'In such a case, I would be even more eager to return it. I could never accept such a large gift without knowing from whom it came, or the reason it was given.'

Richard gawped at her.

'You'd turn down a hundred pound? If you ain't careful, Dr Claybourn will lock you away with the rest of the lunatics!'

With a dry chuckle, he went on his way. Susan went into her chamber. She stopped still in the doorway. Something was not quite right. Her handful of books were aligned with too much perfection, as if someone had rifled through them and set them back a little too neatly. The clasps on her trunk, which she was certain she had left closed, were open. She pulled it from beneath the bed and examined its contents. Susan kept her letters beneath her neatly folded petticoats and undergarments. Excepting Miss Sutcliffe's brief missives, all were from her mother or Florence. She took them up and turned them in her hands. The thin blue ribbon which secured them was intact, but the knot took some dexterity to release. She could have sworn she had tied a bow.

She wondered then what Richard had been doing upstairs, when he wasn't even supposed to be in the main house. Had he been rifling through her things? The idea made her quite ill, but it was impossible to be certain and she couldn't bear the thought of asking him.

Unable to ascertain the provenance of the apples, Susan decided to share them among her class. The dilemma of how to divide four apples among fifteen girls generated a hitherto untapped enthusiasm for arithmetic, motivated by a desire in the breast of each girl to obtain a fair share of the bounty. Without any of them comprehending it, Susan was able to instil some of the basic principles of both long division and fractions, and she considered the day a resounding success.

Autumn turned to winter. The last of the colour leached from the heathers and the moors turned brown and drab. Swirling winds sent icy draughts along the corridors and Susan pleaded with Mrs Claybourn for a fire to be lit in the refectory in the evenings. She was supported by Dr Claybourn, who pointed out the dangers and, more significantly as far as his wife was concerned, the additional costs associated with the girls catching chills.

'I would of course do my best in such an eventuality, but I specialise in sickness of the mind, not of the body,' he said.

Not for the first time, Susan felt him to be her only real ally at Matterdale Hall, and was increasingly ashamed that her first instinct had been to laugh at his appearance. His civility and joviality were welcome distractions from her homesickness and self-doubt. Even his waistcoats, although invariably hard on the eye, were welcome as an antidote to the drab monotony of the rest of her existence. Together Susan and Dr Claybourn won over the reluctant Mrs Claybourn. Yet even with the fire blazing, the refectory was so large that most of the heat was sucked up into the rafters. The girls huddled together on the benches, donning fingerless woollen gloves to keep their hands warm as they scratched out their lines. Any suggestion of heating the dormitories was met with a firm negative. Mrs Claybourn declared it too dangerous to have a fire in a room of unsupervised children. Susan would have applauded such concern for her pupils' welfare had she not suspected it was a smokescreen for saving money. Susan's own chamber was not exempt from this proscription. Each night she wrapped her cashmere shawl around her shoulders, grateful that Dr Claybourn had returned it to her, and shivered beneath her thin blankets until she fell asleep. The wintry weather brought one small comfort. The lingering smell of decay that had haunted the hall had finally disappeared. Mrs Claybourn congratulated herself on the success of her new feline employee, but Susan suspected the rats had run away in search of somewhere more hospitable.

13

In Which Susan Suffers a Disappointment

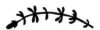

As November slid into December, Susan's spirits began to lift. In a few short weeks she would see Florence and her dear mama. The countryside seemed to celebrate in sympathy as a hoar frost gave the moors a sparkling, crystalline appearance and the sprawling holly in the corner of the grounds burst into a festive profusion of berries. Susan's joy was to be short-lived. Mrs Claybourn stepped noiselessly into her classroom one morning and asked Susan if she would join the family that evening for supper.

'Who will supervise the girls?'

'I think they can do without you for one evening. You are to be congratulated on their behaviour.'

Ever since Isabella's beating, the girls had given no trouble, but, even seeing the benefits, Susan would never be convinced that Marion's approach was right. The girls, and Isabella in particular, were more sullen than studious, and Susan suspected any evils had been hidden rather than banished. Her employer informed her there was no need to change her dress.

'It is an informal family affair and we never change. As you know, we do not keep a maid and Helena finds dressing up beyond her strength.'

The centrepiece for supper was a shrunken joint of gammon that seemed lost on the platter carried in by Mrs Clegg, who struggled even with such a limited load. She was assisted in serving by Tabitha, whose unusual eagerness was explained when Susan saw her picking left-over pieces of gammon and fat directly from the plates and stuffing them in her mouth as she cleared away. Such behaviour would not have been tolerated at the parsonage, but Susan didn't feel it was her place to tell tales. Having herself partaken of the same stinting fare as the girls, she did not begrudge Tabitha her reward. She marvelled at such a change in her own perspective after only a few short months as a schoolteacher and wondered whether any other of her previously held principles were at risk.

She was grateful for Dr Claybourn's presence. Without him, supper would have been an uncomfortable affair. For once, he had forgone his brash waistcoats in favour of a bottle-green smoking jacket and gold cravat arranged in substantial folds and pinned in place with a mother-of-pearl brooch. Marion wore her usual plain black, unadorned with lace or jewellery. Her unsmiling gaze landed so frequently upon Susan that she began to fear her collar might be crooked or that she had food in her teeth. Helena gave off such a profusion of different scents—jasmine, lavender and violet battling with cloves, thyme and other spices—that Susan suspected her perfume had been fabricated by a small child who had been set loose in the flower garden and then been given the keys to the pantry.

'Have you been reading today, Helena?' her father inquired. 'Do you enjoy your latest novel?'

'I scarcely recall. The heroine is a strange creature indeed. I do not think I shall finish it,' Helena said wearily. 'Why must these authors write at such length? Five words, where one would suffice. And such unrealistic characters. The women are always walking, or visiting, or dancing. Such excessive activity seems quite improbable.'

'I do not understand why young people waste their time reading novels,' Mrs Claybourn remarked. 'It fills their heads with impractical nonsense, when there is work to be done. Which reminds me, Marion, we have sheets that need mending.'

'Cannot you ask Helena? I am teaching all day while she is at leisure.'

'You know it is beyond my capabilities, Mama,' Helena protested. 'You might as well ask Marion to attempt a smile.'

'Marion will mend the sheets and we shall have no more discussion on the matter.'

A muscle in Marion's cheek convulsed.

'Do you read, Miss Claybourn?' asked Susan, feeling compassion for her fellow teacher. Their days were arduous enough without additional chores in the evenings. Marion looked as if something sharp had wedged itself between her teeth and was snagging her cheek.

'I prefer instructional volumes.'

'That's a fib!' Helena protested. 'Why, only last week you stole my *Lady Audley's Secret*, which I had only just received from

Marianne Ratcliffe

the publisher. Don't think I didn't notice the pages had been cut.'

'I took it by mistake,' said Marion, a hint of pink rising upon her cheeks. 'I have no interest in such lurid tales, full of reckless coachmen and foolish young women.'

'You know a great deal about it for someone who claims to read only instructional volumes,' Helena remarked. Susan was amused at the idea of Marion being a lover of romantic novels, but, feeling her eyes upon her, she suppressed a smile.

'Only a fool would find pleasure in such things,' Marion returned stiffly. 'I'm sure Miss Mottram is too sensible to be entertained by such nonsense.'

'I thank you for your compliment, but I'm afraid it is undeserved,' said Susan. 'I delight in a well-told romance or novel of intrigue. Our own lives can sometimes feel so dull and constrained—what could be more enjoyable than escaping to distant realms, or vicariously partaking of some thrilling adventure?'

'To escape, yes,' Helena echoed wistfully, massaging the top of her head with her hand.

'What have you to complain about?' Marion asked bitterly.

'You do not know what I suffer!'

'To be sure, it is hard to keep track. You have listed symptoms enough these past weeks to fill an almanac.'

'Enough,' said Dr Claybourn sternly. For an instant, although his cheeks were as rosy as ever, his expression was so altered that Susan might have mistaken him for a man of temper. By the time he turned towards her, his habitual good humour had returned.

'I understand that you have been attempting to teach Mary

Martin. I fear you are wasting your time on such a defective child, heh-heh.'

'I am convinced the only thing wrong with Mary is her hearing. She learns words at a great rate.'

He listened attentively as she explained the principles of sign language.

'Well, well, I commend you. I beg you will keep me apprised of your progress. I am eager to hear whatever the child is able to convey.'

Susan, grateful for his interest, assured him that she would be delighted to do so.

'However,' continued Dr Claybourn, 'I should warn you that impaired children such as Mary have difficulty comprehending the difference between reality and their own imaginings, heh-heh. When she is at last able to communicate, it is most likely to be nonsense.'

'Speaking of Miss Martin,' interjected Mrs Claybourn, who had been listening to their discussion with ill-concealed impatience, 'her parents have written to ask if we might keep her over the holidays. They have house guests and do not want Mary in the way.'

'Poor Mary,' Susan exclaimed. 'What a sad fate, to be left all alone when the other girls return to their families.'

'Isabella Brownloe and Anne Fordyce are also to remain here. They must be supervised.' Mrs Claybourn looked to her husband, who cleared his throat.

'Miss Mottram, since you have become such a good friend to Mary, we were hoping you might be persuaded to undertake the role.'

Susan couldn't hide her dismay.

'But I am to go home!' she protested. 'It was agreed.'

'We cannot leave the girls unattended,' said Marion. 'They will run wild.'

'Will you not be here?' Even as Susan asked the question, the thought of any girls left under Marion's care over Christmas made her tender heart swell in sympathy. Not even Isabella deserved such a fate.

'We have been invited to Harrogate by my cousin,' said Dr Claybourn. 'He is a man of wide acquaintance and we hope to secure additional pupils from among his set. I also plan to speak at a meeting of medical colleagues. I am hoping one of them might be able to refer me an interesting case—something aligned to my area of research. And, who knows, I may find myself a patron at last.'

'Who will care for your patients?'

'Richard has his instructions. Have no fear, he will ensure they remain safely within the infirmary.'

'You will be content with mutton for Christmas dinner, I'm sure,' said Mrs Claybourn. 'And since your pupils are too young for wine, you would not expect us to open the cellar merely on your account.'

Susan was dismayed to realise they had already presumed upon her agreement. Dr Claybourn placed his hand on hers.

'It is an imposition on your good nature, Miss Mottram, but our visit is necessary for the continued success of the school.'

'We need more students, and wealthier ones, if I am to continue to justify the expense of a junior teacher,' added Mrs Claybourn.

Susan wrestled with her conscience. She had been looking forward to seeing her mother and sister for weeks. To be home, among those she loved, and who loved her in return. She had a thousand questions to ask them, and so much to impart. Not everything could be said in a letter. However, her duty was clear.

'I trust there will be a supplement to my stipend to reflect the additional time worked,' Susan said at last, for she refused to be taken utterly for granted. Mrs Claybourn's mouth tightened.

'Of course there will, heh-heh!' exclaimed her husband with a chuckle that even a glare from his wife could not suppress. After some negotiation, it was agreed that Susan would be given an additional pound for each week of the holiday period. Susan retired at once to write to her mother, so that she and Florence might have fair warning of her change in plans. She enclosed her full quarterly allowance after deductions made by Mrs Claybourn for the broken slate, keeping nothing back for herself. The additional money she would be paid over Christmas could cover any small expenses of her own.

Hiding her own disappointment, she explained to Mary, by a mixture of drawing and signing, that the little girl would not be going home. Mary's lip began to tremble but when Susan made her understand that she, too, would be staying, Mary broke into a smile and threw her arms round Susan's waist. After such a demonstration of affection, Susan could no longer be sorry that she had acquiesced to the Claybourns' request.

14

The Claybourns Depart for Harrogate

The holidays arrived and those girls that were leaving did so on foot, by traps or aboard carriages, according to their relative fortunes. Susan stood in the doorway and watched them leave with undisguised envy. As soon as the last girl had left, the Claybourns began preparations for their own departure.

'Now, remember, Miss Mottram,' said Mrs Claybourn, locking all the family rooms except the second parlour, 'the good conduct of my pupils is in your hands. Mrs Clegg has my keys and strict instructions regarding the use of sugar. For Christmas day itself, I've ordered you half a leg of mutton.'

Susan dipped her head in acknowledgement, for Mrs Claybourn clearly wished to be thanked for such unaccountable generosity.

'I put by a dozen candles, which should be sufficient. At my husband's suggestion, you may use the second parlour. I shall be examining it for damage on my return.'

Dr Claybourn hurried past, followed by old Mr Clegg, who was bent double, a large trunk on his back.

'My dear, the trap has not yet arrived.' Dr Claybourn took out his pocket-watch with a worried frown. 'I fear we will miss our train.'

'I ordered it not to arrive until the quarter hour,' replied his wife complacently. 'Mr Smith charges by the hour and I refuse to pay his driver to sit idle on my driveway. Where are the girls? We must be ready to depart the instant the trap arrives.'

'Miss Helena's still in her bed,' croaked Mrs Clegg as she shuffled blindly past, her vision obscured by the tall stack of hatboxes she carried in her arms.

'Fetch her, Henry,' said Mrs Claybourn. Her husband headed obediently towards the main stairs. He had been gone no more than five minutes when the clip-clop of horse hooves could be heard on the driveway.

'Marion!' Mrs Claybourn called out in annoyance. 'Helena! We must leave at once!'

Marion emerged from the second parlour.

'Marion, you have not even got your coat! Whatever have you been doing?'

'I would much prefer to stay,' Marion said. 'I believe I would be more useful here, assisting Miss Mottram. She is very inexperienced to take on such a responsibility.'

Susan was surprised at the offer, and aggrieved it had not been made sooner, for then she might have returned home herself.

'Marion, I insist you come. Miss Mottram doesn't need you

hanging about her like some gloomy spectre at the feast,' said Dr Claybourn, from the top of the stairs. Susan gave him a grateful smile. Helena was leaning heavily against her father. The buttons on the front of her bodice were misaligned and her hair hung loose and uncombed. As they reached the foot of the stairs, a strong floral scent filled the corridor, underpinned by something much less pleasant.

'Helena insisted she was not well enough to travel, but when I mentioned the handsome countenance of my cousin's ward it effected a miraculous cure,' said Dr Claybourn. 'If I could only prescribe a pretty young woman or handsome fellow instead of pills and ointments, I would not want for clients.'

'That is not true!' Helena protested weakly, her face extremely pale behind the rouge smeared on each cheek. 'I am a dutiful daughter; that is all. And you threatened to carry me out in my nightgown if I did not dress.'

Susan stepped forward to assist Dr Claybourn and together they helped Helena into the trap.

'Your prescription has no effect on Marion, I see,' Susan remarked, as the elder Miss Claybourn proceeded to examine their coachman through narrowed eyes, no doubt looking for signs of recklessness.

'If only we *could* find a suitor to Marion's taste. Such an exceptional character is more likely to be met amongst the hordes of Harrogate than here at Matterdale Hall.' He lowered his voice so that only Susan could hear. 'Wish me luck, for I face heavy odds.'

'Miss Helena, you have forgotten this.' Richard hurried forward with a purple hatbox.

'Not another hat?' Marion protested as Helena seized Richard's offering eagerly.

'You may be content to look like a haggard old widow Marion, but one of us should make a respectable showing.'

'Your current state can hardly be called respectable.'

'How should one describe such an example of sisterhood?' Dr Claybourn asked, of nobody in particular. 'Were I to devise a collective noun, I would steal from the crows and call them an argument of sisters. That would do capitally, would it not, heh-heh?'

His daughters did not share his amusement.

'I think it might be murder,' mused Susan.

'Good grief, I hope it does not come to that, heh-heh!' Dr Claybourn exclaimed. Susan put her hand over her mouth to hide her smile.

'Of what are you speaking?' snapped Mrs Claybourn, already perched on the trap.

'The collective noun. I have heard it called a murder of crows,' said Susan.

'Is it really, heh-heh? Of what was I thinking, I wonder? Helena, that hatbox is occupying my seat.' The rickety trap groaned as Dr Claybourn added his considerable weight to that of his family and their many possessions. 'If you had only let me order a carriage, my dear, as I suggested,' he said, looking for somewhere to sit.

'At twice the cost? I do not think so.'

'I shall carry it on my knees,' said Helena, lifting the hatbox so her father could sit down. 'It is my very favourite bonnet, I would not part with it.' She clutched it to her chest in the way a small child might clasp a beloved doll.

'Carry on driver, and be sharp about it,' snapped Mrs Claybourn. 'I expect to be recompensed if we miss our train.'

'Have a safe journey,' Susan said brightly, as the poor cart-horse strained valiantly against its harness until it coaxed the overloaded trap into motion.

Dr Claybourn doffed his hat and Susan waved back before returning to the house. She made for the second parlour, eager to explore her new domain. A cottage piano sat in one corner and Susan rushed forward with a cry of delight. Alas, after playing only a few notes, she discovered it was horribly out of tune. The rest of the parlour was in a similarly unhappy state. The yellow wallpaper was peeling and mottled with mould. The floor was bare planking, excepting a threadbare hearthrug and, besides the piano, there was only a small table and a scattering of mismatched chairs. A pasteboard box wrapped in a pink ribbon sat on the table, with a card addressed to 'Miss Mottram' in block letters. Inside the box was a glazed fruit cake that smelled of cinnamon and brandy. With a cry of delight Susan hastened back to the courtyard to thank Dr Claybourn, for such a thought-ful gift could only have come from him, but the trap had already disappeared over the gentle rise towards Hustanton.

The hall seemed vast and empty without the girls. Mary had disappeared during the hubbub surrounding the Claybourns' departure. Isabella took up station in a lumpy old armchair and pretended not to hear when Susan suggested any activities. Anne's eyes were red from weeping. If this was to be the pattern for the holidays, they would be miserable indeed. Susan tried not to think of the previous Christmas, filled with singing and laugh-ter, her family all about her. How much her life had changed. She comforted Anne who, after a gentle probing, owned to being homesick.

111

'I love our little park, especially at this time of year,' she sobbed. 'I wish I was pretty, like my sister. She's Mama's pet. Papa says I'm so pale and sickly-looking, he can scarce believe we are sisters. I suppose that's why they don't want me at home. I wish I was there.'

It said much for the bleakness of Matterdale Hall that Anne preferred to be somewhere she was neglected and despised. Susan attempted to cheer her.

'Is there nobody at home who is kind to you?'

'Oh yes! Stephen, my eldest brother. He taught me to read and gives me the best gifts. We always put up the decorations together when he comes back from school. I suppose he must do it alone this year.'

Her lip began to wobble.

'Decorations? Why, Anne, what an excellent thought. Let us do what we can to brighten up the place.'

Anne's face lit up, and Susan was no less satisfied with her idea. She and Florence had always transformed the front parlour of the vicarage into a splendid emporium, glittering with candles and coloured streamers. If they could make Matterdale Hall half as festive, the holidays need not be so gloomy after all. Mrs Clegg, however, did not share her enthusiasm.

'I do not know what can be done. The missus never puts out a penny for decorations. If Miss Smythson's class hadn't made them paper ornaments last year, the hall would've been as bare as my Jack's head.'

'I'm surprised Mrs Claybourn permitted paper to be used for such a frivolous purpose. Perhaps it was this recklessness that led to Miss Smythson losing her position?'

'Oh no. They used old copybook pages, already written over.

The missus even praised Miss Smythson for her engine, or something like that. I wasn't sure what she meant.'

'Do you mean ingenuity?' Susan asked.

'Aye, that was the word. Why can't folks just speak plain?'

'Were the decorations kept?'

The housekeeper tipped out a basket of walnuts on the kitchen table.

'Mrs Claybourn never likes to throw things away. They'll be in the attic.'

The attic was accessed by a small door just beyond the servants' quarters. Mrs Clegg, after some demurring, was persuaded to lend Susan the household keys.

'You'll bring them back, won't you? The missus said I weren't to let them out of my sight, but them stairs play the devil with my poor knees.'

Anne and Mary were eager to search for the decorations, although Isabella refused to move from her chair. The attic was filled with boxes, stacked in tall columns. Cobwebs hung from the cross-beams and sent out white threads that formed slender bridges between the stacks. Susan lit a candle from her precious allowance and they began to search. A sudden, shadowy movement along the floorboard made Anne scream, and Susan's own heart palpitated until she held forth her candle and saw it was just the cat. It carried half a dead rat in its mouth and paused to eye Susan balefully. Susan felt a mixture of disgust and apprehension. She had a momentary fancy that the cat was a familiar for Mrs Claybourn, for with that pale glare and the half-moons beneath its eyes it certainly had something of her employer's countenance. She collected herself. Such superstitious imaginings were for little children, or those touched with madness. Even so, she was vastly relieved when the cat slunk away with its furry treasure.

Mary attracted Susan's attention by waving. She had found an old trunk, so battered and scratched that the initials could barely be made out. Susan brushed away the dust to reveal the initials H.V. She supposed it might have been Mrs Claybourn's before her marriage. Inside was an untidy pile of dresses, a confusion of check patterns and paisley prints. Such bright colours did not seem Mrs Claybourn's style, nor Marion's. Perhaps they had belonged to Helena, before her infirmities had got the better of her. Lifting a dress with a green and red check pattern, Susan saw a large square of material had been cut away from the skirt, and she recalled Dr Claybourn wearing a waistcoat in the same material. Mrs Claybourn never liked to waste anything. She closed the trunk and moved on. In amongst a stack of old hat boxes, they found their treasure—sheets of paper folded into flowers, the black lines of writing giving their petals a pleasing variegated appearance. Susan was filled with admiration for her predecessor, who was clearly a woman of resourcefulness. Whatever fault had led to her dismissal, it must have been grievous indeed, for Mrs Claybourn did not give praise lightly. However, when she lifted the flower from the top, it wilted in her hand, spotted with blight. She dug further down, but the entire box was ruined.

'Oh, that's a shame,' said Anne. 'They would have been very pretty.'

'Well, ain't we busy little sparrers?'

Anne yelped, and Susan was no less dismayed to turn and find Richard leaning casually against the doorjamb. Although he had denied it, she still suspected it was he who had rifled through her possessions. Was he now following her about? He folded his arms.

'Need some help? I'm always happy to assist a lady.'

'There is nothing to carry,' Susan said. 'Miss Smythson's decorations are ruined. I'm afraid they'll have to be thrown out.'

'I'll take 'em.' Richard lifted the box from her hands. She was forced, out of politeness, to thank him.

'I expect you'd rather be in Harrogate, Miss, attending fancy parties and dances with the Miss Claybourns,' he said, as they descended the servants' stairs. 'I bet they're having a right royal time.'

'I suspect Miss Marion finds little pleasure in such entertainments.'

His eyes settled on hers.

'But you think Miss Helena would like 'em?'

'I do not know her well enough to speculate on her feelings.'

'You'll put in a good word when they get back, won't you? Tell old Grundiguts how helpful I've been?'

'I would be delighted to tell Dr Claybourn you have diligently attended to your infirmary duties,' she said stiffly, 'but I could only do so if I believed it to be true.'

That got rid of him. She hoped to see him no more. Although she had few expectations for her own happiness over the next few weeks, Richard's society would certainly do nothing to improve it. She pitied Amelia and the other inmates of the infirmary, spending Christmas in his care.

At Susan's request, Mr Clegg cut them a basketful of holly from the tree in the grounds. Susan hung a sprig in each corner of the parlour but, since the rest of the walls remained bare, the holly only seemed to emphasise the paucity of their decorations. Susan considered asking Mrs Clegg to save the walnut shells, hoping the girls could gild them and make decorative little objects, but Mrs Clegg informed her that she had already thrown them out and, besides, there was nothing to paint them with.

'You should stop trying, Miss. It is our fate to be cold and miserable,' said Isabella, with a pained glance at their feeble fire, kept low due to their limited daily allotment of coals. When Mrs Clegg confirmed that Mrs Claybourn had provided neither money nor ingredients to make a plum pudding, Susan decided that urgent action was needed and ordered the girls to wrap up as warmly as possible.

'We shall go to Hustanton,' she said, resolving to sacrifice the precious pound note that she had received from Mrs Claybourn as an advance on her holiday pay. 'We cannot have Christmas without plum pudding.'

The sky was overcast and a cold drizzle hung in the air. Cloaked and bonneted, Susan and the girls walked the two miles along the muddy track to Hustanton. The village was equipped with a grocer's, a haberdasher's and a post office, as well as a bakery. Yet, as Susan examined the items on display, she was dismayed at the prices. She had hoped that, in addition to the pudding ingredients, she might have money left over for some decorations. However, it seemed they could eat well, or deck the parlour with some style, but not both.

As they passed the post office window, Mary stuck her nose against the glass and pointed to a selection of greetings cards that were displayed there.

The lady, she signed. *The book of hands. Say thank you.*

'You mean Miss Sutcliffe?' Susan asked, forgetting for a moment that Mary could not hear. The girl pointed to a card with a puppy lying on its back in the snow.

That one.

Susan smiled as she remembered the little beagle with the limp. She had thought often of its owner, filled with regret that her own naivety had scuppered any hope they might become friends. She doubted that Miss Sutcliffe would welcome any attempt at communication; Susan had written to thank her for the books, but had received no reply. However, Mary was insistent and so Susan purchased the greeting card on her behalf. She returned to the grocery shop to buy butter, spices, dried fruits and sugar for the plum pudding. She had just enough money left to buy the girls a stick of candy each. The candy was devoured during the walk home, and Susan wondered if she had really achieved anything. Christmas Day looked set to be a disappointing affair. After a simple luncheon of bread and butter, Mary opened the card and took great pains to write a message in her best hand. It was still little better than a scrawl.

To pretty lady. Thank for pictur book.

She signed it with her name and looked at Susan expectantly.

Writing—very good, Susan signed encouragingly, before adding an 'e' to complete 'picture'.

Lady we go visit. Now? Card give to her.

Susan tried to explain to Mary that Miss Sutcliffe didn't wish to be visited, but it proved beyond both their signing skills. Mary left the parlour and reappeared a few moments later wearing her coat, her arms filled with a large bundle which she thrust towards her teacher. It was Susan's own cloak and bonnet. Although they had not long returned from Hustanton, Susan hadn't the heart to discourage such a positive inclination. Anne declined to join them. Her delicate health had been taxed by the walk to the village, and Isabella, after looking out of the window at the grey clouds, said she would rather stay with Anne. Leaving Mrs Clegg in charge, Susan and Mary left via the kitchen, it being more convenient than the main door. Leaning with his back against the wall of the infirmary was Richard, one hand in the pocket of his frock coat, a pipe in the other. Mary tugged at Susan's hand, forcing her to increase her pace. Richard gave them a sardonic salute before tapping out his pipe against the wall and disappearing inside. Only when they were outside the grounds did Mary let go of Susan's hand and start to trot across the frozen moor, her precious card clutched against her tummy.

15

An Uninvited House Visit

Susan blew on Mary's hands, which were ice cold, and rubbed them as they waited before the ornate door of Heathersage Manor. She had knocked three times, the last loud enough to startle a pair of crows perched on the nearest gable. She was reaching towards the heavy knocker for a fourth time when the door was opened by an irritated Mrs Grainger.

'Oh.' She looked at Susan in disapproval. 'It's you, is it?'

Susan gently nudged her shy charge forward.

'Miss Mary Martin wishes to call upon Miss Sutcliffe.'

'Miss Sutcliffe does not receive visitors. I thought that had been made clear to you.'

The beagle emerged from behind Mrs Grainger's skirts, its bottom waggling in excitement. It lowered itself on its belly at Mary's feet and then rolled over. Mary bent down and rubbed the proffered tummy.

'Eppy, that is not polite!' Mrs Grainger protested, but Eppy writhed in delight under Mary's tickling. She then bounded up and scurried back inside, stopping just inside the threshold to look back, as if proffering an invitation. Mary ducked under Mrs Grainger's arm and ran in after her new friend.

'Mary!' Susan remonstrated futilely.

'You had better collect your student.' Mrs Grainger opened the door a fraction wider, her expression making it clear this concession was made most unwillingly.

'We will not disturb Miss Sutcliffe for long,' Susan said quickly, not wishing to be taken for one of those people who forced their acquaintance on others. 'Mary only wishes to thank her for the sign language books. They have been most helpful. I—' She stopped in her tracks. The spacious entryway was filled with a dense cornucopia of statues, pottery and other exotic objects. Species of stuffed animals and birds that Susan had never seen, either in life or in books, surrounded her, standing or crouched, their jaws and beaks parted in a silent chorus. Amid this profusion, the beagle jumped up at Mary so excitedly that all four paws left the floor. Mary was attempting to pat it on the head with one hand whilst holding the precious card safely above her head with the other.

'Eppy!' Mrs Grainger repeated, but her remonstrance had no effect. A door opened and Miss Sutcliffe appeared, accompanied by a blast of deliciously warm air. She looked left and right as if she had lost something. The instant her eyes lighted on Eppy, she ran forward and lifted the dog into her arms. Eppy began to lick her face, her white-tipped tail wagging so fast it was almost a blur. Delight spread across Miss Sutcliffe's face, elevating her handsome features to an almost ethereal beauty. However, when she caught sight of Susan, her expression clouded instantly.

Books. Mary wishes to thank you, Susan signed swiftly.

Miss Sutcliffe examined Susan with a baffled look. Concerned she had made a mistake with the signs, Susan repeated them, but Miss Sutcliffe remained as stiff as the marble statues and stuffed animals in the hallway. If not for Mary, Susan would have left at once in the face of such cold reserve, but she went to her pupil and guided her gently towards the young lady of the house. Mary proffered the card with a small curtsey. Miss Sutcliffe accepted the offering cautiously and read it with deliberation. Mary's fingers formed shapes.

Lady, kind.

A hesitant smile spread across Miss Sutcliffe's face. She tucked the card beneath her arm and touched her chin with the tips of her fingers, moving it towards Mary as if she were blowing a kiss, but from her chin instead of her lips. Susan recognised the sign as *thank you*. The young woman turned towards Mrs Grainger with a questioning look and there was an exchange of signs, too rapid for Susan to follow. Mrs Grainger turned towards Susan.

'I suppose you expect some refreshment,' she said sourly. Susan would have declined such a reluctant invitation, but Eppy disappeared through the open door and Mary ran after her. Miss Sutcliffe followed them, leaving Susan uncertain whether she was supposed to remain in the hall or had been invited to join them. Mrs Grainger offered no advice before disappearing down a corridor. Deciding she could not abandon Mary, Susan followed her into the parlour. Like the hallway, it was crammed full of exotic objects. Glass-fronted cabinets contained pottery and other knick-knacks. Rare and unusual items spilled out onto every surface, not excepting the windowsills. There was no order to the profusion. Delicate Japonica sat side by side with African totems, and the penchant for taxidermy was as evident as it had been in the hallway. Even Mary had stopped playing with Eppy to peer at the collection, her mouth gaping in awe and not a little apprehension. Susan gave her shoulder a reassuring squeeze.

Their hostess had retreated to one of the windows and stood clutching her elbows with her back turned to them. Mary, having gingerly touched the beak of a stuffed peacock and ascertained that it was not alive, turned her attention back to the beagle. Susan was left standing awkwardly in the centre of the room. A generous fire crackled in a large hearth and Susan took a few steps closer to its glorious warmth, just as Miss Sutcliffe turned towards her. Susan felt obliged to explain herself.

'Miss Sutcliffe,' she began, in formal tones, but that young lady gave an impatient gesture toward her ears and Susan stopped, chastising herself for her error. Speaking would do no good, yet the handful of phrases she had learned to sign with Mary were unequal to the task of explaining her unwelcome intrusion. Her hostess glanced repeatedly towards the door, as if anxious for Mrs Grainger to reappear. She made a step towards Susan, but then backed away, wringing her hands together. After pacing up and down a few times, she perched on the edge of a chair and gave such a sad, pleading look that Susan was prompted into action.

F-o-r-g-i-v-e she finger-spelled slowly, her fingers stumbling over the letters.

Miss Sutcliffe's hands flicked so quickly, Susan was forced to shake her head. The long, delicate fingers moved again, more slowly.

You walked here?

Susan nodded.

Cold.

Unsure if it was a statement or a question, Susan nodded again. Another glance at the door was followed by a flurry of signals, from which Susan discerned 'tea' and 'cake'.

Susan touched the tips of her fingers against her chin. *Thank you.* There was yet another awkward pause. Susan had reached the limit of her signing skills and for the first time she realised how much she relied on conversation to make a good impression. She felt Miss Sutcliffe's eyes on her and became aware of the chalk dust on her cuffs and the ring of damp that ran around the hem of her skirts. She was as relieved as Miss Sutcliffe when Mrs Grainger reappeared.

'I've ordered tea,' that lady said, her fingers relaying what Susan assumed was the same message to her young charge. There followed a flurried exchange that Susan was at a loss to understand.

'Cassandra says you sign like a child,' Mrs Grainger remarked.

'That seemed a lot of signals for such a short sentence.'

'I paraphrase.'

Mary and I have much to learn, Susan addressed Miss Sutcliffe, resorting to finger-spelling individual letters.

'I suggest you let me interpret,' said Mrs Grainger. 'Or else the tea will be cold before we can establish whether you take cream or sugar.'

'If it would make Miss Sutcliffe more comfortable,' said Susan, chastened. The tea things were brought in and the atmosphere became less awkward in the established process of giving and receiving cups and cake. Little was required other than polite smiles and nods and Miss Sutcliffe's shoulders, hitherto tense and hunched, flattened into a more relaxed pose. Yet, once they had drunk their tea, she made no move to make conversation. She folded her hands onto her lap, her fingers intertwined so they were locked together. On the table next to her was a bowl of apples, the same shape and colour as those that had been left on her table a month or so previously.

'Did you happen to send me some apples?' Susan blurted out.

Mrs Grainger directed some abrupt signals to her companion, who shook her head firmly before her features creased into an expression of doubt and confusion.

'No,' said Mrs Grainger, sharply. 'There could be no reason for such a gesture. You must have some kind of follower.'

Susan's brow furrowed. She had met no-one in Yorkshire who could be remotely described as an admirer. Who then, had sent her that gift? Was it the same person who had rifled through her things? A chill ran down her spine to think of it.

'You have an interesting collection,' she said to Mrs Grainger, gathering herself and nodding towards the cabinets.

'They belong to Mr Sutcliffe,' said Mrs Grainger, without recourse to her companion. 'He was a great traveller in his younger days, and even now he often goes abroad on business.'

'Is your father at home?' Susan asked, addressing Miss Sutcliffe and attempting to sign the words, for she felt they were excluding her.

'Mr Sutcliffe is in Harrogate on business,' said Mrs Grainger, before her companion could respond. Susan's relief must have shown on her face, for Miss Sutcliffe's slender fingers began to dance energetically.

'She says you must not think ill of her father. He is very pro-tective of her.'

'So I observed,' Susan remarked with a wry smile. 'Does he return for Christmas?'

'Yes,' was Mrs Grainger's blunt response.

Will you be with family at Christmas? Miss Sutcliffe had slowed her hand movements and Susan understood enough not to wait for Mrs Grainger to translate. Via Mrs Grainger, she explained the situation. Miss Sutcliffe seemed surprised.

The four of you, left all alone?

Mary had squatted down on the rug to watch Eppy as she completed a circuit of the room. The puppy then bounded towards Mary and jumped into her lap. The young girl gave out a squeal of laughter. Her joy was so infectious, Susan could not help joining in.

Mary, you are laughing! she signed delightedly.

Happy. Mary fingered back. Even Miss Sutcliffe's lip quirked in amusement.

'I have never heard her laugh before,' Susan said to Mrs Grainger. 'Indeed, it is the first time she has made any sound at all.'

Miss Sutcliffe looked questioningly at her companion, who made a few quick signs. A lengthy response was translated thus by Mrs Grainger: 'People think the deaf cannot laugh. To some, we are less than human. But we have feelings every bit as tender as the rest of mankind.'

Susan adjusted her skirts, recalling with shame the behaviour of Gwendoline and Agnes.

'Anyone who has seen your drawings cannot doubt your sensibility. Are you self-taught, or did you have a tutor?' she asked, looking to Mrs Grainger to translate. However, that lady did not deign to do so, instead responding directly to Susan.

'Miss Sutcliffe's father provided for her education. She lacked for nothing in that department. Other young women appear to have been less fortunate.'

Eppy nudged Susan's ankle, demanding attention. Looking down, Susan recalled quite suddenly the little pug with one eye they had taken in when Florence was still a child, its ugliness rendering it unwanted by its previous owner. It was a happy memory—why then did she feel as if a pebble had lodged itself in her throat? She reached down and scratched behind the beagle's ears.

'Miss Mottram?' Susan was roused from her memories to find the others staring at her. How long had she been distracted? Miss Sutcliffe was looking very serious and signing something that Susan was unable to comprehend.

'I'm sorry…' Susan began, as Mrs Grainger rose to her feet.

'It appears we are fatiguing you, Miss Mottram. Miss Sutcliffe insists we detain you no longer. This unexpected visit has been most wearisome for us all.'

Susan and Mary were swiftly ushered into the hallway, their bonnets thrust into their hands, and with little ceremony they were back in the wintry outdoors. As the door of Heathersage Manor clanged shut behind them, Susan rebuked herself for her inattentiveness. Miss Sutcliffe had been beginning to thaw, she was certain of it, before Susan had become lost in her own memories. How discourteous she must have seemed to her reluctant hostess. Her regret at her own behaviour was tempered by the abrupt way they had been shown the door. Any incivility on Susan's part had certainly been repaid in kind.

16

Susan Receives an Invitation

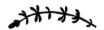

There was more than a week to go before Christmas Day. Isabella drifted around the corridors, complaining of boredom, yet was unwilling to settle to any activity. Anne joined Mary and Susan to pore over the sign language books, practising until their fingers ached. Susan was eager to improve her knowledge, deeply regretting her inability to make herself understood at Heathersage Manor. She felt a strong wish to communicate with Miss Sutcliffe without Mrs Grainger coming in the middle of things. Her smile, when she had lifted Eppy to lick her face, suggested a warm and vibrant nature lay behind that icy reserve, one that Susan longed to know better. And she had spoken, via her companion, of tender feelings. Susan was curious to understand what, or who, might raise such emotions, yet it seemed unlikely she would get another chance to investigate the mystery of Cassandra Sutcliffe. She wondered what sort of Christmas they would have at Heathersage. There had been no sign of decorations but with such a collection of curios, the house needed little to enliven it.

As Christmas Day approached, Susan felt as if the joylessness of Matterdale Hall had begun to infect them all. To lift everyone's spirits, she sacrificed Dr Claybourn's cake to make a tea party, but that provided only a short-lived pleasure. Susan took the last slice to Mrs Clegg and asked her what ideas she had for Christmas dinner itself.

'It's never been my place to have ideas. The missus don't encourage it.'

'What shall we have with the mutton?'

'Tatties and turnips. Or I might boil a leaf or two of cabbage, instead of turnips.'

'Let us be reckless and have both,' said Susan brightly. 'I wonder, dare we attempt a sauce?'

'I could ask Jack to cut us some mint to go in the tatties,' Mrs Clegg suggested doubtfully. 'I suppose you'll be wanting gravy an' all?'

'If it isn't too much trouble.'

No further concessions could be obtained, and Susan resigned herself to a plain affair. A letter from home, rather than raise her spirits, served only to depress them further. Her mother and sister were saddened she would not be with them. They, too, planned a frugal Christmas. Indeed, had Mr Potts not offered them a plucked chicken, they would have had nothing for dinner but roasted vegetables. Yet Susan knew that, had she been at home, the lack of luxuries would have been allayed by the warmth of the company. Here, she could not expect such happiness.

A few days before Christmas, everything was turned upside down by a letter that arrived by the penny post. From the neatly written direction, Susan knew at once it came from Miss Sutcliffe. Vastly surprised to receive a letter from such a source, she opened it immediately, even though Isabella was hanging over her shoulder with ill-concealed curiosity.

Dear Miss Mottram,

My father is returned from Harrogate and sends his compliments. I informed him of your visit with Mary and he is anxious to make your acquaintance. Understanding that you are left alone over the holidays, he asks whether you might be persuaded to celebrate Christmas Day at Heathersage Manor. Eppy would add her own pleas if she could speak, for she has positively pined after her young comrade and is forever running to the door in the hope that little Mary will appear. If neither Eppy's pleadings nor my father's are sufficient, then let me add my own, for I am sure the presence of you and your charges would do much to enliven our little party. I look forward to your prompt reply, that I might give the servants notice of any change in our arrangements.

Yours etc

Cassandra Sutcliffe

'What is it, Miss?' cried Isabella eagerly. 'You look surprised? Is it a nice surprise, or an unpleasant one?'

'That is a very good question.' Susan relayed the contents of the letter. Anne was all for declining the invitation, being extremely shy, but she was outvoted by Mary, delighted at the idea of being reunited with Eppy, and Isabella, who insisted anything would be an improvement on Matterdale Hall.

'Do you think we shall have goose?' she asked eagerly. 'And mince pies? Will there be a tree? Oh, I do hope there will.'

Susan could answer none of her questions. Despite Mary and Isabella's enthusiasm, she was uncertain whether to accept. The invitation was quite unexpected. Mr Sutcliffe did not seem the sort of man to invite people willingly into his house and Mrs Grainger had made her disapproval of Susan quite clear. Miss Sutcliffe had added her own pleas to the invitation, but Susan suspected her words were a matter of form. She had seen how uncomfortable Miss Sutcliffe was in company and could not imagine the scheme was likely to please her. Yet she could find no good reason to decline. As she hesitated, Mary and Isabella looked at her entreatingly.

'Shall I accept?' she asked.

Mary nodded vigorously and Isabella thrust paper and pen into Susan's hands.

'You should reply right away, Miss.'

But there was still Anne to convince, an object achieved by Susan describing some of the interesting objects at Heathersage Manor and mentioning that Mr Sutcliffe kept a library. Susan then wrote Miss Sutcliffe a short, business-like note, accepting the invitation. At the very least, their Christmas promised to be more interesting than anticipated. It would certainly be a whole lot warmer. Mr and Mrs Clegg were informed they might have the half-leg of mutton to themselves, as well as the afternoon off.

'But what about the plum pudding? I spent yesterday after-noon chopping and grating the spices. Felt like I were scrubbing my eyes with onions!' Mrs Clegg protested.

'You may have some yourselves, and we shall have the rest later in the week,' said Susan. 'Or perhaps Richard might take some to Dr Claybourn's patients?'

Mrs Clegg sank into her chair with a look of utter bemuse-ment. Her mouth dropped open but no words came out. Susan suspected that, without something to complain about, Mrs Clegg's conversational topics would be distinctly curtailed. Amused by the thought of poor Mrs Clegg forced into a state of unexpected happiness, Susan began to look forward to the coming celebrations with some impatience, her curiosity regard-ing Heathersage Manor and its occupants overcoming her initial misgivings.

17

Christmas Arrives at Last

Christmas Day arrived, as always, too sluggishly for eager children, yet too soon for those tasked with making preparations. Susan woke to find ice crusting the inside of her window. Despite the cold, it was a happy quartet that donned gloves and bonnets to walk along the rutted track to Hustanton church, breath steaming from their nostrils like dragon-smoke as the frost-rimed heather crunched beneath their feet. They were to attend the Christmas service and there join up with the Sutcliffes, who would take them on to Heathersage.

They arrived at the same time as the Sutcliffes' carriage and Susan received a stiff greeting from Mrs Grainger as Mr Sutcliffe handed her down. The gentleman tipped his hat to Susan, but his countenance was as severe and forbidding as she remembered. Miss Sutcliffe followed them out, dressed in a wool coat the colour of ripe blackberries, with a matching hat. Her eyes flicked towards Susan, but she removed her gaze so quickly that Susan could not tell if her signed greeting—one that she had spent some time practising—had been seen.

The bells were ringing the call to worship and the entire population of Hustanton appeared to have massed outside the church door. Labourers in drab suits and hobnailed boots stood with wives who wore thin cotton caps and blankets for shawls. Some of the children were barefoot, carried by their fathers to prevent their toes from freezing. Standing apart from the poor, the more affluent shopkeepers mixed with genteel ladies, who hid their colourful gowns beneath fur-lined capes. As Miss Sutcliffe reached the gate, both groups began to point and whisper. The young lady raised her eyes just enough to observe all the faces that were turned towards her. She stopped dead, her mouth dropping open in terror. Without thinking, Susan stepped forward and took her by the arm, supporting her as they walked through the gauntlet of the local gaze. Miss Sutcliffe was trembling and Susan squeezed her gloved hand in reassurance. She found her own hand pressed so eagerly in return that she lost feeling in her fingers. *Good heavens,* thought Susan, *it is not reserve, but painful diffidence!*

When they reached the door of the church, she felt her companion inhale with relief, and her hand was released. Miss Sutcliffe then followed her father and companion to their family pew at the front of the church, while Susan and the girls took a seat towards the rear. Throughout the service, Susan's eye was drawn to Miss Sutcliffe's back, the swell of her shoulder-blades visible through the material of her coat. She did not turn her head, or move except to stand with the others at the singing of hymns, and Susan wondered what she must make of the service, hearing none of it.

After the service came the giving of alms. Susan disbursed

the few pennies she had left among the poor, wishing she had more to give. She looked around for Miss Sutcliffe and glimpsed a blackberry-coloured hat amongst the supplicants. She hastened towards it, thinking that Miss Sutcliffe might require assistance. The sky had clouded over during the service and a stiff gust of wind stole her breath, forcing her to stop for an instant and turn her head away from its icy fingers. In so doing, she found herself face to face with Mr Sutcliffe.

'Miss Mottram, I noted your service to my daughter earlier. I hope you will accept my sincerest gratitude for such a kindness.' His face was as grave as ever, but his words were spoken earnestly.

'Anyone would have done the same thing,' Susan insisted.

'Yet it was only you that acted.' He gave a dry cough. 'I am very glad that you accepted our invitation.'

Susan couldn't hide her surprise at his politeness, so far removed from his demeanour at their previous encounter. He raised an eyebrow.

'You doubt my sentiments?'

'After our last meeting, I was unsure of my reception.'

'How fierce you must have thought me! But you can have no idea how many poachers and vagabonds I have to chase off my land. Every young ruffian from the village comes to ogle at my poor girl. I make no apologies for scaring them away.'

Despite the icy wind, Susan gave a wry smile.

'I make no particular claims regarding my own appearance, yet I would be sorry to be mistaken for a ruffian.'

'No, indeed!' he protested gallantly. 'You are certainly very neat and tidy.'

A compliment worthy of Mr Potts, Susan thought. But that only reminded her of home, and she fell silent. Mr Sutcliffe cocked his head.

'I fear I played my part rather too well. Is that why you refused my offer of assistance when you fell?'

Susan thought back to the moment she had tripped and he had reached for her. She had thought he was about to strike her. Now she recalled his palm had been upwards.

'I mistook your intention,' she admitted. 'I was startled out of good sense.'

'One should not judge by appearances. You are proof of it, Miss Mottram, for in accepting our invitation you have shown unexpected courage for one so small in stature.'

'A courage much fortified by the anticipation of a warm fire and a generous dinner,' Susan said with a smile. 'I was surprised to receive Miss Sutcliffe's letter. After the absurd notions I entertained regarding your daughter's welfare, you would have been fully justified in wanting nothing to do with me. Does this mean I am forgiven?'

'After witnessing your kindness to Cassandra just now, I could forgive you anything,' he said, smiling in return. Susan could scarce believe she had been afraid of him. His expression thus softened, she believed she could trace some of his daughter's features in his own.

'Should we try and find her?' Susan looked anxiously over his shoulder. 'She must be distressed to be among so many people.'

'I have her!' cried Mrs Grainger. 'I have rescued Cassandra from those impertinent wretches.'

She dragged her charge forward by the arm. Miss Sutcliffe's other hand was engaged in keeping her hat on her head in the ever-stiffening breeze, and so, though their eyes met, she was prevented from responding with more than a nod to Susan's signed salutation.

'I have sent for the carriage,' Mrs Grainger continued. 'It is too inclement for Cassandra to walk back to the manor. However, I am not sure how we will all fit in.' She grimaced at Susan and the three girls who had gathered behind her, shivering, their faces white with cold. The sky was growing angrier by the minute.

'I'm sure we shall manage, Hester.'

Yet when the carriage arrived, Mrs Grainger's fears proved well-founded. The covered carriage was intended for four people and although Isabella, Anne and Mary might be squeezed together on one seat, the other would by no means accommodate the rest of the party.

Susan owned herself quite happy to walk. Mr Sutcliffe offered to be her escort and Cassandra indicated that she would join them. Susan was quite satisfied with the arrangements, as she was eager to learn more about her hosts and felt she would do better without Mrs Grainger's interference.

'I will not hear of Cassandra walking in this wind,' insisted Mrs Grainger. 'And Mr Sutcliffe, think of your lungs. They have been weak ever since you had that African fever. Miss Mottram might follow us. A teacher must be well used to such exercise.'

'My lungs be d---d,' protested Mr Sutcliffe. 'I will not ride in a carriage while Miss Mottram walks.'

The business was settled by Mary. When she realised the plan was for Susan to walk, she sprang from the carriage and clung to her teacher's waist, refusing to be parted from her. Miss Sutcliffe moved her gloved hands with slow deliberation.

You must go with Mary in the coach. I will attend my father.

But you are shivering! Susan protested.

It is not the cold that makes me tremble. Miss Sutcliffe gave her an expressive look. Mrs Grainger then offered to exchange places with her young ward. Her offer was steadfastly refused, and Susan found herself on the rear-facing seat next to a dissatisfied Mrs Grainger, watching through the window as the carriage moved off and Cassandra and her father receded into the distance.

'I hope you are pleased with yourself,' Mrs Grainger muttered. 'Mr Sutcliffe has delicate health. If he catches pneumonia, I will hold you responsible.'

It was a comment that Susan felt deserved no response.

'You do not choose to speak, Miss Mottram. Perhaps you consider a mere companion beneath you?'

'I assure you, madam, I do not.'

'You will find that I am treated very much as part of the family.'

'I quite believe it.' Susan wondered why Mrs Grainger felt the need to make such declarations.

'You hold yourself quite high for a schoolteacher, yet you must have suffered some disgrace to end up in an establishment such as Matterdale Hall.'

It was such an impertinent observation that Susan once again declined to respond.

'Your father had debts, didn't he, Miss?' said Isabella. Susan looked at the girl with absolute astonishment.

'How can you know such a thing? Unless you've been reading my letters. Good heavens—was it you, in my room? You looked in my trunk!'

Isabella shrugged carelessly.

'You haven't written anything to be ashamed of, Miss. It's

good of you to send money to your family and I would not be so polite about Mrs Claybourn if I were to write about her.'

'If anyone should be ashamed, it's you, Isabella,' Susan returned severely. 'It is wrong to read private correspondence. You would not like it if someone did the same to you, I'm sure.'

Isabella ran her finger through the thin layer of ice that clung to the inside of the carriage window.

'I haven't any letters, so it doesn't matter.'

'It matters to me,' said Susan. 'You must promise never to do it again.'

'I see your ability to instil discipline in your charges has not improved, Miss Mottram,' said Mrs Grainger, with great satisfaction. The rest of the short journey passed in silence.

18

A Christmas Party

They were shown into the parlour with the glass cases, a tall, dark-haired footman taking their cloaks and bonnets. Anne wore a fetching tartan dress that came down to her mid-calf. Isabella had decided she was old enough for a full-length gown of violet satin, which hung loosely about her as-yet undeveloped figure. Mary's parents had provided her with nothing but shapeless smocks. Susan had helped her into the one with the fewest tears and patches and made a pretty sash for her waist by stealing the gold ribbon from her own summer bonnet. As before, a healthy fire roared in the hearth and everyone migrated towards it. Mrs Grainger perched on the front of a chair and made no effort to converse. The girls were too busy admiring the collection of oddities to notice, but Susan felt the force of the older woman's neglect. She felt it was directed towards her and wondered at the cause. It seemed to run deeper than mere protectiveness of her companion.

Mr Sutcliffe and his daughter at last appeared, accompanied by a flash of fawn and white. Eppy bounded into Mary's arms, and Anne and Isabella joined her in admiring the puppy. Mr Sutcliffe's breath came in wheezing gasps. Susan stepped away from the fire, so that he and his daughter might have a clear path to its reviving warmth. Miss Sutcliffe led her father to the hearth and then attempted to drag forward a heavy leather armchair. Susan hastened to her aid, and together they carried the chair onto the hearthrug. Mr Sutcliffe sank into it and Cassandra flashed Susan a grateful smile, revealing a glimpse of soft raspberry flesh inside her bottom lip. Once she was assured Mr Sutcliffe was comfortable, Susan retreated from the fire, her blood strangely heated by her exertions. Mrs Grainger fussed around her employer, attempting to drape a blanket over his shoulders.

'This is too much,' he protested irritably. 'I shall soon be well. Leave me be.'

'My dear Mr Sutcliffe, you have overexerted yourself. You should have heeded my advice and stayed in the carriage. I will have Jones make up a posset at once.'

'I have no need... for possets,' he wheezed. 'A moment's peace is all I require. You would serve me best, Hester, by attending our guests.'

'Pah! It is on their account that you are indisposed,' Mrs Grainger muttered, continuing to worry at the blanket. Mr Sutcliffe glanced imploringly at his daughter and made a sign with his hands. She clutched her skirts and shook her head almost imperceptibly, but he nodded encouragingly and tilted his head towards Susan and the girls.

Miss Sutcliffe reluctantly approached her visitors, raising her hands before dropping them again. Susan waited patiently, understanding how nervous her hostess was. Cassandra's fingers began to twist and twitch, but if she was communicating something Susan could not make it out.

I do not understand, Susan signed with a self-deprecating smile. *Please be patient. I have much to learn.*

Miss Sutcliffe took a steadying breath.

Your signing is much improved since your last visit, her fingers said. The grammar of signing was different from spoken English, but Susan was finding with practice that she could follow it. She was not too proud to take instruction on this from Anne, whose gift for languages extended to the unspoken one.

Mary is a hard taskmaster. They both looked towards Mary, who was giggling as she hugged Eppy to her breast. Miss Sutcliffe put a hand across her mouth but it did not completely hide her smile. Her shoulders and face became animated, as well as her hands.

A hard taskmaster indeed. You are to be pitied.

I do not mind, for I am... Susan paused. She wanted to say that she was eager to make herself understood, but did not know the sign for 'eager'. She tried again. *I do not want to be wrong.*

You wish for a life without mistakes? Cassandra raised an eyebrow. Susan shook her head ruefully. She responded slowly, forced by lack of knowledge into finger-spelling some of the words.

My inexperience and imperfect nature make that impossible. I meant only that I do not want to be... misinterpreted.

Cassandra's expression softened. *That, I understand.*

The tall footman reappeared to inform them that dinner was ready. Mr Sutcliffe had recovered sufficiently to offer Susan his arm, and they led the party across the hallway to a dining room whose table was so loaded down with food that it was difficult to make out the plate and cutlery beneath the profusion. The girls gasped in wonder at the centrepiece: a vast cake in the shape of a swan, its white feathers delicately sculpted from icing. Fanning out from a large tureen of steaming gravy were plates of oyster patties, stewed cabbage and salsify, hams glazed with thin slices of orange, and numerous other delicacies. A vast punchbowl was filled to the brim and Susan counted no fewer than four decanters of wine. Mr Sutcliffe sat at the top with Cassandra and Susan either side of him. The girls were placed further down with Mrs Grainger opposite the master of the house. A hissing joint of beef was brought in on a silver dish so large it needed two footmen to carry it. Hot juices flowed from the centre as Mr Sutcliffe carved.

'It smells lovely,' said Susan.

'I am something of an epicure,' said her host. 'I cannot justify such extravagance when dining *en famille*, but for guests I permit myself some indulgence. You did me a great favour by accepting our invitation.'

He signed everything as he spoke so that Cassandra was included in every conversation, even if it meant putting down his knife and fork. Susan noticed they added facial expressions to alter words or provide emphasis. She suspected that the difference between their fluent communication and her own tentative efforts must be like that between singing and mere talk and longed to be more proficient. Mr Sutcliffe begged his guests to help themselves to whatever they wanted. When he noticed Mary staring blankly at the mountains of food in front of her, too afraid to put anything on her plate, he sprang from his seat and lifted a plate of oyster patties, raising a questioning eyebrow. Mary nodded shyly, and he spooned three onto her plate.

Reaching for a dish of glazed carrots, the pantomime was repeated until Mary's plate was quite full.

'She reminds me of Cassie when she was a little girl,' he said to Susan as he returned to his seat. 'So uncertain and confused by everything.'

'It is good of you to put Mary at her ease.'

'Mr Sutcliffe is a liberal man,' Mrs Grainger remarked. 'Too generous for his own good.'

Once everyone was served, the meal passed quietly, since eating and signing at the same time was impossible. Yet it was a contented, easy silence. Mr Sutcliffe, although not given to smiles, was attentive to even the hint of an empty plate or empty glass. He looked often to his daughter to ascertain that she was happy, and Susan was moved by the eloquent communication that passed between them. After a few glasses of wine, even Mrs Grainger entered into the spirit of the occasion and was gracious enough to insist Susan try some brandy sauce with her plum pudding.

When Mr Sutcliffe could find no takers for further refreshment, they retired to a large drawing room, whose walls were filled with framed pictures, all drawn in the delicate style that Susan recognised as Cassandra's. A magnificent fir tree stood in one corner, so tall its crown was bent crookedly against the ceiling. Its branches were weighed down by candles and glass baubles, with crimson ribbons strewn generously about. Opposite the tree stood an ebony grand piano. Eppy, who had been banished from the dining room in disgrace after stealing a pie from the table, emerged from beneath the tree, crashed into Mary and began to lick her face furiously. Cassandra rescued Mary by gently lifting Eppy away.

Mr Sutcliffe coughed and indicated that he had taken the liberty of getting a little something for each of the girls.

'For there must be gifts at Christmas,' he said gravely.

Isabella tore open the wrapping of what turned out to be a pretty bonnet. Anne was the delighted recipient of a stack of books. Mary, when she could be distracted from Eppy for long enough, opened hers to reveal a skipping rope. She dropped it at once and returned her attention to Eppy.

'I fear she is not happy with her gift,' said Mr Sutcliffe mournfully.

'It's very kind of you,' Susan said, smiling. 'But it is difficult to surpass a puppy.'

'This is for you. Cassie helped me choose it.' Her host handed Susan a heavy box wrapped in gilt paper. Susan hesitated. In years past, as the daughter of the parish vicar, she herself had given gifts to the deserving and the poor. That her hosts might consider her as needing charity was a painful thought. For some reason, it felt worse than any of Mrs Claybourn's impositions.

'I did not expect… really, you should not…' she stammered.

'It would upset my daughter greatly if you did not take it,' Mr Sutcliffe said in a low voice, his hands still.

Within the folds of the thick paper was a lacquered writing set, complete with pens and ink, as well as paper, envelopes and a blotter. There was even a sheet of penny stamps. Susan closed her eyes. It was the perfect gift.

You do not like it? Cassie signed anxiously.

No. Yes. It is… I am… grateful. Susan's fingers stuttered through the words and she prayed the Sutcliffes would ascribe her confusion to lack of fluency in sign language.

'Knowing you are far from home, Cassie thought you would be often writing to your family,' Mr Sutcliffe said, a little stiffly.

'It is a thoughtful gift, but you should not have gone to so much trouble.' Susan recovered herself. 'Your invitation today was generous enough. You saved us from what would have been a very dull affair.'

'No occasion would be dull if Miss Susan Mottram were of the company, I'm sure,' returned Mr Sutcliffe politely. Susan was becoming used to his old-fashioned gallantry and wondered how she could ever have feared him. True, he smiled little, but there was thoughtfulness in every action. He looked towards his daughter. 'It gladdens my heart to see Cassie so comfortable in company. I had given up hoping it was possible. She has always been nervous of strangers. Yet it is often mistaken for pride.'

Susan coloured and was silent, for she could not deny she had initially thought Cassandra reserved.

'To make judgements based on outward appearance is a common fault,' Mr Sutcliffe added, as if reading her mind.

'I cannot deny that I have made such mistakes,' Susan admitted, 'although it is not only appearances that have led me astray.' She recalled Mr Sutcliffe's fierceness on her previous visit. How she had thought him ill-tempered. Wicked even. But he had only been protecting his daughter. 'I have always believed that the way people behave gives the best insight into character. Yet this does not entirely serve the purpose, I find.'

'Anyone can fool the world by acting a part. Even the devil can give alms,' said Mr Sutcliffe.

'But how can we determine character, if not by actions?'

'We must look for the intention behind the deed.'

'But why mislead at all? What is to be gained?'

'Sometimes we act a part to protect ourselves, or those we love,' he said, with a grave look at his daughter. Susan couldn't help a smile. 'Does something amuse you, Miss Mottram?'

'For all your protestations, appearances do not always lie. At this moment you are the very picture of a devoted father, and you will not convince me it is an act.'

'Who could not love such a dear girl?'

Cassandra looked up as if sensing their gaze. A flush spread across her cheeks, and Susan was sure it was not just the heat from the fire. Discerning that Cassandra was uncomfortable being the centre of attention, Susan rose quickly and began to admire the pictures on the wall.

'Your daughter is extraordinarily accomplished. These drawings capture the very essence of their subjects.'

'It is interesting you should say so. Some African tribespeople refuse to have their likenesses taken, for fear their souls will become imprisoned.'

'Superstitious nonsense,' said Mrs Grainger.

'People fear what they do not understand, in England as much as anywhere else.' Mr Sutcliffe looked again at his daughter and his face fell into a thoughtful frown.

'Surely that cannot be a universal truth?' Susan protested. 'Else it would be impossible to love God. Or German opera. Although it would explain my pupils' aversion to algebra.'

'You saw how it was at the church. My poor girl suffers doubly; from the colour of her skin as much as her deafness.'

'Yet with such devoted companions, she has many reasons to rejoice. I wish others were so fortunate. Mary's parents seem almost ashamed of her.'

A trace of Mr Sutcliffe's former ferocity flashed across his features.

'It is common to scorn those who are different. When Cassandra was a child, several physicians suggested I commit her to an asylum. Interfering busybodies insisted she was an aberration and therefore dangerous. We had to move to the country to escape such persecution.'

'I cannot imagine Dr Claybourn acting in such a manner,' Susan protested loyally.

'Because he has rosy cheeks and a fat belly, he must therefore be harmless? Have you forgotten my earlier lecture?'

Susan laughed.

'It is difficult to believe evil of a man who wears such waist-coats, I confess. More significantly, he has been nothing but affable and kind to me.'

'Oh, the fellow can smile and smirk with the best, but he is a dis-sembler. He attempted to get money out of me by a gross deception. Claimed he wished me to sponsor an infirmary when it is nothing but an asylum. I could never support such an abomination.'

'Miss Mottram's employers will be disappointed,' said Mrs Grainger, who had been hovering about them for some time. 'I suppose they sent you here to beg for money? Or else to pry into our affairs.'

'I cannot deny that there is much within this house that intrigues me,' Susan said.

'It is as I thought—you have come to spy on us!' exclaimed Mrs Grainger.

'The creatures in your hallway, for instance. I have never seen such an interesting collection.'

Mr Sutcliffe clasped his hands together.

'With Cassie so afraid of the world, I strive to bring it to her, in all its wonderful variety.'

'What is this?' said Isabella, straining on tiptoe to reach for a painting of a reed bunting.

'Isabella!' Susan cried. Her warning came too late. Isabella knocked the picture from its hook and it crashed to the floor. The glass in the frame shattered. With a cry of dismay, Cassandra rushed over to pick up the pieces.

'It was an accident!' Isabella protested, before bursting into tears. Susan hurried to offer Cassandra assistance. Together, they gathered up the broken glass and set it aside.

It is only an old picture, Cassandra signed. *Do not be angry with the child. She suffers a deep torment.*

'What does she say?' Isabella said, sniffling.

'She says you're a wicked girl,' Mrs Grainger remarked acidly. Susan wondered if Mrs Grainger often misinterpreted her young companion's words. Eppy took that moment to seize Mary's discarded skipping rope between her jaws and retreat beneath the piano where she crouched with her bottom in the air, tail wagging. Mary couldn't resist following and there began an energetic game of chase between the piano legs. Concerned for the safety of the instrument, Susan retrieved the toy from Eppy in exchange for an ear scratch.

'Thank you for your prompt actions,' said Mr Sutcliffe. 'I would hate to see our pianoforte damaged. It belonged to my wife.'

'It is a fine instrument,' said Susan with a wistful sigh.

'Do you play?'

Susan found it easier to sign than to speak.

We sold our own piano after my father died.

In an instant, Susan's hands were clasped between warm fingers and pressed against a pair of soft lips. The warmth of the gesture, together with the deep sympathy of Miss Sutcliffe's gaze, caused tears to prickle at the back of Susan's eyelids. Resolutely, she blinked them back.

'My condolences for your loss,' said Mr Sutcliffe gravely. 'Was it recent?'

'Easter.'

'Within the year? You must feel his loss acutely.'

Their kindness was too much for Susan to bear. She pulled away from Cassandra and fled into the oddment-filled hallway. There was a burst of heat as the door opened behind her. Gentle arms enclosed her from behind and a warm cheek rested against hers. No words were spoken, but none were needed. It was the first time she had been held, Susan realised, since she had left home, and that thought alone was enough to unlock the grief she had kept suppressed for so long. She turned and buried her head in Cassandra's shoulder and sobbed until she could weep no more.

She was roused by an awareness that her cheek was pressing against Cassandra's breast. It sparked something within her, a kind of yearning ache. She pulled back with a self-conscious gasp.

Thank you. The simple sign was a poor expression of what she felt.

Mama died when I was very young. I comprehend loss. But to lose a beloved father… I cannot imagine the agony.

I have been afraid to feel it, Susan admitted, the revelation surprising her. *Afraid that grief would make me incapable of doing what I must.*

Cassandra smiled tenderly.

I know nobody more capable than you. Except my father.

Susan laughed through the remnants of her tears.

Then you must have few acquaintances. I am a poor teacher. The girls do not listen to me and have no wish to learn.

You will make them love you. I know it. Have faith in yourself.

Susan was embarrassed by such undeserved praise, yet grateful for it all the same.

You are very kind. I am much recovered—shall we return?

The girls, entranced by Eppy, did not appear to have noticed their absence, but Mr Sutcliffe strode instantly towards Susan and clasped her hands in his.

'My dear girl…'

'This is a poor return for all your kindness,' said Susan. He presented her with a handkerchief which she accepted gratefully.

'I'm sure I was upset when Mr Grainger died,' said Mrs Grainger as Susan dabbed her eyes. 'But I never made such a fuss about it.'

'I beg you will play for us,' said Mr Sutcliffe, as soon as Susan had recovered. He opened the lid of the pianoforte keyboard. 'It is past time the house was filled with music.'

Susan brushed her fingertips across the ivory keys.

'It doesn't seem right when there are those who cannot enjoy it.'

Cassandra's hands fluttered eagerly.

I would take much pleasure in watching you.

Any doubts that she might have forgotten her skill after months without practice disappeared as Susan's fingers flew across the keys in long-remembered patterns. Without thinking, she played a mournful, contemplative air, full of feeling. The cover was propped open and Cassandra reached in and brushed her fingers against the strings as they vibrated, closing her eyes as if she might feel what she could not hear. Mary followed her lead, her own eyes widening as the piano wires danced under her small hand. Even Isabella approached to listen. Susan found herself so wrapped up in the music that when she finished the room seemed oddly bright and clear, as though she had gone into a darkened room and then returned.

'That was quite…' Mr Sutcliffe began, but then he turned away.

Papa is sad?

Not sad. Recollecting.

'A strange choice of tune for Christmas Day,' said Mrs Grainger. 'Reminding poor Mr Sutcliffe of his dead wife. I see what you are about and, mark my words, you shall make an enemy of me if you persist.'

'Play something jolly, Miss,' urged Isabella. 'Something we can dance to.'

Susan began a lively Scotch reel. Isabella grabbed Anne by her hands and proceeded to twirl her about the room. Out the corner of her eyes, Susan saw Mr Sutcliffe clutch his daughter to his breast, and she followed the reel with another to divert attention from such a private moment of grief. It was a grief she understood, for she had only to close her eyes to see her dear papa, watching her play as he had so many times before.

The second reel finished, she switched to a country dance but was stopped within a few bars by Mr Sutcliffe who informed her that his daughter, intrigued by Isabella and Anne's dancing, had asked to be shown the reel. Might she repeat the tune? Susan was happy to oblige, watching with interest as Mr Sutcliffe led his daughter into the dance. Although Cassandra could not follow the music, she mimicked his movements, and was soon laughing delightedly as he flung her about. Susan was entranced by the sight. It was as if Cassandra danced to her own, internal music. A melody so ancient it was beyond hearing and could only be felt in the thrumming of a heart, or the beating of a pulse. As the music reached its peak, Cassandra closed her eyes and threw back her head, her back curved as she danced round her father. It must, Susan thought, be how the Greeks had danced at bacchanals, lost in the ecstasy of that unheard rhythm. Not wanting to break the magic, Susan extemporised a coda to extend the dance. However, Mr Sutcliffe became breathless and was forced to call a halt.

'Enough!' he said, sinking into the nearest chair.

'Oh, but I was hoping you might ask me to jig,' said Mrs Grainger. 'I was quite the dancer when I was younger.'

'I'm sorry, Hester. Until I am recovered, Cassandra must be your partner, or one of the girls.'

Mrs Grainger disdained any other partner and contented herself by sitting next to her employer and fanning his brow.

After a lull, Isabella asked if they could play charades. Instead, Susan suggested a game of *The Sculptor*. Since it required no words, all might participate. Neither Mr Sutcliffe nor Cassandra knew the game. Susan explained that they must nominate a sculptor whose task was to place the others in strange poses, from which they must not move, laugh, or make any sign.

'I shall not be party to such nonsense,' Mrs Grainger said. 'Mr Sutcliffe, I'm sure, will not relish such childishness.'

Mr Sutcliffe owned he was still a little breathless but would happily watch from his chair.

'I shall begin,' offered Susan, setting Isabella, Anne and Mary into the form of the three Graces. She made them each balance on one leg. Cassandra seemed ill at ease as Susan reached out to pull her towards the others.

Do not be alarmed.

As carefully as if she were working with precious marble, Susan guided Cassandra into a position with her slender arms stretched out in supplication. She stepped back and examined her living statues thoughtfully. Cassandra's eyes flicked towards Susan who wagged her finger with a smile.

No moving.

Susan then began an elaborate pantomime, pretending that she was an old woman, bending over as if her back hurt and waddling comically about the room, her grimacing face low to the ground. Eppy decided this was a delightful addition to her game and jumped up to lick Susan's face. Susan tried to brush her away, but Eppy stood up on her back legs and continued to lick Susan's nose. Cassandra burst into unconstrained laughter and the Graces collapsed inwards, clutching each other to stop themselves falling.

'Miss Sutcliffe laughed first,' said Isabella.

You are now the sculptor, Susan explained. Cassandra raised an eyebrow. She worked first on the girls, bending them into hoops with their hands touching the ground. Susan waited her turn. For some reason, her heart began to flutter wildly. Cassandra turned to her and rested her hand lightly on the small of Susan's back, spinning her round so that Susan was facing away from her. She then moved her hands to encircle Susan's wrists. Susan felt a tremor run through her. There was a divinity in Cassandra's touch beyond her comprehension. She felt like the Promethean clay statues, breathed into life by Athena. Every hair on her body prickled and she could feel every pulse of blood as it throbbed through her veins. As Cassandra's fingers brushed against the nape of her neck, easing her head down, Susan gasped at the tumult that raged beneath her skin. Yet the rules of the game prescribed she must stay motionless. It was a moment of exquisite torture. She sensed Cassandra behind her but, even had she been permitted to look, she would have been too afraid, for such was the strange sorcery swirling around the room, she feared that the merest glimpse of her sweet tormentor might transform her, like Danae, into a shower of rain. Or was it Zeus that was the rain? She couldn't remember. One of the girls must have moved, because there was laughter.

'My turn!' Isabella exclaimed, but Susan, her legs weak and trembling, begged they would continue without her. She retreated to a window seat to compose her body and her thoughts. So difficult did this task prove, she was barely mistress of herself before becoming aware that Mrs Grainger had ordered the carriage to take them back to Matterdale Hall via Hustanton. Mr Sutcliffe protested that it was too early, but Mrs Grainger insisted that his health was too important to be trifled with, and the party was broken up.

19

In Which we Discover the Cause of Isabella's Behaviour

In the days immediately following the party, the residents of Matterdale Hall were noticeably subdued. Isabella complained that there was nothing to do and became sulkier and more withdrawn than ever. Mary seemed bereft without Eppy to play with. Susan's own reflections were more complex. That she had enjoyed her visit could not be denied. Mr Sutcliffe's attentions had been most agreeable. It had been a pleasure to converse with someone of wit and intelligence. And she was grateful to his daughter for her generous expressions of sympathy. To feel that someone understood her grief was an unexpected comfort. But what was she to make of the peculiar indisposition that had afflicted her during the game? She had no patience for those who accused Cassandra of witchcraft, yet Heathersage Manor contained a magic to which she had no resistance. If it was sorcery, it was of a remarkably enlivening and pleasurable kind. Her letter of thanks to Miss Sutcliffe received a prompt reply.

My dear Susan,

Your kind note drives me to an instant response, for any gratitude must fall entirely upon myself. I have never experienced such a merry Christmas! So full of liveliness and feeling. We are all pining in your absence, Eppy most of all. My dear father was quite charmed by you. To hear that beloved instrument played once more was a delight to him and I thank you for it from the depths of a grateful heart. My only regret was that I was not able to appreciate it as he did, for he tells me you play quite beautifully. Would that I could understand the mysterious force that moved my papa to tears and my dear friend also! I hope it is not presumptuous to refer to you in such a manner? Forgive me if I am impertinent. I have so few acquaintances that I am uncertain of the appropriate customs. I only know what I feel, and beg to be known henceforth as

Your affectionate friend,

Cassandra

P.S. You will forgive me that I do not call on you. Father was greatly fatigued by the excitements of our party, and I attend him until he is recovered.

Although I own that, even with the enticement of seeing such a dear companion, I find the idea of visiting so difficult that I have not the courage for it. Your sympathetic heart, I know, will acquit me of any neglect. Know that you would always be welcome at Heathersage, and I beg you will come as soon as you are at liberty to do so. I will look for you every day.

To think that Susan had once thought the writer cold and proud! Here was nothing but warmth and ardour. To offer friendship on such a short acquaintance showed a generosity of spirit that delighted her. Her first few months at Matterdale Hall had been marred by homesickness and dismay at her own incompetence. With such a friend close by, she could look forward to the coming term with brighter hopes. She looked at the clock. It was only just past noon. Not too late to pay a visit to Heathersage, if they left within the hour. This pleasing notion was interrupted by Anne, sobbing heartily because Isabella had upset her. Isabella loudly protested her innocence and ran off before Susan could get to the bottom of the matter.

'Anne, whatever has happened?' Susan asked.

'Isabella… she said that there are ghosts in the infirmary,' Anne sobbed. 'When I said I didn't believe her, she told me I was mad, and that Dr Claybourn would lock me up.'

Susan reassured Anne that nobody was going to lock her away, and certainly not someone as kind as Dr Claybourn. The girl was so distressed that it took some time to console her. At length, Anne cried out her tears and, after fetching her a cup of cocoa, Susan went in search of Isabella. She found her in the dormitory, sitting on a bunk, clutching her knees against her chest. She looked so fragile that Susan hadn't the heart to scold her. Cassandra believed that Isabella was suffering in some way. Perhaps that was at the root of her behaviour. Uncertain how to proceed, Susan sat beside the girl.

'I didn't do anything,' Isabella protested, rubbing her snub, button-like nose.

'I know you didn't *do* anything. But you *said* something that upset Anne very much. Why?'

Isabella only shrugged.

'Come, it is not like you to be silent.'

'She said I was lying, but I wasn't.'

'Lying about what?'

'The ghosts in the infirmary.'

Susan couldn't help but raise an eyebrow. Isabella reddened.

'I heard them. Last summer. Everyone had gone, except me and Mary. There was screaming fit to make your ears break.'

'Come, Isabella, you are too clever a girl to believe such nonsense.'

'Nobody believes me,' she cried, turning away. 'Nobody ever believes me. But I'm not a liar, I'm not!'

She burst into tears. Susan snaked her arm around the girl's shoulders.

'Isabella, won't you tell me the cause of your distress? This grief cannot be for a ghost, surely?'

She waited patiently until Isabella's shoulders stopped jerking up and down.

'M-my father,' Isabella blurted out at last. 'He thinks I drowned my little brother, but I didn't. I swear I didn't!'

Susan looked at her in shock.

'You don't believe me!' Isabella wrenched herself from Susan's grasp.

'I do believe you,' Susan assured her. 'I'm just… to lose your brother. You poor dear child. And then to be blamed for it! How awful.'

Isabella buried her head in Susan's chest and wailed.

'Tell me what happened,' Susan prompted gently.

'M-Matthew wanted me to play with him, but I was reading and I told him to leave me alone. He didn't listen. He never listened. He kept throwing his ball at me. When it landed on my book and tore a page, I got angry and threw the ball away. I didn't see it had gone in the pond. He must have run after it. When I looked up, he… he was lying in the water. I jumped in and pulled him out, but it was too late.'

'Oh, you poor dear girl.'

'One of the servants told Papa she'd heard us arguing and Papa thought I pushed Matthew in. He sent me to this horrid place to punish me.' She began to sob again. 'But I… I deserve much worse.'

'It was an accident. You were not to blame.'

'I-I should have been watching him. I should have played with him. I'd give anything to tell him how sorry I am,' Isabella sobbed.

'But you can, Isabella. We can tell him right now.'

Isabella wiped her nose with the back of her sleeve and looked at her. 'What do you mean?'

'Do you believe in heaven?'

Isabella nodded uncertainly.

'That is where Matthew will be, for all little children go to heaven. All we need to do is pray, and he will hear us. Come, let us do it together.'

They knelt down beside the bed and Susan closed her eyes and prayed to God to take care of little innocent Matthew and said that his sister was sorry she hadn't played with him, that she missed him every day and hoped that he had lots of playmates in heaven.

'Amen,' sniffed Isabella. They rose to their feet. 'Thank you, Miss.'

'Now, about this ghost…'

'I did hear something, I did!'

'Could it have been the wind?'

Isabella bit her lower lip.

'There is a lot of wind hereabouts,' she admitted.

'I wish you would apologise to Anne for saying you would lock her up.'

'I didn't. I said the Claybourns would,' Isabella protested with a hint of her usual sulkiness.

'Which is even worse, for you can have no reason to make such an unfounded accusation against Dr Claybourn. Come, make things right. You will feel better for it and make Anne happy too.'

It was soon done. Anne was quick to accept Isabella's apology and, seeing the older girl's reddened eyes and tear-stained face, even gave her a hug. Susan was glad to see them reconciled. She marvelled at Cassandra's insight. Whereas Susan had only seen an obstinate girl who refused to do as she was told, Cassandra had seen beneath the surface to the heartache within. She longed to ask Cassandra how she had acquired such an interesting talent but it was too late now to contemplate a visit to Heathersage. Her questions must wait until another day.

20

At Home with Cassandra

Ever since she had been a girl, Cassandra Sutcliffe had known she was different. It was one of the few things she understood absolutely, along with the enveloping love of her father. The rest of the world was not so easy to comprehend. She barely remembered her mother, although there was a sense of something missing, something soft and loving. She felt safe only with her dear Papa, for other people were a mystery to her. Their faces, contorting into such odd shapes, to what purpose? Complete strangers would point and stare at her, and children of her own age would prod her with their fingers, or pull her hair, as if she might be teased into behaving as they expected. She soon came to dread such exchanges, her fears accompanied by physical symptoms. Head pounding, chest constricting, she would run away from visitors, hiding in the shadows until she was herself again.

Yet she was curious and began to observe people from a distance, hoping to understand them. She started to detect those slight changes in expression, those unconscious movements of the body that betrayed the inner person. She understood the emotions of those around her long before she could communicate with words. When she was five years old, her father brought a young widow into his household to teach Cassandra to understand the world around her. Mrs Grainger had a deaf brother and was therefore experienced enough to instruct Cassandra in sign language. This was a blessing, but also a curse, for as she learned to understand the world Cassandra began to comprehend that her deafness was not the only reason, nor even the most important one, for the hateful looks and insults aimed at her. Her aversion to strangers grew to such a pitch that she was reluctant to leave home. When she did venture out, she did not go beyond the land immediately around Heathersage Manor, from whence she might swiftly retreat to her refuge should she spy anyone coming. The Christmas and Easter visits to church were a torture borne only out of duty to her dear father.

Despite distancing herself from others, Cassandra never lost her ability to read the inner person. Her intuition sensed goodness inside Susan Mottram, even at their first meeting. Although distressed by the familiar mockery of the girls, Cassandra had observed the young teacher's embarrassment, and had understood her compassion. When Susan had first come to Heathersage, Cassandra had been awed by her courage. To venture forth, uninvited and alone, to such a forbidding place as Heathersage Manor, to make her apologies, was something quite remarkable to Cassandra. As she saw more of Susan, other emotions stirred within her. She had believed herself content with her life. She had Mrs Grainger for company as well as a succession of beloved pets, the most recent a beagle puppy with a bad leg that the local huntsman would have put down. Cassandra had loved Eppy instantly, welcoming into her heart a creature that, like her, had been fashioned imperfectly. Until Susan's arrival, Cassandra had not realised how dull and secluded her life had been. When Susan had played the piano at Christmas, Cassandra felt the strings vibrate beneath her fingertips. In the same way, her own heart-strings had thrummed into life beneath Susan's gentle touch. What pleasure it was to think that she might at last have a friend of her own age, with whom she could share her thoughts and hopes. And so Cassandra waited, each day, hoping that Susan would appear.

21

A Visitor Blows in from the Sea

The next morning it was snowing. Susan and the girls took breakfast in their parlour. Although wood and coals had been laid in the grate, the fire had not been lit. Rather than ring for Mrs Clegg, who had been forced to retire to bed early the previous evening due to her aching joints, Susan thought she might attempt to light the fire herself, watching in satisfaction as the kindling caught and the flames sprang to life. For some reason, such little self-sufficiencies delighted her. Isabella asked if she might borrow Mary's sign-language book and some paper.

'I want to practise drawing hands,' she said. Anne and Mary decided this was an excellent plan and the three girls settled down together on the hearthrug. Mary had brought her little basket and opened the lid so that the mouse might run around between them. Susan went to the window. The sky was that odd mixture of brightness and menace that came with snow-fall. She watched the flakes of snow as they landed, holding their shape for a few moments before melting away. Would it settle? If the moors remained clear by late morning, she believed she might walk to Heathersage Manor. Her boots were stout enough and the cold did not frighten her. In the meantime, she took up a pen and began a letter to her mother, but she found it difficult to keep to her task. Her attention was too often drawn to the window. The snowflakes had become larger and more plentiful, leaving a thin covering on the ground. Yet she still thought the moors might be passable if she were to set off before noon. Suddenly, there was a fretful knock, followed by Mrs Clegg's head appearing between the door and jamb. Susan supposed it was beyond her strength to get her entire body through the gap.

'There's a… a person who insists on speaking with the master or mistress of the house. I told him they weren't here, but he asked who was in charge and now he wants to speak with you. He's a rough and surly fellow. I don't know what the missus would say about it all.'

'Where is he now?'

'I left him at the door, Miss. I daren't let him in without permission.'

'You left him outside? In such weather!'

Susan went herself, concerned that their visitor would freeze to death in the time it would take Mrs Clegg to drag her aching bones back down the corridor. The moment she opened the door, a man with sun-darkened skin forced his way past her and into the hallway, dropping snow from his short jacket and boots. 'My sister—is she here?' he demanded brusquely.

'Pray compose yourself,' said Susan, alarmed by the roughness of his manner. 'To whom am I speaking?'

He paid her no heed, striding down the corridor and seizing the handle of the first door he came to. It was the main family parlour. Finding it locked, he rattled the doorknob so furiously that the door shook against its hinges.

'Kitty, are you there? It is Josiah!' When there was no answer, he gave out a great sigh. 'Oh, please God, let her be safe!'

'I assure you, that room is empty,' Susan said, her heart touched by such obvious distress. 'Whom do you seek? Most of our girls are gone for the holidays.'

He seemed to see her for the first time. He scraped off his battered and shapeless cap.

'My name is Josiah Smythson, first mate of the *Titan*, a cutter out of Liverpool.'

'You are related to Miss Smythson, perhaps?'

'My sister.'

'Then I am sorry, for you have had a wasted journey. Miss Smythson is not here. I understand she was let go.'

She kept her tone steady and was relieved to observe that he had calmed a little, although his brow remained creased.

'I knows it. My sister wrote to our mother saying she was to come home. But she never arrived.'

'Good heavens, you must be greatly concerned!'

He rolled his shapeless hat in his hands.

'Concerned—yes. I've come straight from my ship—three days afoot, for I would not wait for my wages. My 'pologies if I was abrupt just now, but I thought I was to be turned away.'

'After such a long journey you must be fatigued. Won't you take some refreshment? You will not take it amiss, I hope, if I receive you in the kitchen? It is the warmest room by far, and I will ask Mrs Clegg to make you up a negus.'

He permitted her to lead him to the kitchen, but declined her invitation to sit.

'I prefer to stand,' he said, looking about him as if he expected any moment to be jumped. He continued to worry at his hat, which was so battered and pulled about that Susan suspected it must often suffer such treatment. She began to wonder if it had been wise to admit a person whose address and appearance did not speak of gentility. Her natural sympathy had overcome her good sense. There was a yowl and a mottled grey shape sprang onto the kitchen table. Susan started back with a cry, for she had not noticed the cat at all.

'Shoo!' she said, with an ineffectual wave of her hand. The cat hissed at her, tail up and hairs rising on its rising back. Mr Smythson grabbed it. There was another high-pitched yowl and Susan's visitor dropped the cat instantly, swearing loudly. He then began to suck on the back of his hand.

'You are bleeding?' Susan cried.

'It's nothing. A scratch.' He shook his fist at the cat. 'That's a wicked creature, that one.'

His fierce demeanour prompted Susan into brisk activity. The sooner she got rid of Mr Smythson, the sooner her charges would be safe.

'Mrs Clegg, I beg you would make up a negus for our guest. Your husband is close by?'

This question was entirely for the benefit of their visitor. Susan wished him to know they were not without protection. There was, of course, no need to mention Mr Clegg's age. Or his rheumatism. Mrs Clegg's aurora of hair wobbled furiously in testament to her disapproval of the situation.

'I shall fetch him at once,' she said in an unusually decided tone. 'And I'll get Richard an' all.'

'I'm sure there is no need,' said Susan, who felt the idea of Mr Clegg might be more of a deterrent than his actual presence. And she wanted no favours from Richard. Their visitor shook his head.

'You've no need to fear me, Miss. I would never hurt a lady. Although there's not a man alive I wouldn't be afraid to stand up with, if it comes to it.'

He twisted his hat as if wringing it dry. Susan noticed white scars across his knuckles next to a thin red line where the cat had scratched him. Mrs Clegg huffed and puffed like a worn-out steam engine as she made up the hot drink of port, sugar, lemon and spices.

'I fear there is little I can tell you,' said Susan. 'Your sister was gone by the time I arrived.'

Mrs Clegg placed a steaming pan on the table and then wandered away without thinking to bring cups. Susan retrieved a metal tankard from a shelf and poured the negus herself. Mr Smythson accepted the tankard, his eyes continually assessing every entrance.

'Do you know why she was dismissed?'

'I know only that the Claybourns found her in some way unsatisfactory.'

He placed the tankard on the table with some care, its contents untasted.

'How so?' His voice was soft but dangerous.

'I do not know the details. It may not be any reflection on your sister. Mrs Claybourn can be a difficult employer.'

'And what of the husband? You hear of such things, in these remote houses. Could he have done her violence?'

The notion of Dr Claybourn cast in the character of a villain struck Susan as utterly ridiculous.

'Dr Claybourn? I cannot believe it!'

'You're young, Miss, if I may say so, and I can see you have been well brought up. I wonder if you know aught of the darkness that lurks in certain corners of the world.'

Susan stiffened.

'I may be young but I am not without sense. I know better than to listen to unfounded insinuations about a man who has shown me nothing but kindness. I would stake my life on Dr Claybourn's character.'

Mr Smythson reached inside his jacket and drew forth a folded paper.

'Then what am I to make of this? It's from my sister. The last my mother had from her.'

He pressed it on her and Susan's curiosity was stirred sufficiently for her to open it. The letter was written in a large, energetic hand.

Dear Mama,

Well, I am to be dismissed. Although Mrs C, penny-pinching as ever, insists I serve out the rest of my time and stay until the last of the girls have gone, or she says I shall not have my money. Thrice the pittance she gives me would not be recompense for the tasks they heap on my poor shoulders. But I shall have the last laugh, for I believe I have found out Dr C's secret, and if I am right, I shall have my dues out of his wife for my silence. I await a letter from Hustanton to confirm my suspicions and then we shall be rich. Someone as miserly as Mrs C must have a vast pile of money hidden away. I shall be glad to leave this dreary place. When I come home, you shall have a new shawl and Josiah shall have a new sea-chest.

Your dearest Catherine.

Susan could not approve of such a letter and she returned it to Mr Smythson with a frown. He refolded it and placed it once more inside his jacket.

'It don't show my sister in the best light, but she's my kin, and I'll have vengeance on any man who's done her harm!'

His eyes sparkled dangerously. Susan felt it time to bring the interview to a swift conclusion.

'Mr Smythson, I fear your understandable concern for your sister is leading your imagination down a wild and dangerous path. Have you any evidence that your sister did not travel home? Have you asked at Hustanton, or enquired at any of the nearby train stations?'

'I came directly here.'

'Then I recommend you do, before you make such unworthy accusations against a well-respected gentleman. Perhaps… I beg your pardon, but is there any chance… might your sister be visiting a friend? A gentleman friend? I understand there were rumours.'

The sorry hat was subjected to such a furious tugging and twisting that Susan was certain the fabric must tear.

'I'm sorry if the suggestion causes you pain,' she said quickly. 'But, in the circumstances, I feel it best to keep nothing from you, no matter how distressing, if it may help you find her.'

Mr Smythson shoved what was left of the hat in the pocket of his jacket and gave her a short bow.

'I reckon you're right. I may have put the wind before the ship. I shall make enquiries.'

'I do hope you find your sister safe and well,' Susan said earnestly. 'Indeed, I am sure you will, for I cannot believe any harm befell her within these walls.'

'Thank you, Miss. I 'pologise if I've been rough in my manners, but I've seen things in this world that would send shivers down your back. God send that you are right and my sister is safe somewhere. Good day.'

Susan saw him off with relief. Although it had stopped snowing, she did not feel she could leave the girls unattended with such a fierce and intemperate man in the neighbourhood. With regret, she put off her anticipated visit to Heathersage Manor for another day.

22

A Promise is Made

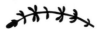

S usan was delighted to rise and find the light dusting of snow from the previous day had vanished. The sky was clear and there was no sign of Mr Smythson. There was nothing to prevent her visiting her new friend. At breakfast, she mentioned her scheme. Isabella and Mary were keen to accompany her, but Anne owned she was fatigued and would prefer to remain at Matterdale. Susan left Anne in Mrs Clegg's charge while she and the other two girls headed across the moor.

Eppy's greeting was as enthusiastic as ever, but Cassandra seemed ill at ease. The visitors were shown into the drawing room by James, the tall footman Susan remembered from Christmas. The fir tree had been taken down and the room seemed bare without it. Cassandra retreated to a distant chair, her hands clasped together on her lap, and made no movements towards conversation. It was almost as if the Christmas party had never happened. Mr Sutcliffe, after a quizzical look towards his daughter, greeted Susan with ceremonial politeness. Susan took care to frame her words with her hands as well as her voice.

'I hope you are recovered from your indisposition, Mr Sutcliffe?'

'I am tolerable, thank you. I have an excellent nurse.' He smiled fondly at his daughter.

'I like to think I do my best,' said Mrs Grainger, complacently.

'Pair of nurses,' said Mr Sutcliffe swiftly, offering his daughter a look of encouragement, as if urging her to join the conversation. She declined to take the hint, instead taking up a sketch pad and pencil and starting to draw.

'It was all that foolishness on Christmas Day,' said Mrs Grainger. 'Little wonder you were taken ill. For myself, I like nothing better than quiet companionship, among individuals with similar tastes. At our time of life, that must be our best hope for contentment.'

'I am not yet so old as to forgo pleasure altogether, Hester. Did you not enjoy our little party?'

'I take no pleasure in seeing you ill.'

'A few days a-bed is a small price to pay for such delights. I believe Cassie enjoyed herself immensely.' He directed a flurry of signs towards his daughter, who could ignore him no longer.

I did, she returned, after placing the sketchpad and pencil reluctantly on her lap. *Very much. But it seems so long ago.*

'We thought you might call on us sooner, Miss Mottram,' Mrs Grainger remarked icily. 'I suppose the inclement weather kept you indoors?'

'I do not mind the cold,' Susan replied. 'I took great pleasure in our walk here. Though it is winter, there is still much to observe in the countryside. I was delighted to glimpse a kestrel as I came past the lake.'

'I see. Then you have been ill, perhaps?'

Susan frowned in confusion.

'Not at all. I am fortunate to enjoy very good health.'

'Then I can only think that, without the inducements of a fine meal and exceedingly generous gifts, you prefer the society of servants and children to that found at Heathersage?'

'No, indeed!' Susan protested, looking towards Cassandra in alarm. Was this the reason for her reticence? Cassandra glanced up, her expression one that Susan could only describe as painful hope.

I wished to come sooner, Susan assured her. *But I am not always at liberty to follow my own desires.*

'The world is full of those who are happy to accept kindness but are reluctant to make any efforts in return,' said Mrs Grainger.

'I hope I am not one of those!' Susan protested. 'I fully intended to come yesterday, but we had an unexpected visitor.'

'A gentleman, perhaps?' Susan was glad Cassandra could not hear the insinuating tone of Mrs Grainger's query.

'He was not what I would call a gentleman.' Before the words were out of her mouth, Susan realised her admission would do her no favours.

'Indeed.' Mrs Grainger directed a meaningful glance at Mr Sutcliffe.

Susan swiftly recounted the circumstances surrounding Mr Smythson's visit. Mr Sutcliffe leaned forward.

'Smythson, you say? That name seems familiar to me, although I cannot recall why. What can Claybourn be thinking, leaving you so defenceless?'

Cassandra drew her chair forward, her eyes playing across Susan's face.

It must have been most distressing.

'Mr Smythson's manner was rough, it is true, but I believe it was only out of concern for his sister.'

'I admire your charitable inclinations,' said Mr Sutcliffe, 'but since you could not be assured of your visitor's character, you would have been wiser to deny him entrance until Dr Claybourn returned. I think only of your safety and that of the girls. Sailors are not always the most temperate of men.'

His rebuke was so gently given that Susan could resent it no more than she could disagree with it.

'I hope Miss Smythson is not in any trouble,' she said.

'As do I. But Claybourn seems exactly the sort of fellow to be hiding something.'

'I cannot fathom what it could be,' Susan said dutifully.

Unfathomable mysteries are the most fearful. Cassandra shivered. *What lies beyond our worst imaginings is troubling indeed.*

Susan raised an eyebrow.

'I recently made false accusations without evidence and was rightly chided for it. You would not wish me to make the same mistake again?'

'Smythson!' Mr Sutcliffe clapped his hand to his thigh. 'Was not that the name of the young person who imposed herself upon us?'

'Oh yes!' cried Mrs Grainger. 'Knocked on our door, bold as brass, begging for a glass of water. Said she felt faint, but she recovered swiftly enough to ask a good deal of impertinent questions. Cassandra, do you remember? She had red hair.' She signed as she spoke.

Cassandra shook her head. *I must have been taken ill.* She looked at Susan regretfully. *I am often so when strangers come.*

'What did she want?' Susan asked.

'To satisfy her vulgar curiosity of course. Wished to know about the lady of the house. Did she have any friends? Did she ever visit Hustanton? Was she of age?'

'A fortune hunter, plain and simple,' said Mr Sutcliffe. 'Doubtless she intended to befriend Cassie in the hope of preying on her kindness.'

'Can there be such people?' Susan exclaimed in disbelief. Although she couldn't help but remember the letter Mr Smythson had shown her. His sister had certainly shown a grasping, avaricious tendency.

'You will not countenance the number of young men, or old men for that matter, that I've turned away. Women too. All after my daughter's fortune. I will not let Cassie fall prey to such vultures. Whoever woos my dear girl… must be able… to provide for her.'

He had roused himself to such a pitch that he began to cough, his face reddening with the strain. Cassandra rushed to his side in alarm.

'You must rest,' said Mrs Grainger, also rising. 'I will assist you to your chamber.'

'Don't fuss, Hester. I can manage… perfectly well.'

But Mrs Grainger persisted, and he was persuaded to retire. In her father's absence, Cassandra's anxiety returned. She turned this way and that, hands clutching at her slender neck, before she took up the sketch book again and retreated to the safety of a comfortable-looking armchair. Susan saw the ploy for what it was—an excuse to avoid the difficult task of conversing.

She rose instantly and sat down on an ottoman by Cassandra's feet.

You are offended that I did not come sooner.

She had to repeat herself twice before Cassandra would raise her eyes and set aside her book.

Offended? No. Cassandra shook her head decidedly.

Wounded then? If so, I am very sorry for it. I would not upset you for the world.

Cassandra bit her lip.

I was afraid. I thought… you did not wish us to be friends. That I had been too forward and you wished to draw back.

Never! Susan protested. Cassandra met her gaze at last.

I wondered what I had done to make you dislike me. The writing set—I could see you did not wish to accept it.

Shame coloured Susan's face.

My foolish pride was hurt, she admitted. *I have been accustomed to giving charity, not receiving it.*

It was not charity! I wished only to make you happy.

I know that now. Your friendship pleases me more than any gift.

Cassandra's lips parted in a tentative smile.

I would not blame you if you did wish to draw back. I know so little of the world. I have so little to say, so little to contribute.

That is not true. You are a loving, dutiful daughter, full of compassion for others. You have an open, loving heart and draw quite beautifully. I would rather ask why, with all your accomplishments, you would wish to be friends with a penniless teacher, neither pretty nor elegant, and with a head full of all manner of foolish notions.

Cassandra's smile deepened. *That is not what I see.* Her eyes were as depthless as the peat-stained waters of the lake near Heathersage, and something powerful and warm rooted itself in

Susan's breast. Behind them, the sound of the door opening made Susan jump up. It was Mrs Grainger, returned from attending Cassandra's father.

'How is Mr Sutcliffe?' Susan asked, striving for composure.

'In danger of suffering a relapse. I do not think he has got over that walk on Christmas Day. I should have insisted he go in the carriage.' She turned to Susan. 'I suppose we will see little of you, these coming months. You will no doubt be kept busy.'

'I will come on my half days, if I may?'

You must! Cassandra signed. *Would that I, too, had some purpose.*

You are the daughter of a gentleman, Mrs Grainger responded. *There is no requirement for you to be useful.*

Susan is a gentleman's daughter, too. As were you, Hester.

That is quite different. You are wealthy. There is no need for you to engage in drudgery.

Cassandra gave a small smile.

Is it so onerous a task to be my companion?

'Of course not. I did not… I mean that… You are… I could not love you more if you were my own child.' Mrs Grainger was so flustered that she forgot to sign, but Cassandra smiled at her fondly, understanding the sentiment, if not the words.

'Why, Miss Sutcliffe, that's a very fine likeness!'

Isabella had taken up the sketch book that Cassandra had set aside. Cassandra's hand went to her throat and her features twisted in dismay.

'Isabella, return that book to Miss Sutcliffe at once!' Susan commanded, without any real expectation that Isabella would heed her.

'Here's a picture of you, Miss Mottram. Why you look quite… I don't know how to describe it.'

'Let me see, girl.' Mrs Grainger thrust out her hand. Isabella looked questioningly at Susan, who nodded gravely. To her amazement, Isabella relinquished her prize at once. Mrs Grainger glanced at the drawing before casting it aside and looking towards Cassandra.

You can do better. I do not think it very like. Miss Mottram's complexion is not so fine.

'You must not blame the artist for deficiencies in the model,' Susan remonstrated good-humouredly. She took up the book to return it to Cassandra and in so doing caught a glimpse of the picture. It was only partly complete, but still a flattering likeness. Cassandra had caught Susan with her lips parted in the ghost of a smile. Her eyes seemed to shine out of the page. She looked almost pretty. If these were the benefits of a brisk walk in cold weather, she resolved to attempt the exercise more often. She returned the book to its owner.

You are too generous, she signed.

I draw what I see. Cassandra seized the book and hugged it against her chest. Isabella tugged Susan's sleeve hesitantly.

'Please tell Miss Sutcliffe I am sorry if I upset her.'

Susan translated. Cassandra's expression softened. She held out her hand to Isabella before looking at Susan.

She is much changed. You have spoken with her, I perceive? Your kindness has been well rewarded.

I deserve little credit. I did not see what you did.

'Cassie is very perceptive,' said Mrs Grainger. 'In some things, at least. In others, she is inexperienced and easily taken advantage of. But her father and I know how to protect her.'

Mrs Grainger's frowning presence deterred any further exchanges. As the conversation died, Cassandra's discomfort returned. Seeing her distress, Susan rose to take leave.

I will come again, tomorrow, she signed.

Tomorrow? Cassandra's face contained as much doubt as hope. Susan gave her a reassuring smile.

You have my word, and I was taught never to break a promise.

23

A Promise is Kept

As soon as light began to leak round the sides of her thick damask curtains, Cassandra flung aside her bedcovers and stepped lightly towards the dresser, where a bowl of gently steaming water awaited her. There was a lightness in her step, an ease to her breathing that made her feel capable of anything. It was the same feeling she had whenever her father wrote to tell her he was returning from his latest travels. On this occasion, however, the exhilaration arose from the knowledge that, for the first time in her life, she had a friend of her own age. A friend who, with an expression of absolute sincerity, had promised to visit that very day.

She rang for Hannah, her maid, who began applying oil to Cassandra's thick tresses before untangling the knots using a wide-toothed amber comb that had once belonged to Cassandra's mother. In general, Cassandra found the painstaking process soothing: a time to compose her thoughts and gather her courage before facing the day. Today, she chafed beneath Hannah's tweaking and plucking. It seemed an age before her hair was combed through and then arranged in an elaborate chignon. Now it only remained to dress. It felt like a special occasion, so Cassandra chose one of her favourites, a peacock-blue velvet day dress whose cuffs and hems were embroidered in arabesques of silver thread.

Next, she proceeded to her father's chamber to see how he did and was delighted to find him sitting up and partaking of a small breakfast from a tray on his lap. The peachy aroma of his favourite Oolong tea mingled with the salty tang of fresh oysters. Around his shoulders he wore a crimson-dyed blanket of Danish wool, one of a pair he had brought back from Odense five years ago, simply because Cassandra had admitted to having cold toes during a particularly icy January night. She had insisted he use it while he was ill. At her entrance, he immediately set aside his tray to answer her inquiries.

I am much improved, thank you.

Yet not well enough to join us in the breakfast room?

He widened his eyes and contorted his face into a grimace. *Hester.*

No further explanation was required. Cassandra knew how much her father hated to be fussed over by anyone other than his daughter.

You look lovely today, her father continued. *So like your dear mother*. Cassandra flushed with pleasure, hoping that his words were more than those of an indulgent father.

Hannah has worked wonders, she signed. *I shall give her my old tartan dress. If she took it up, it would suit her very well.*

An excellent notion.

Not wanting to overexert him, Cassandra rose and wagged her finger at him.

Since you are such a cowardy custard, I must face Hester alone. For which I shall, in due course, extract suitable penance.

He only gazed at her fondly. Cassandra knew that she could ask for almost anything in the world, and her dear father would move heaven and earth to obtain it.

Hester was in the breakfast room, wearing a sour expression.

How is your father? He will not let me see him.

Much improved, Cassandra signed brightly. *Might we walk out, after breakfast? Eppy would like it and we could meet up with Susan on her way here.*

Hester's lips formed a thin line.

I must speak to cook about luncheon. Who knows how many extra mouths we shall be expected to feed? I would not be surprised if Miss Mottram is brazen enough to invite the whole school.

James entered with a rack of toast and a pot of golden butter. He looked very smart in his double-breasted coat. As always, his first action was to look for Cassandra, to whom he smiled and bowed.

Thank you, Cassandra motioned as he placed the toast beside her. James had been with them since she was very young. Although he never signed himself, he always seemed to understand her.

I do wish you would accompany me, Cassandra continued to plead with Hester. *You know I have not the courage to go alone.*

Instead of answering, Hester spread butter on her toast, pressing down so forcefully with her knife that the delicate triangle fractured. Cassandra, sensing that strong emotions were running through her companion, reached out to touch her arm.

I will never forget what a dear friend you have been to me, these past years. But you must know I have long yearned for a friend my own age.

Hester's expression softened, but still she refused to countenance accompanying Cassandra from the house.

Out of concern for your father, I have sent for Dr Kirtley. One of us must be here to receive him.

It struck Cassandra then how much she had permitted herself to depend on others. How meekly she had let her fears and insecurities restrict her life. She gazed towards the window. The sky was perfectly clear, and the low morning sunlight gilded the moors. Perhaps she might walk to the far side of the lake? She was capable of that, at least. She could take her sketching journal, for on such a fine day, the hares and squirrels were sure to be out. And Eppy really did need a walk.

Cassandra donned a fur-lined pelisse for warmth and set out. Although the air in the shadows was bitingly cold, it was pleasant enough in the sunlight, as long as she kept moving. Nose to the ground, Eppy darted in and out of the undergrowth, wearing a red woollen coat. They soon reached the far side of the lake. Cassandra paused to look at the beaten down path that broke off from the gravel track she was standing on and led out onto the moors. The idea of stepping onto it, alone, terrified her. She glanced backwards in the hope that Hester might have relented and followed her. Although her skittering heart was calmed by the reassuring sight of Heathersage Manor's soot-blackened chimneys, there was no sign of her companion. With a heavy sigh, she turned once more to the path, but even as she willed herself to move, her muscles went limp at the idea. Now she had stopped moving, she grew cold and clutched her journal to her chest for warmth. The tips of her ears were stinging with cold, and she wished she had thought to put on a bonnet.

She had stood in that place for some time when a touch on her arm made her jump. She whirled round, but it was only James, bundled up in a coat and scarf. Under one arm, he carried a tartan blanket, in the other, a knitted tam-o-shanter, yet another gift from her father. Cassandra put it on gratefully, tugging the wool over her frozen ears. James, with a questioning look, placed his fingers against the journal that Cassandra had tucked beneath her left arm. Understanding, she relinquished it.

Did Hester send you?

James only tucked the book under his arm next to the blanket and gestured towards the path. Her blood bubbling with anticipation, Cassandra followed him out onto the moors.

They reached the top of the escarpment, where James laid the blanket across Cassandra's favourite rock. However, instead of sitting down, Cassandra stepped towards the edge so she might look over the rolling landscape below. The sky was clear enough to observe the cold, square lines of Matterdale Hall and its smokeless chimneys. A little further away, Hustanton's church spire rose above stone-tiled roofs. Far beyond, on the horizon, she could just make out the shadowy peaks of the Lakes. Movement below caught her eye. There! Four figures, heading towards the escarpment. Two of the figures broke off, chasing each other into the heather, the other two remaining close, walking together. Susan and Anne, Cassandra guessed, with Isabella and Mary playing. She turned eagerly to James.

Shall we meet them?

James found a narrow path that led downwards. He stepped into it, pausing to reach backwards with a gloved hand. With a last reassuring glance toward Heathersage, Cassandra planted her left hand in his, raised the hem of her skirts with her right and began to descend.

The path was narrow and very steep, but James' strong hand steadied her all the way down, despite Eppy constantly weaving between their legs. Usually, Cassandra would expect to feel cold fingers of dread running down her back at the thought of meeting someone from outside the boundaries of Heathersage, but today all she could think was that Susan was waiting at the end of the path. It was only when they had nearly reached the bottom that it occurred to her the figures might easily be strangers, but by then it was too late.

They broke out onto the plain and, to Cassandra's immense relief, there was Susan, no more than a hundred paces away, her head covered in a plain poke bonnet. As always, she wore a brown wool cloak with a patterned border—an elegant garment that was beginning to show its age in its mended hem and shiny patches where the material was wearing thin. On seeing them, a broad smile lit up Susan's face and she hastened forward, waving furiously. Cassandra was gratified to witness Susan's genuine pleasure at seeing her. Mary, who had been running around with Isabella, broke off to fling her arms around Cassandra's waist before turning to look for her beloved Eppy. Anne and Isabella, although more reticent, approached and signed a greeting. The warmth of their combined welcome did much to settle Cassandra's remaining nerves. Susan started to communicate, but her thick leather gloves made it difficult to discern the signs.

I came to meet you, Cassandra signed at the same time. She wore fingerless woollen gloves, useful when sketching outdoors. They had the added advantage of permitting her to sign clearly.

Susan attempted more signs, equally indistinct.

Your gloves—I cannot see, Cassandra informed her.

Susan's eyes widened and her hand flew to her mouth in an almost comical expression of self-reproach. She swiftly removed her gloves.

What a glorious day. And how brave of you to come and meet us.

As they closed on one another, Cassandra felt a sudden burst of diffidence that prevented her from communicating further, but Susan, of course, knew what do to. She seized Cassandra's arm and gave a squeeze as if to say, *I am here and I am proud of you.*

Don't let go, Cassandra pleaded internally, and Susan smiled and squeezed her arm again. What miracle was this? To understand one another, without words or signs? They walked forward, arm in arm, and the girls fell into step behind them, James bringing up the rear like a sheepdog rounding up his flock.

All too soon, they reached the bottom of the escarpment, where the narrowness of the path forced Susan to disengage her arm and go on ahead. Although she often looked back to see how Cassandra did, Cassandra felt the loss of Susan's presence next to hers and made every effort to ascend quickly. They reached the top, their breath steaming in the cold air, having left James and the girls some way behind. James had left the blanket and journal on the stone and they sat to catch their breath. Susan rested her hand on the journal and looked questioningly at Cassandra.

May I?

Although generally unwilling to share her drawings with anyone other than her father and Hester, Cassandra felt no reluctance in giving Susan permission to leaf through the book. It was only animals and landscapes after all. No intimate portraits to cause confusion. Susan turned each page carefully, smoothing each page with a reverent touch. Cassandra observed her face, noting passing expressions of surprise and appreciation. It charmed her that Susan was unaware of just how clearly her feelings were displayed. Cassandra doubted that Susan could ever tell a lie and not be instantly found out.

Susan pointed out a picture of a Brown Argus that Cassandra had drawn from memory and began to sign.

I love… She stopped with a frown.

Cassandra made the sign for butterfly. To her it was a very simple one, but Susan, in attempting to copy her, made something more akin to 'angel'. Cassandra reached for Susan's hands, so that she might form the appropriate shape. At her touch, Susan trembled and her cheeks flushed. Cassandra immediately released her and bowed her head in embarrassment. Was it wrong to touch someone so, without their permission? She had done so once before, at Christmas, but only because a grieving Susan had been in need of comfort. And how cold Susan's fingers had been, all because she had removed her gloves so that they might communicate. Mortified at having committed, however unwittingly, some grievous error in etiquette, Cassandra began to wish she had waited at home, as Hester had suggested, until a feather-light touch on her arm roused her. She turned to find Susan's clear green eyes examining her with tender enquiry and a hint of confusion that mirrored her own. Before Cassandra could gather her thoughts, Eppy scrambled onto her lap for attention and she became aware that James and the girls had arrived atop the escarpment, their cheeks red and their noses dripping with cold.

We must get everyone home, and into the warm, Cassandra suggested. Although not used to taking the lead, she felt strongly that this was the right course of action and was pleased when everyone instantly agreed. She wondered if it was appropriate to take Susan's arm again. As if reading her thoughts, Susan half turned to her and stuck out an elbow invitingly, making a space just the right size for Cassandra to slip her arm into. Which she did with a glad heart, and off they went.

24

Another Promise is Made

Susan and the girls were shown into the dining room, where a splendid luncheon had been laid out. Plates of cold ham and devilled eggs, freshly baked bread rolls and sliced chicken pie were set next to desserts including mince pies, curd tarts and pickled rhubarb. The girls rushed towards the roaring fire. Susan felt a pang of remorse. Although she had done her best to eke out their meagre supply of coals, their allowance had run out the previous day and Mrs Clegg had refused to fetch more from the coal cellar. Thanks to Susan's poor housekeeping, the girls had become so cold that not even a brisk walk could take the chill from their bones.

Mr Sutcliffe had, on the instructions of his doctor, sent his apologies, and Mrs Grainger also made her excuses, so it fell to Cassandra to perform the duties of hostess. Once the girls had warmed themselves through, she did so assiduously, helping everyone to tea and ensuring each guest was well supplied with milk or sugar or lemon. At first, she seemed anxious, biting her lip as she looked across the table, as if concerned something was missing. Susan made sure to smile reassuringly every time their eyes met. She understood what courage it required for Cassandra to take charge. Anne, who was the most proficient of the girls at signing, asked Cassandra how her father did, and informed their hostess that it was a splendid luncheon. Cassandra responded with a warm smile. As the meal progressed without incident, Susan was delighted to see Cassandra's assurance grow, and her posture become more relaxed. How elegant she looked in her beautiful gown, so well-tailored to her slender frame, its rich velvet tones echoing the smooth purity of her complexion.

Will you try this? Cassandra offered Susan a slice of ginger cake so dark it was almost black. *Our famous Yorkshire parkin.* The rich, sweet flavours danced across Susan's tongue.

Some people find it too rich for their taste, but it is my favourite, Cassandra informed her.

Then henceforth, it shall be mine also, Susan returned with a smile. She was relieved that there was no awkwardness between them after the unfortunate moment on the escarpment. The instant their fingers had met, Susan had felt the same powerful stirring of her blood as at the Christmas party. Overwhelmed by such a strong and unexpected reaction, she had withdrawn and knew this had caused Cassandra great confusion. In truth, she did not herself comprehend what had happened. However, she wished now, with all her heart, that she had not pulled away.

After luncheon, Anne asked Cassandra if she would teach them to draw. Cassandra agreed willingly, and papers and pencil and charcoals were soon obtained. It was agreed that Eppy should be their model and, in response to some signs from Cassandra, the puppy lay down obediently on the carpet and promptly fell asleep.

The girls hung about Cassandra's chair, awed by her confident pencil strokes, from which the face of the beagle began to emerge. As her long, elegant fingers darted across the paper, Cassandra's face glowed with a mixture of extreme concentration and delight. It was the expression of an artist enraptured by her craft and Susan felt as if she could have watched forever.

The clock chimed half past two, startling Susan from her reverie. They must leave soon if they were to get back in the light. The girls displayed their artistic efforts. Mary proudly brandished an indistinct smudge that might just as easily have been a cat, or a mouse, but Cassandra and Susan assured her it was very good indeed. Isabella's attempt was more obviously canine, although poor Eppy had no mouth or whiskers. Anne's attempt was by far the best, but neither Cassandra's expression of delight nor Susan's fervent words of praise could convince her that she had any degree of talent.

The clock chimed the three-quarter hour and, with regret, Susan informed Cassandra that they must go, even though she dreaded a return to the cold, dank corridors of Matterdale Hall. Cassandra plucked at the embroidered sleeve of her day dress, her brow creased as if in some internal debate.

I shall accompany you as far as the escarpment, she signed. *Eppy will benefit from another walk*. That their hostess would make such a heroic gesture on their behalf touched Susan greatly.

You must not distress yourself on our account, she assured Cassandra. However, their hostess would not be put off.

I will come. Within short order they were outside, Eppy looking

197

very fetching in her little red coat. Nose to the ground, she led the way, with Isabella and Mary following. Cassandra clung to Susan's arm as they lagged behind, releasing it only when she spotted animal tracks, such as those of hares or water voles. More at ease than when they had come that morning, she pointed out much that Susan would have missed and spelled out the names of any local birds Susan did not recognise. She laughed in unfettered delight at a redwing taking a bath in a puddle and then plucked a leaf from a stem of mint, rubbed it between her fingers to release the scent and inhaled deeply, before insisting Susan do the same. Susan marvelled at the difference in her companion's demeanour from the timid and restrained Cassandra that had first greeted her. Arm in arm they walked. Although the sun was setting and the air growing chillier by the minute, Susan did not feel at all cold. As they stopped to admire a waxwing with an extravagant crest fluffing its chest feathers, Susan imagined how enlivening it would be to walk across the moors in spring with such a companion. It seemed no time at all before they reached the escarpment. Cassandra dropped Susan's arm.

I dare go no further. While I can still see my beloved Heathersage I can bear it, but when I am alone, I find it impossible to go beyond its sight.

It was kind of you to come so far, and to teach me so much, Susan returned.

You owe me no thanks. I came for my own pleasure entirely. I hope you will return soon?

I will come as soon as I can. I promise.

She reached for Cassandra and this time there was no shrinking away as their fingers touched. They clasped hands for a long moment. Cassandra then looked back at the long, lonely walk that lay before her and a shudder ran through her body. After a last, reassuring squeeze, Susan released her hands so she might communicate.

I will watch you awhile, to see you are safe.

Cassandra, with a deep sigh, turned and headed for home. Watching her leave, Susan felt a wrench, as if something had been torn from her grasp. At the bottom of the gentle slope, Cassandra turned and raised her hand. Susan waved back. She would have waited longer, but the girls grew impatient and started down the steep path that led down the side of the cliff. She had no choice but to follow.

25

The Claybourns Return

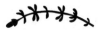

The Claybourns returned from Harrogate. The trunks had barely been lifted from the trap before Mrs Claybourn was inspecting the second parlour for damage.

'This holly must be removed at once. I only pray it has not scratched the paintwork.'

'I hoped to make the room a little more festive for the girls,' Susan explained. 'We would have put up the flowers Miss Smythson's class made, but they were mouldy.'

'You were in the attic?' Mrs Claybourn's head whipped round.

'Yes. Mrs Clegg—'

'Mrs Clegg had no right to give you the key.'

'I assure you, everything was put back in place. You would not have known anyone had been in there.'

'That is not the point. The attic floor is riddled with woodworm.'

'I... I did not realise!' Susan exclaimed, horrified to have put Anne and Mary at risk.

'I make these stipulations for good reason, Miss Mottram. I do not wish to get a reputation for harming my teachers.'

'I am grateful for your concern, ma'am.'

'My mother's primary concern is that you might be rendered unfit for work,' Marion remarked drily. Mrs Claybourn finished making her circuit.

'I had not realised how drab this paper is. These walls must be repainted immediately.' She tugged the bell. It took three more rings before a flustered Mrs Clegg made an appearance.

'We'll take tea in here, Clegg. Bring coals so we might have a fire. You will stay, Miss Mottram,' she added, as Susan prepared to remove the girls. 'We have news that concerns you. Ah, there you are, Henry. I hope all is well?'

'Yes, yes, everything is quite in order. With only four patients, how could it be otherwise?' her husband replied sulkily, as he and Helena joined the others in the parlour.

'You should never have attended that lecture. They always put you in a bad mood.'

'These dabblers with their private fortunes quite exasperate me. They puff themselves up about some trifling advance, but there's not an ounce of real ambition among them. Yet they take me for some country bumpkin and laugh at me behind their hands.'

'You had no luck in finding a patron?' Susan asked. Dr Claybourn fingered his collar as if it were too tight.

'They could not grasp my theory. They quibble over my methods.'

'You had a quiet time here, I am sure,' Marion stated in her customary abrupt manner.

'On the contrary, we had an unexpected visitor.' Susan told them about Mr Smythson.

'Miss Smythson is missing?' Dr Claybourn frowned. 'Her brother must be distraught.'

Susan read nothing but concern in his countenance.

'Not distraught enough to stop him accusing us of malfeasance,' said Mrs Claybourn sharply.

'I assured him I had every confidence in Dr Claybourn's character,' said Susan.

'Bless you, my dear. I do hope nothing untoward has happened.' Dr Claybourn shook his head.

'That false girl deserves no sympathy, after writing such a letter. As if Henry could keep any secrets from me!'

'Most distressing, heh-heh.' Dr Claybourn's customary chuckle lacked exuberance. He took out a handkerchief and dabbed at his brow. 'I wish you had not faced him alone. Had I been here, I could have reassured the poor fellow.' He seemed so upset at the accusation that Susan almost regretted bringing it to his attention.

'Have we any secrets, Marion?' asked Helena with a knowing look.

'I don't know—do we?' Marion returned calmly. Susan could have sworn Helena blushed beneath her rouge and she broke the stony silence that followed by asking the family how they had found Harrogate.

'Most disagreeable,' said Mrs Claybourn. 'The expense was hardly to be believed. So many tickets to be paid for, and every coachman and his dog seemed to expect a gratuity.'

'One must always be travelling hither and thither.' Helena, after looking around in vain for a chaise longue, sank into Isabella's armchair. 'I was forced to decline a dozen invitations. It was kind of Mrs Mollard to let me stay quietly within the house.'

'You gave her little choice,' Marion remarked. 'The servants had to prise you from the sofa every time we took dinner.'

'It is not my fault that my health is poor. My lungs are quite ravaged by the cold from travelling in that horrid trap. Papa, I beg you will send Richard to the apothecary for a tincture.'

'You were well enough to talk nonsense with Mr Finchley.'

'I exerted myself where I could. You know nothing of civility, Marion.'

Marion gave a dry cough.

'You are still upset by our little game?' Helena asked. 'Miss Mottram, you will be diverted, I'm sure. Mr Finchley wagered he could make Marion fall in love with him. I insisted he could not, for without a heart to begin with, she is a hopeless case. You will not be surprised that I returned ten shillings the richer! It was harmless fun, yet you'd think I'd broken all ten of the commandments the way Marion grimaces at me.'

'I think it a cruel sport that plays with human feelings,' said Susan. 'Love most of all.'

'You need not fear for me, Miss Mottram,' said Marion swiftly. 'I am quite unmoved by the likes of Mr Finchley.'

'I found him quite charming,' said Helena. 'But Marion would not recognise charm if it wore a red hat and waved a stick in her face.'

'Cease this confounded bickering!' Dr Claybourn's irritable interjection stilled his daughters into silence. Mrs Clegg had, by this time, completed the almost interminable rites involved in making a pot of tea, although it arrived lukewarm from its inevitable snail-like journey from the kitchen.

'This is not to be borne!' exclaimed Dr Claybourn, setting down his cup so abruptly it clattered against the saucer. 'Cannot a man have a decent cup of tea in his own house?'

'Our sojourn in Harrogate was not without some success,' said Mrs Claybourn, calmly handing Susan some tea. 'A respectable widow of Mr Mollard's acquaintance is great friends with Sir Peregrine Mandrake. He has two spirited daughters, whom a string of governesses have failed to tame. I made an excellent case for our establishment.'

'A single glance at Marion, and those girls will be terrified into good behaviour,' drawled Helena.

'The eldest girl is musical. I mentioned our pianoforte. Miss Mottram, did you try our instrument while we were away?'

'I did. I'm sorry to say it is dreadfully out of tune.'

Mrs Claybourn frowned. 'Your pupils would not mind the odd wrong note here and there. You can still work on fingering, I am sure.'

'I'm afraid it would be quite impossible to give lessons with the piano in its current state.'

'I suppose I must send to Harrogate then, at great expense?' Mrs Claybourn's expression suggested her cup was full of squeezed lemon, rather than tea.

'You might apply to Miss Sutcliffe,' Susan suggested. 'They have a splendid instrument at Heathersage Manor and may be able to recommend a tradesman with the requisite skills.'

'You have been to Heathersage?' Marion asked sharply.

Susan related the Sutcliffe's kind invitation, and her acceptance. Marion's forehead creased into a frown.

'I am surprised you exposed our pupils to such dangers.'

'We all returned with a full complement of fingers and toes.'

'I suppose you had a sirloin,' said Mrs Claybourn sourly. 'I hear they have nothing but the best at Heathersage.'

'We were entertained most generously.'

'Since you are now such a favourite, perhaps you could ask Mr Sutcliffe to send along whoever tunes his piano? We must make a good impression when Sir Peregrine visits.'

Susan acquiesced with alacrity, happy for an excuse to write to Cassandra.

'Miss Mottram should be discouraged from any acquaintance with that house.' If the windows hadn't already been frosted over, Marion's expression would have made them so.

'If the fellow and his daughter wish to make a friend of our own dear Miss Mottram, we should not stand in the way,' said Dr Claybourn, ever Susan's ally.

'But what of the rumours? Of witchcraft and worse.'

Dr Claybourn arced his closed fist through the air as though he carried an invisible sword. 'Rumour brought Mr Smythson to our door, with his violent temper and false accusations. Out Rumour! I dispel thee! Let it have no place here!'

26

A Mistaken Assumption

As had become her custom during the holidays, Susan tucked Mary into bed, and said good night to Anne and Isabella. On leaving the dormitory, she heard raised voices from the corridor that led towards the back of the house. A man and a woman, arguing. Concerned that perhaps Mr Smythson had made a return, she went to investigate. At the end of the corridor, Helena was pressed up against the wall and Richard was leaning over her, gesticulating angrily. Helena seemed to be pleading with him, her palm pressed against his chest. As Susan hurried towards them, she saw that Helena's rouge was runnelled with tears and her skin was grey where the red pigment had been washed away.

'Helena, are you ill? Is Richard upsetting you?' she asked.

Helena slowly turned her head and gave Susan a blank look.

'This is none of your business, Miss Sparrer,' said Richard without looking away from Helena.

'Mrs Claybourn, I am sure, would not approve of you being here,' Susan remarked icily.

Richard tilted his head.

'And I suppose you'll be obliged to tell her?'

'Not if you leave immediately.'

He grinned and put his hands in his pockets.

'Richard, please! Wait. Don't leave me,' Helena pleaded, but Richard sauntered off whistling.

'Why must you interfere in other people's concerns?' Helena asked Susan peevishly. 'I had a particular matter to discuss with Richard, but he is angry with me, and now he has gone!' She turned and rested her pale forehead against the door of her chamber and emitted a low, anguished moan.

'I am only concerned for you,' said Susan, for when she grabbed hold of Helena's hand, it was hot and feverish. 'Can I get you anything? Should I fetch your mother?'

A loud wail, in a minor key, indicated a decided negative.

'Or Marion, perhaps?'

A particularly agonised groan informed Susan that this suggestion was even less welcome than the first. It was impossible to leave Helena alone in such a precarious state and so Susan attended her into her bedchamber, which was in such disorder Susan wondered if a thief had rifled through it. Shoes and gowns were scattered across the floor. A corset hung drunkenly from the back of a chair and the bed was buried beneath a mound of stockings. Helena prised herself from Susan's arms and weaved towards a large dresser, paying no heed as she trod on an open book and tore the page with her heel. On top of the dresser was the purple hat box that Helena had taken to Harrogate. Frantically, she rummaged inside.

There was the sound of clinking glass and Susan peered over Helena's shoulder to see the hatbox was full of tiny brown bottles. Helena scrabbled desperately among them, her hands shaking, but almost all were unstoppered and empty. Then, with a cry of delight she found one that was still full of liquid. She pulled the cork and downed the contents, tilting back her head and shaking every last drop from the bottle. With a sigh, she sank onto her bed amid the mound of stockings and closed her eyes. Still unwilling to leave her, Susan sat by her, and gently stroked her hair, as she had done with Florence whenever she was ill. Eventually, Helena raised her head. Her eyes seemed unusually dark, her pupils bloated.

'I must look a state.' She patted her head distractedly. Her hair was disordered, pins dangling from several loose strands.

'I fear Richard has distressed you in some manner?' said Susan, diplomatically changing the topic.

'Richard? No. It was my own fault, for talking of Mr Finchley. But he must know I meant nothing by it. A little gentle flirting never hurt anyone. What else is one supposed to do in Harrogate?'

'Can it be possible that you have… some kind of an understanding? With Richard?' Susan queried doubtfully.

'You do not approve my choice?'

'He is an odious man.'

Helena's eyes widened, and Susan realised that an honest answer might not have been what was required. 'Forgive me, you asked my opinion.'

'And you made the mistake of giving me a truthful one,' said Helena with a faint smile. 'Perhaps if you loved someone society does not think you should, you would be less eager to condemn.'

'He is a fortune hunter. He admits it himself!'

'At least he is an honest one. You and he have that in common.'

'But does he love you?'

'He has never pretended what he does not feel and has sworn to be a good husband to me. Since he is always truthful, I know that he means what he says. But I suppose that you are one of those foolish romantics that consider love more important than trust?'

'I would have both,' declared Susan. 'But perhaps I have unrealistic expectations.' She certainly couldn't claim any success when it came to romance. Unless one counted Mr Potts, which she certainly did not.

'As for love, I have enough for the both of us. He has a rough type of charm and is quite handsome when he does not open his mouth.'

'Certainly more agreeable,' Susan could not help adding.

'I am not blinded to his faults. In marrying him, I need pretend no longer.'

'Is your life here so dreadful?'

Helena rummaged around in the pile of stockings and came up with a hairbrush. She proceeded to run it idly through her tangled locks.

'You have observed how my mother treats me. And Marion.'

'But your father is good to you, is he not?'

'But it is all because of a lie!' Helena's lip trembled. 'I believe I will tell you. You have compassion, a commodity in poor supply in this house. Tell me, do you think me an indolent creature? One who pretends to be ill to avoid work?'

When Susan did not immediately respond, Helena prodded her in the ribs with her hairbrush.

'Come, where is your candour now?'

'You have displayed an unusual variety of symptoms,' Susan admitted, 'but no-one could doubt the severity of your recent indisposition.'

'I have such terrible headaches—when they come on, as one did just now, they quite blind me. I invent other maladies to hide my true indisposition.'

'Why would you do such a thing?'

Helena's hand fluttered to the top of her head, as if feeling for a wound, or scar.

'I am Papa's greatest achievement. I cannot tell him that his so-called cure served only to replace one cruel affliction with another. He would be heartbroken.'

'Surely if you told him the truth, he would wish to help you? He is a physician, after all.'

Helena shuddered.

'You must not tell him. I could not bear any more of his treatments. If Richard did not bring me laudanum I would be in perpetual agony. He alone cares for my needs. And now he is angry with me. Miss Mottram, will you speak to him? Tell him how sorry I am?'

Susan did not know quite how to answer, but luckily Helena's eyelids had begun to droop, and a few moments later, she fell back onto the bed in a stupor.

On leaving the chamber, Susan bumped into Richard. He appeared so quickly, she suspected he had been waiting for her. Perhaps even listening at the door.

'Well, Miss Sparrer, I see you have found out our little secret. I hope you can be trusted to keep it.'

His confident grin disgusted her.

'What of your boast to always speak the truth?'

'The Claybourns aren't quite ready to hear it. But they will be, soon enough.'

'And how will you accomplish such a miracle?'

'That's my business.' He tapped the side of his nose. 'We're all hiding something. Even you, Miss Sparrer.'

'I am not so interesting, I'm afraid,' Susan said stiffly. 'You should not cast aspersions without any foundation.'

'Poor little sparrer. I suppose you dream of nothing but flowers and butterflies. You're so blind, you could put your head in the noose and not even see it.'

Susan looked up and down the corridor. She longed to be free of him but refused to give him the satisfaction of running away.

'Do you seek to frighten me into keeping quiet?'

'I'm only giving you friendly warning. Man is at heart a beast, who survives only at the expense of others.'

Unable to bear any longer the wolfish way he looked at her, Susan retreated, with as much dignity as she could, to her chamber. A neatly wrapped package lay upon her pillow. It contained a small mother-of-pearl pendant on a silver chain, nestling in a fragment of soft velvet. As with the previous gifts, there was no note to say who it was from. Susan felt distinctly uncomfortable. The apple and the cake had been one thing, but a pendant was a different matter. It was too much like a love token. Her secret benefactor was certainly persistent. She had assumed the cake at Christmas had come from Dr Claybourn and had been happy to accept what she thought an innocent gift, meant to be shared amongst the girls. Could his courtesies, which she had always considered a fatherly concern for her welfare, have a more ardent source? If Dr Claybourn, a married man, was her admirer, it would explain the secrecy, although not excuse it. Such admiration was wrong in every possible way. She must make it clear, in the strongest terms, that she did not welcome his attentions.

The next morning Isabella volunteered to help Susan take down the holly.

'We had such a nice time at Heathersage, didn't we?' Isabella said, placing a stem of holly into the empty basket that Susan had fetched for the purpose. 'I've never eaten so much in my life, nor seen a tree so big. Miss Sutcliffe was agreeable, wasn't she? Not at all like a witch.'

'I'm sure you are too sensible to believe such ridiculous stories,' said Susan.

'People mistake Eppy for her familiar,' said Anne, looking up from her book. 'Which is silly. Everybody knows that witches have cats.'

'She's far too pretty,' Isabella added. 'Witches are ugly old maids with long noses and scowling faces.'

At that moment the door was flung back and Marion strode in.

'Oh!' gasped Anne, and Isabella's mouth hung open in such a comical expression that Susan struggled to keep a straight face.

'Mouth closed, Miss Brownloe,' Marion snapped. 'No need to gawp like a village idiot.'

Isabella's mouth twitched into a grin.

'Does something amuse you?'

'May we help you, Miss Claybourn?' Susan asked, before Isabella could reveal what had diverted her.

'I wondered if you required assistance.'

'Oh, how kind of you. But we are almost done. I suppose this room is to be locked up again when the girls return?' She looked around the parlour with some regret. In the last few weeks, spartan though it was, it had come to feel a little like home.

'You do not welcome the new term?'

'It is an odd creature that prefers work to leisure.'

'Then I am one such, for I welcome a return to my duties.'

'Perhaps you have yet to find the right sort of pleasures?'

'I do not understand you,' Marion snapped. 'Of what pleasures do you speak?'

'Why, only the innocent joy to be found in a book, or in listening to music,' Susan said, wondering why Marion was staring at her so oddly. She placed the last sprig of holly in the basket.

'Allow me.' Marion strode forward and plucked the basket from her hands.

'It is not heavy, I can manage perfectly well.'

But Marion insisted. In the corridor they were met by Dr Claybourn, resplendent in a paisley waistcoat.

'Ah, Miss Mottram, there you are. I must apologise for being out of humour yesterday. Mr Smythson's false accusations wounded me greatly. That, and the fatigue of our journey made me inexcusably abrupt. I hope you will forgive me.'

'Being out of humour is no great sin,' said Susan.

'Marion will be delighted to hear that, I'm sure, heh-heh.'

Susan was eager to speak to him about the pendant but did not want to shame him by raising such a delicate subject in front of his daughter. Unfortunately, Marion stood with the basket of holly in her hands and showed no sign of departing.

'It seems that Christmas is over,' continued Dr Claybourn,

nodding at the basket. 'You and your pupils must be heartbroken.'

'I plan a large dose of Euclid to distract them from their grief.'

He tilted his head.

'Euclid's work as an effective cure for broken hearts? An interesting hypothesis, if it could be proven.'

'Perhaps we might devise an experiment?' Susan suggested lightly. 'Although that would entail dividing my class so that half received the lesson, while the other did not. Such a measure would be bound to cause resentment.'

'I see the problem. Those pupils from whom you withhold the delights of Euclid will be envious of their fellows.'

'I fear it would be quite the other way round.'

At that moment, Mary stuck her head around the door of the parlour. Seeing the three of them together in the corridor, she retreated swiftly.

'Isn't that the little deaf girl?' asked Dr Claybourn, leaning around Susan to see better. 'Did you make any progress while we were away? Has she told you aught of herself, and her history?'

'We progressed a great deal, but she is still very shy. You see how she shrinks from everyone except myself and Anne. I cannot even persuade her to come into the kitchen. Now that the second parlour is to be shut, I thought we might take our leisure there. It is warm and we are not in anybody's way. But she refuses to go in. I suppose she is afraid of the Cleggs.'

'We cannot have you being cold,' exclaimed Dr Claybourn. 'I will ensure there is a fire in the refectory every morning until term begins.'

'I suggested the same thing to Mother only yesterday,' said Marion stiffly. 'But she refused.'

'I think I can be more persuasive,' said her father. 'Marion, is that holly to be removed, or do you plan to hang about in the corridor like the ghost of Christmas recently past?'

Marion's jaw clenched and she disappeared towards the back of the house. Dr Claybourn leaned into Susan and lowered his voice. 'I am glad she is gone. I wish to discuss something with you. A matter that is close to my heart.'

Susan blanched, certain she knew his purpose. Eager to pre-empt any declaration, she reached into her pocket for the pendant.

'If you wish to speak of this and the feelings behind it, I beg you would not. Please, take it. I cannot keep it.'

He started backwards in shock.

'Miss Mottram, what is this? You seek to give me some token?'

Susan flushed. Had she been wrong to suspect him?

'No, indeed. Only to return it.'

'I suppose I should have expected this. A man of my intellect and impeccable appearance is always prone to unwanted admir-ation. Alas, I have many attributes that attract female attention.'

'That is not quite what I meant,' Susan began.

'How could I ever transfer my affection from the divinity that is Mrs Claybourn? A woman of rare purpose, a woman of forti-tude! With a mind so exalted, especially among females, who are so often deficient in reason and logic. Reason and logic, Miss Mottram. Those attributes appear to have deserted you entirely.'

'Certainly, it seems I have been mistaken,' Susan admitted.

'You poor girl, I see how it has been. You have misconstrued my kindness for affection. Or perhaps this delusion is the after-effects of your visit to my infirmary. I did warn you about miasma. Let me cure you of any misapprehension. I assure you, I am quite devoted to Mrs Claybourn.'

'You did not leave this in my chamber?'

'Indeed I did not! It would be most improper!'

'I am relieved to hear it,' said Susan. 'But you have been so kind to me, and when you said you wished to speak to me concerning a matter of the heart…'

'My research!' Dr Claybourn cried. 'I was hoping you might be persuaded to assist me. I had thought you a sensible and intelligent young lady, but it seems we have both been very much mistaken.'

With a last incredulous look at her, he turned away, leaving Susan feeling very foolish indeed.

27

A Letter is Begun

The next day, Susan entered the refectory to find a fire crackling in the grate. Despite her unfounded accusations, Dr Claybourn had made good on his promise. Anne and Mary were sitting on the hearthrug, signing to each other, and Isabella was at a nearby table, sketching with pencils. With them both occupied, Susan was free to write to Cassandra about the piano tuner. She also felt it important to inform her of the Claybourns' return and the consequent restrictions on her freedom.

My dear Cassandra,

I take up pen and paper with a grateful and loving heart. The kindness you have offered me, despite the unfortunate circumstances of our first meeting, fills me with gratitude. In offering me your friendship you have expressed my own dearest hope. I am not deserving of such happiness, but I have never been one to let my own deficiencies prevent me accepting gifts, especially one so pleasing to me. Since I saw you last at Heathersage, the Claybourns have returned and we are busy with preparations for the new term. Yet I can think of nothing but my next half day, when I might visit you, my dearest friend. I——

'Oh, this is impossible!' Isabella crumpled up the piece of paper she had been drawing on and threw it onto the floor. Mary picked it up and presented it to Susan. It was a picture of herself, sitting at her desk. The proportions were awry. Her legs might have served a giantess, and her bosom was so excessively full it defied all laws of anatomy, as well as gravity.

'It was supposed to be of you,' Isabella said forlornly. 'But you've gone a most peculiar shape.'

Susan raised an eyebrow.

'I should certainly turn heads if I looked like that. If I had known I was to be your model I could have sat properly for you.'

'You must have sat for Miss Sutcliffe's picture, for it was a very fine likeness. Why, you looked almost as if…'

'As if what?' said Susan absently, her thoughts still on her letter.

'It's how people look when they are in love. If there was any handsome man within twenty miles, I might suspect you. But there's nobody hereabouts. Besides, you're too poor for anyone to set their cap at.'

Susan laughed and shook her head.

'I admit to being very fond of Eppy. Perhaps I was thinking of her?'

Isabella's shoulders sagged.

'I'll never be as good as Miss Sutcliffe.'

'I'm sure her skill comes from practice as much as natural talent. You saw how many pictures were hanging on the walls. You will never improve if you give up at the first attempt.'

The door opened and the incoming draught almost extinguished their little fire. It was followed by Marion, her expression as forbidding as ever.

'Do not rise, Miss Mottram. I came only to be assured you have a fire.'

'That is very kind,' said Susan. Marion stayed by the door, as stiff and upright as the jamb beside her.

'Do I disturb you? You are writing a letter.'

'I write to ask Miss Sutcliffe if she can recommend a pianoforte tuner.'

'For the piano in the parlour?' Isabella exclaimed. 'Oh, we could dance, just like at Heathersage!'

'There was dancing?' Marion's nose twitched. 'How did you manage for a partner?'

'Miss Mottram did not dance. She played for the rest of us,' Isabella informed her.

'My mother will not encourage dancing here.'

'Why not?' Isabella asked. 'It will be more use than Latin, or any of our other lessons. I am more likely to be asked to dance when I'm grown up than how many King Henrys there were.'

'For such impertinence, I shall fetch my cane.'

'I beg you would not,' pleaded Susan. Marion's eyes settled up on her.

'You remain unwilling to exert discipline?'

'I do not believe that thrashing teaches anything other than

221

repression of spirits. There was no malice in what Isabella said. Some might even call it wit.'

Marion fingered the back of her head.

'Very well,' she said, attempting one of her grimacing smiles. 'I shall be lenient. But Miss Brownloe should learn not to talk back to her elders.'

She strode to the fire and poked it vigorously. Susan took up her pen to continue her letter but had written only one more sentence when a long shadow fell across her desk. Marion's tall frame was blocking out the light from the window. Susan looked up just in time to see Marion avert her gaze.

'Do you need me for some task?' she asked, setting down her pen.

'Yes,' Marion said, after the merest of hesitations. She glanced towards the fire, where the girls were still engrossed in their various occupations. 'Might I trouble you to join me in the second parlour?'

'Is something amiss? I hope you have not found any injury to the skirting boards? I assure you the wallpaper was peeling before we took possession.'

'Come.'

Suspecting that she was to be chastised, Susan left the girls to their amusements and followed Marion from the room. As soon as they were in the second parlour, Marion closed the door behind them, pressed her back to the door and whispered in a low, hoarse voice.

'Do you... Have you ever... sinned, Miss Mottram?' Her pale hands writhed around each other. Susan took a moment to respond.

'I cannot claim to be without fault,' she said. 'It would be an extraordinary person that never erred. Indeed, there is something rather chilling in perfection.'

'Do you... could you stoop to befriending someone who is imperfect?'

'I would not consider it to be stooping,' said Susan, thinking of Cassandra.

'Then,' cried Marion, plunging forward and kneeling at her feet. 'Dear Miss Mottram... Susan... I would beg that you would henceforth see me as your friend. As someone who may confide in you and to whom you could relieve the contents of your heart!'

Susan blinked, disconcerted by the vehemence of Marion's application, as well as utterly astonished by it.

'You do me a great honour,' she began hesitantly.

Marion's cheeks spotted pink and she lifted her chin. 'I see.' She rose to her feet. 'I shall not debase myself further with advances that are clearly unwelcome. Good day.'

Her shoulders were hunched and her fists clenched and unclenched as she strode towards the door. Susan could not permit her to leave in such obvious distress.

'Wait. Miss Claybourn... Marion.'

Marion froze, her fists clenched by her side.

'I see you are suffering,' Susan said gently. 'I would gladly offer my help, but I fear my abilities are unsuited to such a task. Your anguish makes me think you need a true confessor, a person with experience in such matters. A clergyman, perhaps? Or your father?'

'My father?' She grimaced. 'No!'

'Then...' Susan approached and rested her hand on Marion's forearm. 'Perhaps we might visit the chapel together? There can be much consolation in prayer.'

The other woman flinched as if Susan's touch burned her.

'Jehovah will not listen to such a one as I.'

'Marion, such self-disgust cannot be healthy. What can be its source?'

'Look at me! Unnatural creature, so tall and... unwomanly. Even the girls can see it.'

'Who is to say what is natural? As for height, there are many women who might wish to be a little taller.' Susan offered a faint smile.

The door opened, and Mr Clegg came in, carrying a bucket of white paint in one hand and a broad brush in the other.

'Sorry, misses. I thought room were empty,' he said. He backed out, his habitually bowed form making it appear as if he were paying obeisance.

'No one can look at you, Miss Mottram and think anything amiss,' Marion croaked, before following him from the chamber as if she were being whipped.

28

A Letter is Concluded

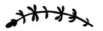

That night, Susan found sleep difficult to come by. Something within the events of the day nagged at her but she couldn't place it. Marion's outburst had certainly startled her. To receive such a fervent request for intimacy from someone who had always avoided her was as strange as it had been unexpected. Yet it was not Marion's behaviour that bothered her, nor Helena's recent confession either, although she felt sorry for any young woman whose future happiness depended on Richard Clegg. It was something else that kept her from her rest. She lay awake for some time until deciding that, since sleep would not come, she might as well finish her letter. She re-read the first lines and instantly knew the cause of her restlessness.

That's how people look when they are in love.

When Isabella had said the words, something inside Susan had shifted. She hadn't acknowledged it at the time, but she had felt something stirring. An echo of those sensations she'd felt first at Heathersage Manor, and then again on the escarpment, when Cassandra's fingers had brushed against her own. She sat up with a gasp. Could she, like Helena, be in love? If so, there was only one person who could be the focus of such feelings—only one person who sent her heart and body into a shuddering thrill. And her recent dreams had been filled, not with flowers and butterflies, but with soft, sepia lips and depthless brown eyes. Once the idea formed inside her head, Susan's innate honesty admitted the truth of it. She was in love with Cassandra. How strange that all the stories and poems suggested that romantic love only existed between man and woman! But there was no room for doubt. She knew those poems well. Only half appreciated before, they suddenly made intoxicating sense.

She paced about her tiny chamber. Should she confess? What would be Cassandra's reaction if she knew the nature of Susan's feelings? There had been so many misunderstandings between them, so many half-communications. Given Susan's inadequacies at signing, how would she ever make herself understood? She had no hope her feelings were returned. What could Cassandra find to love in a naïve schoolteacher, whose figure was too short for elegance, and whose unruly pupils had caused her repeated distress? Attraction between women must be uncommon, for she had never heard it spoken of. It was extremely unlikely that Cassandra would share Susan's desires. Her situation seemed as hopeless as Helena's. In any case, Susan was not free to give her heart. There was her mother and Florence to think of and support. This was no time for reckless honesty. She must keep her secret close. She could not help then, but think of Richard, and his insinuating look. *We are all hiding something.* She tore up her half-finished letter which, on re-perusing, she felt might reveal too much. After many crossings out and false starts she wrote another, much shorter note.

Dear Cassandra,

I regret that my duties here keep me too busy to write more than this short note. I beg you will forgive this seeming neglect and be assured that I hope, as promised, to attend you on Saturday, which is my next half day. Mrs Claybourn asks whether you can recommend a tuner for our pianoforte, as I am to give lessons to some of our pupils and the instrument here is sadly out of tune.

Your affectionate friend

Susan

She re-read it with dissatisfaction for, now she had shorn it of sentiment, it seemed abrupt. More a letter of business than one of friendship. But at least it could not betray her. She sealed it and, when morning came, placed it in the postbag. A few days later, Marion handed Susan an envelope.

'I happened to be speaking with Mrs Clegg when the postman came by. I see the direction is in Miss Sutcliffe's hand. With such exalted friends, I see why you have no desire for others.'

'Thank you,' said Susan, taking the proffered letter. 'But my friendship with Cassandra does not mean—'

'I beg you will speak no more of it.' Marion hastened away. Susan tore open the letter.

Dearest Susan,

Thank you for your note. I will forgive you its brevity since, as a young lady who knows nothing but leisure, I cannot understand the demands that fall upon a schoolmistress. Yet, if we are to be faithful and honest confidantes, I own that I was disappointed not to have more news. Do not think this a reprimand, dearest Susan, only my own selfishness. I have found things so dull here since your last visit. With all our decorations gone, all seems flat and colourless. To comfort myself, I fill my imagination with Matterdale Hall and those occupants who are now so dear to me. I wish to know everything that concerns my new friend. Tell me, have you and Mary learned any more signs? Does Isabella's behaviour continue to improve, now that you have discovered that her heart be more troubled than bad? I'm sure it does, for who could resist your gentle heart? And dear, shy little Anne, how is she? I expect she has read her books twice through already! You must borrow whatever you wish from our library, for the girls, or for your own amusement. I would be delighted to send you anything you should ask for.

Of our news, there is little enough. Mrs Grainger is most attentive to my father, who remains unwell. Nothing is too much trouble for her, although I do believe my father would prefer a few peaceful hours to himself, especially of a morning, for Mrs Grainger is convinced of the benefit of sunlight and an open window, no matter the time of the day. He bids me say that he would be most happy to send along Mr Murray, who trained at Broadwoods, to see to your piano. He is due in a fortnight, and once he has finished here we will send him on to you. Eppy does not like the recent frosts. The instant she sets her paws on the frozen ground she dances back inside the house and hides until she is safe from being asked to go outside. I cannot censure a behaviour that so reflects my own infirmity, and we console ourselves by snuggling together by the window and looking across the lake in the heartfelt hope that our friends might appear. I long to see you here and will count every day until your promised visit. My father says he fears the weather will turn to snow, but I am certain the Gods will not be so cruel.

Your loving friend,

Cassandra

Such an effusive reply to her own short missive filled Susan with shame. It was open and affectionate, whereas Susan's had contained nothing but dissembling politeness. She felt her correspondent's gentle remonstrance acutely. So richly deserved and yet her transgression had been instantly forgiven. She sighed. Every generous sentiment made her more in love than ever. What was she to do? She resolved to make amends by paying Cassandra every possible attention when at last she saw her. If that meant owning the truth, then she would not shy away from it, no matter the consequences. That was the least she owed Cassandra. And yet... The letter had kindled a spark of hope within her breast. Such expressive feelings! Dare she hope they might eventually turn to love? She pored over Mary's sign language book, searching for the means by which she might communicate what was in her heart. She found neither signs nor words that seemed in any way suitable for such a task.

29

In Which Susan Suffers Another Disappointment

Alas, Mr Sutcliffe's reading of the weather proved accurate. On Friday morning, snow began to fall from a leaden sky, growing heavier through the day and continuing into the night. On Saturday, Susan awoke to a blanket of white so thick that the branches of the holly tree drooped beneath its weight. Large drifts had collected beyond the walls of the grounds. The moor, breathtakingly beautiful in its white purity, was impassable. Even the track to Hustanton had disappeared under two feet of snow. Communication with the outside world was impossible.

The girls did not share Susan's dismay. As soon as the morning lessons were completed, they donned bonnets, scarves, gloves and coats, and rushed out into the grounds to frolic in the snow. Susan watched them from the window of her tiny chamber, tying her cashmere shawl around her shoulders in a fruitless attempt to keep warm. At the edge of the property, the harsh lines of the infirmary had been softened by a pristine white blanket of snow, but the girls did not stray near it. Susan wondered if she would be considered mad, to be in love with a woman? Would she be locked away, like Maria, in a padded cell, if her feelings were known?

In the distance, the escarpment burst up from the snowy carpet to form a gaping grey wound. Beyond, a narrow column of smoke rose into the white sky. It could only be coming from Heathersage Manor. She closed her eyes and pictured Cassandra seated on her favourite chair, feet tucked beneath her, with Eppy curled on her lap. The image was so vivid and beguiling that when someone knocked on her door, she started up in surprise. Anne and Mary had come to ask if she would join them, for they needed someone tall enough to put a head on their snowman. To be considered tall by anyone amused Susan enough to jolt her out of her low mood. She put on her bonnet and gloves and went out into the yard. But even though her person was with the girls, pressing fistfuls of snow atop their snowman, her thoughts might roam where they may, and they returned, again and again, to one mistress.

The snow lay for days, muting sound and senses, until at last the sun burned through the clouds and it began to melt. By the middle of the week, pockets of heather started to poke through the white carpet and Susan began to hope she might make her promised visit that weekend. But then a chill spread rapidly through the school. Several of Susan's pupils began to cough and sneeze, their noses red and streaming. Mary was among them and on Friday morning, Susan felt her forehead and was alarmed enough by the temperature to ask Dr Claybourn to give his opinion. He came at once to the dormitory but, on seeing him, Mary instantly shrank under her blanket.

There is no need to be afraid, Susan signed, but Mary would not come out. Dr Claybourn chuckled.

'Come now child, this is taking timidity too far.' He reached towards her. The instant he touched the blanket, Mary began to scream. Her distress was so severe that Dr Claybourn was forced to retreat. Susan volunteered to examine the patient and report back her symptoms.

'You did right to call me, Miss Mottram,' he said gravely. 'She has a fever. I will make up a draught and a plaster must be applied to the chest. The severity of her neurasthenia concerns me greatly—I did warn you that such things were likely. But let us deal with one ailment at a time.'

Since Mary refused to take medicine directly from Dr Claybourn, Susan administered her draughts during short breaks stolen between her other duties. Anne, who had not succumbed to the illness, offered to help nurse Mary, but Susan forbade it. Anne's own health was too delicate for her to risk infection by attending the sick. Evening came and Mary was no better. Susan sat with her through the night, tending to her as she coughed fretfully, unable to settle. Other girls with the same sickness were also restless and Susan attended them diligently, finding extra blankets, cooling their fevered brows and dosing out cold broth or medicine.

When morning came, Mary showed no improvement and Susan felt it impossible to part from her. She asked Tabitha, happily unaffected by the contagion, to take a note to Heathersage in return for sixpence. Susan wrote Cassandra a brief note, offering her apologies and explaining why she was prevented from making good on her promise. The afternoon proved very different from the previous Saturday. Delight and pleasure had turned to misery. Those girls who were not ill were forced into quiet pursuits, so as not to disturb the sick. Dr Claybourn was in constant attendance, but Susan grew increasingly worried about Mary, who still refused to let Dr Claybourn near her. Her breathing had grown hoarse and her forehead hotter than ever. Susan changed the plaster, using hot towels to clean the excess wax from Mary's painfully thin chest, but nothing seemed to help. Isabella came to visit the patient and caught Susan offering up a whispered prayer.

'I'll say one too,' she offered. 'And watch with you.' Susan squeezed her hand.

'I'm sure Mary would like that.'

As good as her word, Isabella stayed with Susan the whole afternoon.

Tabitha returned from Heathersage Manor bearing a square parcel the size of a shoebox, tied up with string. It gave out a strong scent of spices, among which Susan recognised cinnamon and aniseed. It came with a letter that must have been hastily written, for Cassandra's hand lacked its usual neatness.

Dearest Susan,

How the fates conspire against our happiness! Yet I cannot think of censuring you when your absence arises from such a noble cause. I must repress my own selfish disappointment in once again being deprived of your society. I beg you will send Mary my love. I console myself that with you as her nurse she is certain of the best care. I send you some powders for a tisane. My father first brought it back from the Orient when I was a small child, and it proved so efficacious for winter chills that we always keep a good supply. It is to be served with freshly boiled water—one spoonful per cup, well stirred, taken in the morning and again at night. Write to me as soon as you are able, that I might be assured of your own health. Mrs Grainger informs me that Mrs Claybourn is rumoured to be less than generous with her coal and I can't bear to think of you in such a cold, draughty place, surrounded by sickness. I shall do nothing but worry until I hear from you.

Your most concerned and ever affectionate,

Cassandra

How like Cassandra to be so thoughtful and generous. Susan consulted at once with Dr Claybourn regarding the tisane and he offered no objection to anything that might help her sick pupils.

'The empirical method behoves us to try different approaches to determine which is best, heh-heh. By all means, proceed.'

Susan hurried to the kitchens. Mrs Clegg was bent over the stove working a pair of bellows in such a lackadaisical manner she made no impression on the black, smoking coals.

'The fire burned down while I was cleaning the pots and I cannot revive it. What's to be done? With tea to be served in an hour and Tabby run off somewhere. Was ever a creature less fortunate than I?'

Urgent action was needed. Susan plucked a spare apron from a peg and seized the bellows. With a few vigorous puffs, the coals sparked into life.

'You're a sight stronger than you look, Miss,' Mrs Clegg observed, as Susan scooped more coals from the bunker. The pile was lower than before, and she was forced to lean in to get at the coal, hanging onto the edge of the hatch to keep her balance. Cassandra had provided such a generous amount of powder they could have dosed everyone at Matterdale Hall for a month. Nine girls besides Mary were abed with the sickness, so Susan boiled two kettles and made up ten cups. The aroma of the tisane was so enticing that the other girls watched Susan with ill-concealed jealousy as she carried a tray of steaming mugs into the sickroom. Isabella grabbed Mary's cup and took a sly sip.

'Oh, that's divine!'

'It is supposed to be for Mary,' Susan remonstrated.

'I'm showing her that it is safe to drink,' Isabella protested. The tisane made the girls drowsy and even Mary dropped into a restful slumber. Susan sent a silent prayer of gratitude across the moors.

On Monday morning, Mrs Claybourn made it clear that Susan's nursing duties were no excuse for shirking her other responsibilities. Classes must continue for those girls not confined to bed. 'Education must still be given,' she said. 'Matterdale Hall shall not get a reputation for slacking.'

Neither Marion nor Helena offered to help nurse the sick girls. Ever since the heavy snowfall, Helena had remained in her room. Susan suspected her indisposition was related to the fact that the deep snow had prevented Richard from visiting the village apothecary. Marion opined that anyone who lay abed, no matter the reason, deserved little sympathy. Susan felt that her absence from the sickroom was probably a relief for those girls with a more imaginative turn, as Marion, with her grim expression and black attire, might easily be mistaken for death in female form. All she lacked was the scythe.

By midweek, the sickness had run its course. Whether through nature or the beneficial effects of the tisane, Susan neither knew nor cared. When Mary sat up and begged to be allowed to take a short walk, Susan was overcome with relief. Isabella and Anne assisted their little playmate, leaving Susan suddenly free. Her weariness, kept at bay for so long, made itself felt. That evening she took herself early to bed and was asleep the instant she lay down.

30

The Cottage Piano
is Tuned

The arrival of Mr Murray, the piano tuner, caused much excitement among the inhabitants of Matterdale Hall, for visitors were rare and young men even rarer. He was a wiry Scotsman, sporting bountiful ginger whiskers and broad moustaches. To the girls' dismay, Mrs Claybourn instantly bundled the visitor off to the second parlour and closed the door, whereupon strange creaks and groans began to emerge, slowly changing into chords and arpeggios over the course of the afternoon. As she escorted her class to supper, Susan was stopped in the corridor by Marion.

'You are to go to my mother. I am to supervise the girls in your stead.'

Susan found Mrs Claybourn and Mr Murray standing by the piano. The room smelled of paint, the faded yellow wallpaper now gleaming white, its furled edges flattened and reattached with fresh glue.

'Are you the wee lassie that plays?' the Scotsman asked.

Susan owned that she was.

'Yon mistress insists you check ma work. Cannae tell herself whether she's in tune, or no. Why, it wasnae easy work. She needed a dozen new strings. I've never seen the like, not since I was brought to a house that had been flooded.' He patted the top of the upright piano. 'She was wailing like a birthing heifer, but she'll be right now.'

'I won't be swindled,' said Mrs Claybourn coldly. 'I am sure you have strung out the work. Half a day, just to tune a little piano!'

'It wouldn't have taken so long if she'd been properly cared for,' muttered Mr Murray. Susan squeezed past them to take a position on the stool and began to play a few scales.

'It's not like the Pleyel at the Manor, but she plays pretty enough now, Miss.'

Susan agreed. It lacked the resonance and depth of tone of the Sutcliffe's grand piano, but she performed a rising set of arpeggios and was delighted to inform Mrs Claybourn that the pianoforte was, indeed, in tune.

'You'll attend to ma bill now, I hope?'

'Has not Mr Sutcliffe recompensed you?'

'For his instrument, aye. Surely he's nae footing the bill for here as well?'

'Miss Mottram, did you not arrange this with your benefactor?'

'I would not dream of assuming so much upon our limited acquaintance,' Susan protested.

'This is too much delicacy. A man who can afford sirloin for dinner can surely put his hand in his pocket to help a neighbour. Mr Murray must ask him to make good on his next visit.'

'I will not, ma'am,' insisted Mr Murray. 'I've been serving Mr Sutcliffe these past twenty years, and I wouldnae dream of charging him for another's work. It isnae right, is it, Miss?'

Despite significant looks from her employer, Susan felt obliged to agree with Mr Murray. Mrs Claybourn then began to haggle and Mr Murray eventually agreed to accept two-thirds of his usual rate. He was paid and the bell was rung for Mrs Clegg.

'Someone in your dependent position should consider how to please her employer, Miss Mottram, instead of siding with strangers,' said Mrs Claybourn, snapping her purse shut. 'You shall receive not a shilling extra for your lessons until I have recouped this expense.' She tugged the bell again, but there was still no response.

'Shall I show Mr Murray out?' Susan offered. 'If we wait for Mrs Clegg, he might be obliged to charge for another half hour.'

This was such an alarming notion that Mrs Claybourn acceded to Susan's suggestion immediately.

'And they say we Scots are canny with money!' Mr Murray said with a whistle as the parlour door closed behind them. Susan enquired whether he had come direct from Heathersage Manor.

'Aye, lass. It's always a pleasure to run my fingers over such a fine instrument.'

'Did you see anything of Cass… of Miss Sutcliffe?'

'Aye, I did! What a surprise it was, for I have never seen her before, not in all the years I've been visiting. What a bonny lass she is! I've always dealt with Mr Sutcliffe, her being so shy. I pity her.'

'Pity her? Why? I hope she was not unwell?'

'No, no. She was bonny enough, although Mr Sutcliffe said she'd been out of sorts. Only, I pity anyone who cannae hear music. I cannae imagine life withoot it.'

'Out of sorts?'

'Miss Sutcliffe was upset for the poor bairns that were sick, here at the school. She feels things deeply, I believe. Why, I quite forgot, what with your mistress and her shenanigans. The lassie bid me give you this.' He rummaged around in his waistcoat and retrieved a crumpled envelope.

'Good day to you, Miss.'

He tipped his hat and headed down the path towards Hustanton.

The letter from Cassandra was brief.

Dear Susan,

Having not heard from you these five days, I am distraught, thinking only the worst. That my dear Mary is no more, and my dearest Susan perhaps, even now, lies on her deathbed. For why else would she not write to put my mind at ease? Papa says I imagine too much, and that he is sure you will write when you are able, but I beg you to end my suffering and let me know you are well.

Your faithful friend,

Cassandra

Susan let out an exclamation of horror. Had it been five days since Cassandra had sent the tisane? She had been so occupied with the girls that she had completely forgotten to reply. She ran out after Mr Murray and begged him to stop.

'You travel by Hustanton?'

'Aye.'

'Would you do me the greatest service and take a note to the post office, to be delivered at the earliest convenience to Heathersage Manor?'

'For you, lassie, I'll take it to the manor myself.'

'Oh, thank you!'

She invited him to step back inside while she retrieved her writing case. As she opened it, her fingers rested for a moment on the lacquered wood. She could not believe that, through wounded pride, she had almost refused such a wonderful gift. She wrote a quick note.

Dearest Cassandra,

Once again, I must beg your forgiveness. Be assured that I am well, and Mary is almost recovered, although we had some concerns that kept us watchful. Indeed, until yesterday, we were fearful for her safety. Your tisane was most welcome and I am convinced it aided Mary's recovery, and that of the other girls who took it. Mr Murray informs me that you and your father are well, and he has kindly agreed to convey this letter to you, that it may reach you with all possible speed. He waits as I write, and my haste must excuse its brevity and any faults of execution. I entreat you will allow me to make good on my arrears by receiving me this coming Saturday. I rely on your generous spirit to give me one last chance to make amends. I would write more, but Mr Murray begins to tap his thigh and I must not impose any further on his good nature.

She sealed the note and gave it to Mr Murray, repeating her expressions of gratitude. It only remained for her to wait, with the utmost impatience, for when she should have her liberty.

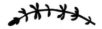

A Baronet Pays a Visit

The next day, a letter arrived from Susan's mother. Susan perused it while the girls were devouring a luncheon of bread and dripping.

My dearest Susan,

How delighted we were to receive your last and hear of your invitation to Heathersage Manor. We were glad you did not have to spend a miserable Christmas alone with those poor little girls. Florence is exceedingly interested in your new friend and begs that you will send more details of Heathersage and its occupants. That Mr Sutcliffe allowed you to play his piano!

If I ever meet him, I will thank him with all my heart for I know what a delight that must have been for my dear Susan. Such a sad day, when we lost our own pianoforte. I can hardly bear to think of it. However, it may not be the last of our misfortunes, for the list of your father's debts is endless. We are so pressed that I have been forced into arrears on the rent of our humble cottage, and only the promise of your next stipend prevents us being turned out into the street. That I must ask such a sacrifice from you, who has done nothing to deserve such misfortune, wounds me to the soul. I thank the Lord every day that he gave me such a precious and dutiful daughter.

I have taken in a little sewing and Florence assists me when she can, but her spirits remain low from the shock of all that has happened. It breaks my heart to see her sitting in our parlour with my old shawl around her shoulders, gazing at the window in the hope of some better fortune. She was not even cheered by a visit from Mr Potts, who is now out of mourning for his third wife. He brought us a basket of turnips and was very attentive to your sister. However, she made no return for such kindness and barely spoke to the poor man. I would have scolded her, for with so few friends we cannot afford to neglect those who could do us some good, but I am concerned about her nerves. My greatest fear is that she will fall ill, for we have no means to pay for a doctor. I am glad you have such a learned physician as Dr Claybourn at Matterdale Hall and that your health is in such good hands. I pray you will write as soon as you are able, for your letters never fail to cheer us.

God keep you well, my dearest girl,

Your ever-loving Mama

Susan set down the letter with a trembling hand. To think that her mother and Florence were in such danger, and she was not there to strengthen them with her love. Yet reason told her that she could help them best by staying where she was. That evening, she wrote a reply, and enclosed the two pound notes that remained from her holiday earnings. Of her time at Heathersage, she was happy to recount all that was interesting and happy.

When it came to the school, it became more difficult to find cheerful topics, but she wrote of Mary's progress and of Isabella's much improved behaviour. She dared not write of Mrs Claybourn's reprimands, nor of her secret feelings for Cassandra. No good could come from raising topics that would only cause worry and uncertainty. Susan was unused to keeping confidences from her family and her lack of candour weighed heavily on her heart, although not as much as the thought of poor Florence being an unwilling recipient of Mr Potts' attentions.

Thursday and Friday progressed at such a sluggish pace that Susan took down the clock in her classroom to check that it was fully wound, for she was convinced the hands must be sticking. Each tick and tock felt like the tortuous drips from a leaky tap. She would not have been surprised to learn that, by some strange twist of fate, Mrs Clegg had taken a spell as Father Time.

Saturday came at last. Dawn rose with bright promise, cheerful expanses of blue sky emerging from behind mounds of billowing clouds as they eased their way across the moors, driven by a playful wind. Only a few patches of snow remained. Knowing that after the morning lesson she would at last be free to visit Heathersage, Susan found it impossible to be still. She devised a game for the girls to practise their spoken French. They were to act the parts of shopkeepers and customers, walking up and down the gap between the desks as if it were a Parisian thoroughfare. Susan joined in, prompting and offering suggestions. The girls were delighted by the lesson, their voices rising in their excitement. The activity proved somewhat efficacious in calming Susan's blood until the door crashed open and a scowling Marion stood in the frame.

'Miss Mottram, pray tell me how my class are supposed to

concentrate on their Latin grammar with this hullabaloo coming through the walls?'

Susan quickly ushered the girls back to their seats.

'I apologise if we disturbed you. The girls are conversing in French.'

'To what purpose? I do not approve of the current fashion for the languages of other countries. Every civilised person should be able to speak English.'

'But there is great delight to be found in French literature, or in following the libretto of an Italian opera.'

'I do not feel the lack,' Marion said. 'Good heavens, what is occurring now?'

In the corridor behind her, older girls were passing and re-passing in haste. Some held brooms while others carried mops and buckets. Mrs Claybourn appeared, tying an apron around her waist.

'Marion, why are you not in your classroom? Never mind. We have more important concerns. A letter has just arrived from Sir Peregrine Mandrake. He is coming this very afternoon, with his wife and daughters. The senior class are to dust and sweep each room. Marion, you must have your girls fetch coal and make up the fires.'

'What about their grammar?'

'Latin has existed for thousands of years. It will still be here on Monday. Miss Mottram, you will ensure that your class are washed and presentable. Mrs Clegg is preparing the hot water now. Put on your best dress, for we must make a good showing when the Baronet arrives.'

'But I am engaged!' Susan protested. 'I am expected this afternoon at Heathersage Manor.'

'Out of the question. You are needed to demonstrate the pianoforte.'

'I have broken a firm engagement twice already,' Susan cried. 'I dare not disappoint them a third time.'

'It cannot signify. If the Sutcliffes' friendship does not extend to the trivial expense of tuning our piano, they cannot expect any undue courtesy.'

Susan felt as if she were being cast adrift at sea, with no way back. She feared that Cassandra's fragile confidence would not survive the blow if Susan were to break her promise. And there was so much she needed to say to Cassandra.

'But my not coming today will appear like deliberate neglect!' she cried.

'Miss Mottram, you gave up the freedom to make engagements when you took on paid employment. You are no longer a young lady of leisure. Must I remind you that your livelihood depends on the success of our establishment?'

Susan would have had great satisfaction in throwing off an employment that made such unfair claims upon her, but with Mama and Florence situated so precariously, she had no choice but to comply.

'At least let me send Tabitha with my apologies,' she pleaded, her stomach twisting in knots as she imagined what Cassandra would think of her.

'Absolutely not. She is assisting Mrs Clegg along with two of the older girls. A baronet will expect sandwiches and cake with his tea. Without help, Mrs Clegg would provide nothing but bread and dripping. Bread and dripping for a baronet! Imagine!'

Susan continued to plead her case. Observing her agitation, Mrs Claybourn relented, although with poor grace.

'Very well. I will ask Henry to send Richard with your message. Now attend to your duties. Once the girls are made presentable, you will find out their best needlework. And be sure to put away all but the very neatest copybooks.'

With everyone set to work, Matterdale Hall was soon transformed. Once they had performed their tasks, the girls were scrubbed until their faces were pink and glowing and then herded into the refectory, where Marion was to watch over them. Fires blazed in every hearth and the freshly painted second parlour, in which the Baronet and his family were to be received, had been enlivened by the addition of the best furniture and rugs from other rooms. Sprigs of greenery were arrayed artfully on the windowsills and a lace cloth, only slightly yellow at the edges, had been freshly pressed and laid across the table. Even Helena had been prised out of her beloved chaise longue to make her toilette. Her mother had insisted she apply less rouge than normal, lest she be mistaken for a character from a burlesque. Without her disguise, Helena's face was as grey as old dough. Susan thought that her parents must surely notice their daughter's unusual pallor, but their attention was fully engaged by the impending visit. Dr Claybourn was resplendent in his favourite mustard waistcoat and his boots were polished to a sparkling sheen. Mrs Claybourn had donned a silk evening gown of egg-shell blue, her bosom covered with a black lace chemisette. She was noticeably agitated, stepping into the hallway every few minutes to see if the visitors had arrived. If Susan had not been distressed at missing her appointment at Heathersage, she might have been diverted by Mrs Claybourn's antics.

'They're here!' Mrs Claybourn cried at last, returning

breathlessly from her latest foray. 'A barouche, with a coat of arms on the door, drawn by four horses. And two footmen attending. Sir Peregrine's estates must be doing very well indeed. Helena, sit up straight, for goodness' sake.'

Mr Clegg, attired in his Sunday best, led the visitors into the parlour, his bald dome as polished as Dr Claybourn's boots as he presented their illustrious guests.

Sir Peregrine was well past his best years, yet dressed in the very height of fashion, with a cravat so extensive his neck might have been encased in plaster of Paris for all the movement it allowed. His much younger wife was also dressed very finely, her figure pinched in exceedingly at the waist and her skirts ballooning out in such an abundance of purple pleats that Susan estimated there was enough silk within it to run the entire length of the parlour, were it to be stretched out. Their daughters followed behind; a sulky looking child of about twelve in a white pinafore and a slightly older girl who carried herself with the confident bearing and full-length skirts of a grown up.

'That's a powerful waistcoat, Sir,' Sir Peregrine remarked, raising an eyebrow at Dr Claybourn. 'What peculiar fashions you have in this part of the country.'

The oldest girl, introduced as Georgiana, circled the parlour disdainfully.

'No flowers?' she drawled. 'I suppose they do not have hot-houses in Yorkshire.'

'We have two hothouses,' Mrs Claybourn informed her swiftly. 'But we only grow useful items such as fruit and vegetables.'

'What a devilish poor track you have here, Claybourn.' Sir Peregrine was forced to turn his whole body in order to face his host. 'We almost threw a wheel. I've never been so bumped about in all my days.'

'I apologise for any inconvenience, heh-heh.'

'Why does the fellow laugh? I see nothing amusing in being shaken about like pepper in a pot.'

Mrs Claybourn broke in to perform formal introductions.

'And this is Miss Mottram, our junior teacher,' she concluded.

'Where?' Sir Peregrine's eye line was fixed at the level of the picture rail by his tortuous cravat, and Susan was far beneath his gaze. At last, by stepping backwards and looking down the length of his nose, he was able to make her out.

'Good Lord, what a drab little thing.'

Susan was wearing a grey silk dress, the most elegant she retained after selling her finest gowns to pay her father's creditors.

'Miss Mottram is still in mourning for her father,' Mrs Claybourn explained. 'A respected clergyman and very much the gentleman.' Susan was surprised at her employer knowing such a thing, for she had never once enquired after Susan's family.

'A vicar's daughter, eh?' Tipping his head backwards, Sir Peregrine examined Susan more closely. 'I suppose she has the look of a gentlewoman. Was you acquainted with the Bishop of Lambeth? They say he is quite the man of fashion.'

'I have not had the pleasure,' Susan said composedly. 'But our parish was in the country and we rarely went to town.'

Sir Peregrine snorted with such violence, he nearly choked. Georgiana sat down at the piano and picked out a few notes of a popular song with a forceful hand.

'My eldest girl is musical, as you see,' said her mother

indulgently. 'Lord Pembroke says she has a great deal of natural talent.'

'We Mandrakes are blessed with many natural gifts,' agreed her husband, glancing complacently at his own reflection in the nearest window.

'We believe in encouraging the talents of our pupils,' said Mrs Claybourn. 'Miss Mottram is our musical instructor.'

'Well, young lady, what say you to my Georgiana's playing?' Sir Peregrine demanded.

Feeling the eyes of Mrs Claybourn on her, Susan observed that the young lady played with spirit, but her natural honesty led her to add that she might benefit from instruction on fingering, as well as emphasis. Georgiana broke off her tune to look at Susan with undisguised venom. Her sharp nose and narrow mouth were very much suited to that expression.

'Perhaps you might show Miss Mandrake what could be achieved under your tuition,' Mrs Claybourn suggested, ushering Susan to the instrument. Susan began a concerto. She had barely finished the exposition when Sir Peregrine interrupted her.

'What was that opera we heard in town this spring? It was quite the thing. Georgiana, you will recall the composer's name?'

Georgiana shrugged peevishly.

'I believe it was Sir Julius Benedict,' offered Lady Mandrake. 'Do you know anything of Sir Julius' music, Miss Mottram?'

'A schoolteacher cannot know anything of fashionable music,' said Georgiana. Susan stopped playing and placed her hands carefully on her lap. For this, she had given up an afternoon with Cassandra!

'I was fortunate once to be lent the sheet music for one of Sir

Julius' concertinos,' she said with extreme politeness. 'Would you like me to play it for you?'

'Very well. Let's have it,' commanded Sir Peregrine.

Susan was only a few bars in when Sir Peregrine again spoke over her.

'You do not sing?'

'Since this is a concertino and not an opera, you shall escape that particular torment,' said Susan. After only a few more bars, Sir Peregrine interrupted her again.

'What else can my girls expect to be taught?'

'Everything that is required of a young lady,' said Mrs Claybourn rising. 'Perhaps you would care to examine some of their needlework?'

Sir Peregrine flicked his hand dismissively.

'After such an intolerable journey I am far too fatigued.'

Mrs Claybourn persisted.

'The handwriting of a Matterdale girl is much admired. I have set aside some copybooks in the main parlour, if you would care to step through. Or perhaps you would prefer a tour of our premises?'

'I would much rather take tea.'

Mrs Claybourn smiled weakly and pulled the bell to summon Mrs Clegg. Susan could only pity her. Such a vast quantity of coal burned to no purpose, if Sir Peregrine did not intend to go beyond this chamber.

'Handwriting and sewing,' mused Sir Peregrine. 'Any village school would teach as much.'

'They will also learn cyphering, and Latin and Greek, as well as modern languages,' said Mrs Claybourn. 'Just this morning, I heard Miss Mottram's class speaking Italian like natives.'

'That is not very encouraging, for they were supposed to be speaking French,' Susan remarked with a smile. 'But they have only just begun to learn,' she added, after a sharp look from her employer. She resumed the concertino, which seemed her safest course. The tea at last arrived. Dr Claybourn hurried to assist Mrs Clegg with the tray, and Mrs Claybourn lost no time in serving her guests while the tea yet retained a little heat. There were insufficient teacups, and so Susan was not invited to join the party. She continued to play, resolving to take pleasure where she could.

'Tell me, how do your pupils eat?' said Sir Peregrine, eyeing a plate of irregularly cut sandwiches with suspicion. 'My daughters are used to the very best.'

'You have nothing to worry about there, Sir Peregrine. We offer apples as regular treats, and those that stayed here over Christmas had sirloin for their dinner.'

Susan's fingers stumbled over the notes, so shocked was she by such mendacity and half-truths. Fortunately, nobody was paying her any attention.

'We also provide spiritual education,' Mrs Claybourn continued. 'We have our own chapel and the girls attend Hustanton church every Sunday.'

'The village we passed on the way here? How the deuce do you ferry them all across?'

'They walk.'

'Walk!' Georgiana exclaimed in horror. 'Why, it must be five miles!' Her sister, who had been staring blankly into the fire the whole time, looked up in disbelief.

'It is not quite two,' responded Mrs Claybourn with a tight smile. 'My husband, as a medical man, approves the exercise as beneficial to good health. Is that not so, Henry?'

'Ahem, yes,' said her husband who, after Sir Peregrine's earlier reprimand, had been studiously maintaining the most sombre of bearings.

'What of discipline?' Sir Peregrine asked. 'My Georgiana has lively spirits and Roseanna needs prompting to apply herself.'

Mrs Claybourn leaned forward eagerly. Here, at least, she was on solid ground.

'Tell me, Sir Peregrine. What do you hear?'

'Why, nothing at all.'

'The place is like a coffin,' Georgiana muttered sourly.

'The girls are not two doors away, and currently engaged in quiet study,' Mrs Claybourn said with great satisfaction.

'You are to be commended,' said Lady Mandrake. 'If I may inquire—what about… um, I hope there will be no opportunity for… um… unsuitable…'

'My wife means boys,' said Sir Peregrine briskly. 'I will not have my name attached to scandal. Nor place my daughters where they might be prey to fortune hunters.'

'I assure you, I permit no such scoundrels to approach Matterdale Hall,' said Mrs Claybourn decidedly. 'Nothing disgusts me more than men who prey on rich young women for their money.'

'What was that?' Sir Peregrine swivelled round as a strangled sound, something between a sigh and a cough, emerged from the chair occupied by Helena.

'Ah… nothing,' muttered Helena weakly.

'Your daughter does not speak much,' Lady Mandrake said, with a quirk of her eyebrow.

'Not all young women can be blessed with the natural

vivacity of a Miss Georgiana Mandrake.' Dr Claybourn's swift response earned him a look of approval from his wife.

'Quite, quite,' agreed Sir Peregrine.

'All our girls enjoy extremely good health,' added Mrs Claybourn, encouraged by such promising signs. 'The moorland air is so wholesome, I am sure Miss Mandrake will feel the benefit.'

'Is she insinuating that I appear unwell?' asked Georgiana with a look of disbelief.

'Georgiana's complexion is universally admired!' cried Lady Mandrake. Mrs Claybourn instantly realised her error.

'Pardon me, I meant only to assure you that the air here is so conducive to health, we rarely have any sickness among the girls, even in winter. My own daughters are always in excellent health.'

Helena, whose posture had begun to sag, jerked upright.

'And,' finished Mrs Claybourn, 'should your girls suffer any indisposition at all, they would be certain of the best care. My husband is an eminent physician. His work has been published in the Transactions.'

'Yes, indeed, heh-heh,' said Dr Claybourn, unable to restrain himself any longer. 'I am a specialist in neurasthenic disorders. I am at present looking for a patron. Indeed, Sir Peregrine, I was hoping I might speak with you—'

His wife was swift to interrupt him.

'Henry, are you not needed in the infirmary?'

'No, dearest. Richard is taking care of things.'

'Richard?' Susan stopped playing. 'But you promised to send him to Heathersage with my apologies.'

'I received no such instruction, heh-heh.'

'I must have forgot to ask,' Mrs Claybourn said with a dismissive wave of her hand. 'It cannot be helped.'

Susan leapt up in horror. To think that Cassandra had been waiting for her, all this time. How wounded she would be at such apparent neglect!

'I must go at once to Heathersage and explain!' she exclaimed.

'Dear me, no. It cannot be countenanced.' Dr Claybourn glanced at the window. 'It will be dark before you return, Miss Mottram. The moors at night are no place for a young lady, heh-heh.'

'I forbid it, absolutely,' added his wife. 'What sort of example would that be to the girls?'

'Quite,' said Sir Peregrine before Susan could press her case further. She stood, undecided, a righteous anger rising in her breast. She began to doubt whether Mrs Claybourn had ever meant to send her apologies at all. Such a suspicion was very unlike her, but the evidence was compelling.

'Perhaps, Miss Mottram, you might see if Marion needs assistance,' suggested Mrs Claybourn. With a firm hand in the back, she escorted Susan from the parlour. 'If you wish to retain your position here, I expect to find you in the refectory once our visitors have departed,' she added in a firm tone, before heading back to the parlour. Such was Susan's resentment at her mistreatment, she was tempted to take up her bonnet and shawl and disobey Mrs Claybourn's instructions. However, the light was fading quickly, and it was clear she could never have made it to Heathersage and back before nightfall. And she could not afford to lose her position. Not long after Susan had joined Marion and the girls, the sound of the barouche departing was followed by the entrance of a delighted Mrs Claybourn.

'Excellent news. Sir Peregrine's daughters will be joining us as soon as they have completed their visit to his friend. Think of that—a baronet's daughters at our school! I shall be able to double my prices. And they shall both have pianoforte lessons at four shillings apiece. You shall have half, Miss Mottram,' she added indulgently, 'once we have recouped Mr Murray's expenses.'

Any additional money that could be sent to her family was of course welcome, but Susan could not share Mrs Claybourn's delight. She fled to her chamber, her eyes stinging with tears. Those at Heathersage Manor would justly condemn her. To have failed, yet again, to make her appointment, and with no word of apology. To know that Cassandra would be feeling spurned and doubtless blaming herself as much as Susan was the worst torture imaginable.

32

Sunday Service

Sunday brought the usual trip to church. Susan had always appreciated a stirring sermon. Even a mediocre one could usually be relied upon to soothe any anxieties, or fortify her resolution to be as good a person as was possible for someone with her imperfections. But that morning she felt like a violin whose strings were being simultaneously plucked and scraped with a bow. Her nerves were in constant vibration, set off by every word or action. Guilt and shame, as well as a feeling of injustice all played their part in the discordant symphony within her.

'Did you attend me, Miss Mottram?' Marion asked.

'What? Am I needed?' Susan was jerked back into the present.

'I have spoken to you thrice, but you do not hear. I asked to you to round up the stragglers.'

'Forgive me. I will do it at once.'

As Susan escorted the crocodile of girls along the track to Hustanton, she determined to ask Mrs Claybourn if she might be released for an hour or two after the service to make her apologies at Heathersage Manor. She simply must explain herself and throw herself on Cassandra's mercy. By great good fortune, Mr Sutcliffe's carriage drew up outside the church just as Susan arrived with her charges. Without recourse to her employer, Susan ran to greet the occupants. Mr Sutcliffe handed Mrs Grainger out of the carriage. Susan looked past them eagerly, but the carriage behind was empty.

'Miss Mottram.' Mr Sutcliffe bowed with grave propriety. 'We had thought you must still be ill, having failed once again to make your appointment. Yet I observe you are quite recovered.'

'You must think the very worst of me,' Susan began miserably. Mr Sutcliffe spoke over her.

'I will not have my daughter's heart trifled with. I am soon to go away on business, and I had hoped… But it seems I must leave my daughter friendless.'

'Never friendless, when I am here,' said Mrs Grainger, maintaining a firm grip on his arm at the same time as casting a malevolent glare at Susan.

'Oh Mr Sutcliffe, Mrs Grainger, you must allow me to explain!'

'No explanation will recompense me for the distress suffered by my daughter. She waited for you all afternoon, so full of hope and tenderness, often rising to the window to look for you. She even went out onto the moors, alone, to find you. She was gone so long we were all concerned for her. To raise the hopes of my dear girl, and then dash them so unthinkingly. It is unforgivable.'

Susan was too choked by his words and the severity of his countenance to make any defence.

'Miss Mottram! Your assistance is needed,' Marion called. The girls required herding into the church. By the time Susan was at liberty to return her attention to Mr Sutcliffe and Mrs Grainger, they had settled into their family pew near the front. Never had Susan been more reluctant to attend to her duties, relegated to the back of the church with a pew of fidgeting girls. She could barely attend the sermon, which was on the topic of beauty. The preacher explained how women should aim to be beautiful in God's eyes by submission and obedience. Susan was lost in contemplation of a different kind of beauty altogether; that of a slender figure and lustrous brown eyes. She could not bear for Cassandra to believe her capable of deliberate neglect. The instant the vicar signalled the end of the service, Susan was on her feet and making her way against the general traffic towards the front of the church, hoping to catch Mr Sutcliffe's eye. She fidgeted impatiently as he spoke to the vicar. When it seemed that others were about to approach him, she could bear it no longer and thrust herself into his presence, without thought of how it might appear.

'Mr Sutcliffe, I beg you to hear me,' she cried. 'I would never hurt Cassandra for the world.'

'And yet you have, most gravely.'

Despite his fierce expression, she was about to launch into an explanation when Dr Claybourn and his wife arrived at her shoulder.

'You may recall, Mr Sutcliffe, that I visited you a few months ago regarding my infirmary, heh-heh,' Dr Claybourn began.

'You, sir, give leeches a bad name. I told you then, and tell you again now, I will have nothing to do with your confounded asylum.'

'But you do not understand the good I might do, were you to agree, heh-heh, to be my patron. Such discoveries at my finger-tips! I would be delighted to offer you a tour of the premises. The progress I have already made—you would be quite astonished, heh-heh.'

'You must look elsewhere,' said Mr Sutcliffe abruptly. 'And I beg you will no longer send your teacher to inveigle her way into our hearts, in the hopes of securing access to my fortune.' He glanced at Susan with such disdain she felt quite ill, and then led Mrs Grainger to their waiting carriage. Susan watched it drive off, her cherished hopes and chances for happiness disappearing with it.

'Come, Miss Mottram. You are lackadaisical today,' remonstrated Mrs Claybourn, as they rounded up their charges. Susan walked in a daze, heedless of her surroundings, wrapped up in her own misery. They had covered just above half the distance to Matterdale Hall when her attention was claimed by Mrs Claybourn.

'Who are these fellows following behind? They do not look trustworthy.'

Susan looked behind. A swarthy man in rough clothes and a rotund fellow in a wide brimmed planter hat were closing on them.

'I believe it is Mr Smythson,' said Susan, rousing herself. 'I do not know the other.' Mr Smythson doffed his battered hat to her, but his eyes were fixed on a different person.

'Be you Dr Claybourn?'

Dr Claybourn had placed himself protectively in front of his wife and Susan.

'I am.'

'I demand you tell me what you have done with my sister.'

'You are Mr Smythson, I collect?'

'Yes, and I will have an answer to my question.'

'There is no need to speak roughly. She was safe and well when she left my wife's employ, heh-heh.'

Dr Claybourn's habitual chuckle was ill-timed.

'This is not a matter for laughter, Sir!'

'Please, do not rush to judgement,' said Susan, sympathetic to any who bore the stain of false accusation. 'Let him speak.'

'Girls, come away,' Marion commanded, but with little effect. The column had ground to a halt and the girls gazed upon the exchange with eager interest. The rosy hue on Dr Claybourn's cheeks spread up to his forehead and down to his neck.

'You will act like a gentleman, my good fellow, when ladies are present.'

'You've no call to look down on me. My mother was a Vasey, who have been squires in my parish for centuries. I come with the constable.' The portly man who accompanied him nodded, still attempting to catch his breath.

'Ah, Jennings. Good day to you,' said Dr Claybourn complacently. 'I hope your family are well? Your wife has fully recovered from that little episode last year?'

'Ahem, yes, Dr Claybourn, Sir, quite recovered, I thank you,' Mr Jennings wheezed, his face florid. He removed his planter and cleared his throat apologetically. 'I've been asked to investigate, by this... um, gentleman, the disappearance of a young lady.' He spoke sedately, as if each word were weighed and counted. 'I am sure it is nothing, but I am bound to look into the matter.'

'Of course, Jennings. Let me invite you both to Matterdale Hall, where I will answer any questions you wish to put to me.

Mr Smythson, I hope you will excuse any incivility on my part, but I am protective of our female charges.'

'You see, Smythson? I told you Dr Claybourn was a reasonable man,' said Jennings.

The girls resumed their march on Matterdale Hall, disappointed that, despite such promising portents, there was to be no argument or physical altercation. Susan felt a tug at her sleeve.

Who is that man? Mary signed. *With the dark face and crumpled hat?*

He is the brother of Miss Smythson.

Mary looked at her blankly.

Who is she?

Your teacher—before me.

Mary's mouth flopped open.

Red hair? Pretty dresses?

Susan nodded.

He is angry. Why?

Miss Smythson has disappeared.

Mary's eyes went as wide as saucers, and for the rest of the journey her attention passed back and forth between Mr Smythson and Dr Claybourn. When they reached the hall, Mrs Claybourn offered Mr Jennings refreshment in the parlour.

'How very kind…' he began.

'We will take no refreshment, only answers,' Mr Smythson exclaimed.

'Let us not be hasty,' said Mr Jennings. 'A man works better with fuel in his stomach.'

'Hasty? Do you know what that word means? You're as sluggish as a Spanish galleon with three years growth on her keel.'

'Miss Mottram, Marion, please take the girls to dinner,' snapped Mrs Claybourn as the girls circled the visitors like ducks after a piece of bread. The constable took out a handkerchief and wiped his brow, which was glistening with sweat after the walk. He leaned conspiratorially towards Dr Claybourn.

'You will forgive the intrusion, Claybourn. But the brother, I'm afraid, will not be satisfied until I have searched the house.'

'I will not,' insisted Mr Smythson, as Susan and Marion ushered the girls away. Dr Claybourn opened his arms in an expansive gesture.

'I have no objection. We have nothing to hide, heh-heh.'

Susan heard no more, for the last of the girls had entered the refectory and she had no excuse for lingering further in the corridor. There was a long wait for luncheon to arrive, and the girls were fidgeting by the time Mrs Clegg brought in a dinner of rabbit stew and dumplings, blowing so hard that Susan feared she might collapse on the spot. She hurried forward to help.

'Bless you, Miss. When Mr Jennings turned up with that other fellow, I was sure Dr Claybourn would ask them to stay for dinner and even Lord Jesus could never stretch out such portions among six. My poor nerves are like cabbage that's been got at by caterpillars. And all for nothing, because they've gone.'

'So soon?' Susan exclaimed.

'Mr Smythson wanted to search everywhere, even the infirmary. The master stood firm, I'm proud to say. Said that his patients weren't to be disturbed. Them poor folk suffer enough without being gawped at. Mr Smythson started hollering and accused t'constable of being too idle to investigate properly, just because Mr Jennings said that, without evidence, he'd take the word of a gentleman over a fellow like Smythson. Well, Mr

Smythson grew so violent the constable and Richard had to take him away.'

'Did not you hear him, Miss?' said Tabitha. 'Calling out "Kitty, Kitty," as they dragged him out. As if Miss Smythson could have been locked up in this house without us knowing it!'

'Well, I suppose that's the end of that,' said Susan distractedly. Something in Tabitha's tale stirred a memory, but she could not place what it was.

'Maybe not, Miss, for Mr Smythson said he'd be back, even if he had to hire a detective himself. I reckon we've not heard the last of it.'

33

Ghosts and Monsters

Susan awoke in the middle of the night, heart thumping against her ribs, certain that something had disturbed her. She had the sense it was a scream, or similarly high-pitched noise. She sat up. Outside, the wind whistled and whined as if a herd of cats had been locked outside. A distant crash made her start. She rose, pulling her shawl tight around her shoulders and looked out of her small window into the yard. A fingernail of moon provided a faint glow that was reflected by a thin layer of fresh snow. Susan's hand went to her throat. She blinked, uncertain of what she was seeing, for it seemed as if a black shadow had just slithered across the white ground. A creature from a nightmare, it bulged at the front but dragged a fat tail behind, like some giant slug. Susan rubbed her eyes and the shadow disappeared. Could she have imagined it? She watched a little longer, but all was still. There followed a loud crash, so close Susan wondered if it were inside the building itself. Heart pounding, she opened her door and stepped into the corridor. A scraping sound came from so close that Susan's thumping heart leapt into her throat.

'Who's there?' she cried out.

'Is that you, Miss?' came the tremulous response. Susan recognised the voice.

'Isabella?'

'Yes, Miss. We're so afraid. We heard screaming, and then bones rattling. Those poor children that died—they've come to strangle us in our beds!'

Isabella's superstitious nonsense brought Susan back to her senses. She was not a child. She would not mistake a few innocent noises for something sinister.

'There's no such thing as ghosts,' she said, returning to her room to retrieve a candle. Its light revealed Isabella, clutching the door frame of the nearest dormitory, dressed only in her nightgown.

'I'm sure it is nothing,' said Susan briskly, her courage returning with the candlelight. 'I expect it's only the wind.'

She tried not to think of the inhuman creature from the yard. Most likely a trick of the shadows, or else her own imagination. An ominous rumbling from the direction of the kitchen drew a squeal from Isabella, who darted back into the dormitory and closed the door.

Despite telling herself that there was nothing to fear, the candle trembled in Susan's hand as she made her way slowly towards the stairs. There was something menacing in the way the shadows in the stairwell seemed to dart towards her and then recede, held at bay only by the flickering candlelight. She proceeded carefully down the stairs and into the entranceway. She checked the front door and was relieved to find it securely locked. The windows stared back at her like black mirrors, reflecting her illuminated face as she forced herself to make for the kitchens. As she passed the refectory, the gritty floor chafed her feet through the thin soles of her slippers. Being tangible and familiar, it reassured her. The door to the kitchen was ajar and something glowed faintly behind it. Susan reached to push it fully open. At that moment, the door was yanked backwards and she almost dropped her candle in fright. Mrs Claybourn stood before her, a shaded oil lamp in her hand.

'Good heavens, you startled me!' Mrs Claybourn raised her hand to her throat, her face pale and ghastly.

'And you me,' Susan said, taking a steadying breath. Dr Claybourn emerged from behind his wife, his cheeks ruddier than ever and a sheen across his face. Richard hovered a few steps behind, like a long, thin shadow, his features partly obscured by the darkness.

'I… the girls—we heard something,' Susan said.

'As did we,' replied Mrs Claybourn. 'It seems that Mrs Clegg forgot to latch the kitchen door. It was banging when I got here. It is all secured now.'

'When the wind is up, this place creaks and groans like an old woman, heh-heh,' Dr Claybourn chuckled. 'I wonder we get any sleep at all.'

'You'll catch cold, Miss Sparrer, coming down here like that,' said Richard, his predatory eyes glinting in the lamplight. Susan pulled her shawl tighter round her neck, suddenly aware she was only wearing her nightgown beneath it. The others, she noted, were fully dressed and their feet were ringed by dark pools of water.

'You have been outside?' she exclaimed.

'I wanted to make sure everything was secure,' said Mrs Claybourn. 'And I was frightened to go alone. I insisted Henry come with me.'

Susan had never imagined Mrs Claybourn capable of fear. Unless it be of an unexpected demand for payment.

'I also heard a noise, and came to help,' Richard added.

'Did you see anything—in the yard?' Susan asked tremulously, unable to dismiss the image of the slug-like creature from her imagination.

'Nothing at all,' returned Mrs Claybourn. 'You must return to the girls and tell them there is nothing to fear.'

Susan returned to her chamber, stopping by the dormitories on her way to reassure the girls that the noise had been nothing but a loose door. Yet, as she returned to her room, she couldn't help wondering if anyone would really get fully dressed in the middle of the night just to investigate a banging door. She was certain there was something more to this affair, even if she didn't believe in ghosts. Had the Claybourns been lying to her? If so, why? What had they really been up to, out in the yard? She tossed and turned, unable to sleep. Images of Cassandra weeping and Mr Sutcliffe frowning and shaking his fist tumbled around her dreams, in which a hulking, creeping creature lurked behind, waiting.

34

A Father Takes Leave of his Daughter

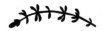

Before she had met Susan Mottram, Cassandra had been content with her own company. Now, her books remained half-read, her sketchbook tossed aside as her fingers became too restless for the fine draughtsmanship required. And with every passing day that Susan failed to make good on her promise, the more anxious Cassandra became. Despite all appearances to the contrary, she refused to believe Susan false. When Susan did not appear on her half day, Cassandra had taken her shawl and, with a deep breath and desperate courage, made her way past the lake and on to the moors in the hope of meeting with her new friend. She had been forced to go alone, for James had been sent to Hustanton on some errand and Mrs Grainger refused to join her. Susan, she had signed, deserved no such efforts.

Cassandra had retraced the route she had taken with Susan a few weeks earlier and as soon as she broached the top of the escarpment she looked eagerly across the moors. There was no sign of her friend. She had remained for some time. She even contemplated descending the escarpment and making her way to Matterdale Hall herself, an idea that was rapidly chased away by the usual treacherous thoughts. What if she were refused admittance? Or fended off with signs meant to ward off the devil, signs she knew all too well? And all those girls—so many eyes, staring at her. Cassandra's throat closed off and a sharp pain lanced through her breast. The next thing she knew, she was lying on the ground atop the escarpment, her side cold and damp, her fingers numb with cold. How long had she been there? The light was fading, and she guessed she had lost maybe an hour. Horror gripped her when she considered what might have happened had some stranger come across her, lying in a helpless stupor. She fled home, sneaking in through the kitchens and retiring to her chamber, unable to face the love and concern of her father.

The next morning, she had asked her father and Mrs Grainger to attend Hustanton church, that they might ascertain news regarding her friend. Susan must be ill, or detained somehow, to have not kept her promise. They had returned with painful tidings. Her father, unusually grave, had informed her that Susan had seemed in good health, and could provide no reasonable excuse for shunning Cassandra's company. Mrs Grainger insisted she should give no further thought to such a fickle friend. Despite feeling hurt, and even a little betrayed, Cassandra could not bring herself to blame Susan. The fault must be hers. She had so little to recommend her, so terrified of everything, so unpractised in social conventions. Susan, despite her small stature, walked so confidently in the world she would surely choose more interesting society than Cassandra, who had been too eager, too presumptuous—it was no wonder that Susan was withdrawing. Although Susan had denied it, she may have been sparing Cassandra's feelings. Or perhaps Susan's expressions of tenderness had been genuine but the weeks of separation had given her time to reconsider. Other society may have presented itself. From her vantage point on the escarpment, Cassandra had glimpsed a carriage in the grounds of Matterdale Hall. If only she had the courage to visit the place herself, she might find out the truth, but such an undertaking was beyond her powers. Small wonder she had no true friends, excepting her father and Mrs Grainger.

Worse was to come for, as her spirits were at their lowest, her father had been called away.

Do not dwell on it, her father signed. *A true friend would not trifle with you in this way.*

I do not believe she meant to hurt me.

We were all taken in. It seems her goodness was all on the outside.

Do not say so, Papa. Do not think ill of her.

I cannot help it, for she has hurt you deeply.

Once his bags were packed and the carriage called, her father drew Cassandra to him, and then released her with an earnest look.

Do not go, Cassandra begged. She never enjoyed saying goodbye to him, but the idea of parting at that moment seemed more awful than ever.

He looked at her tenderly. *If you truly cannot bear me to leave, I will not go.*

She shook her head, regretting her earlier plea. She was not so weak as to demand her father pander to her every whim. He never went away unless it was important.

I have Hester to keep me company. I will be well. Keep safe.

I will return as soon as I can. Is there something I can bring you, to cheer you?

Cassandra shook her head. She let him kiss her and watched the carriage until it disappeared into the gathering mist. Only one thing could raise her spirits, and that was beyond her father's power.

35

Dr Claybourn Makes a Request

Susan woke to find Tabitha standing over her. The morning sunlight infused the ice crystals on her window with a bright amber glow. She knew at once she had overslept.

'You weren't at breakfast, so Mrs Clegg sent me to fetch you,' said Tabitha.

Susan pulled her blanket up to her neck. By curling up beneath her blanket she had created a cocoon of warmth and was loath to leave it. If she went back to sleep, she could forget that Cassandra and her father believed her a capricious friend, utterly without remorse. The previous day she had attempted to write a letter to Cassandra, explaining everything, but after many crossings out and second attempts, she had given up, unable to find words that did justice to her feelings. Recalling that, she stirred herself. With a new day, came new hope. Today, she would do better.

Once she left the warm bed, the chilly air in her chamber encouraged her to dress quickly. As she pinned her hair into place, she glanced down into the yard from her window. A muffled figure in a green coat was sweeping away the snow with brisk motions, his broom scratching against the frozen ground. *Richard.* Most of the yard had been cleared, the trodden down mud appearing almost black against the piles of shovelled snow. She recalled the shadowy beast of the previous night. Any tracks it might have made would be long gone, supposing it had even been real. In the light of the morning, the presence of such an unnatural creature seemed unlikely. As she watched, Richard glanced up at her window and gave her a mocking salute. Susan withdrew and hurried downstairs, barely in time to join her class as they filed into the classroom. The visit of the constable and Mr Smythson had set all the girls chattering. Susan struggled to make them attend her, and her voice soon became hoarse with reprimands. It was a relief to release them for luncheon. Mary approached her, carrying her basket, her lips wobbling, her eyes pink.

What is it? Susan asked.

Mouse, gone!

She showed Susan the basket which was empty. They searched the room, looking in every corner, but there was no sign of the little creature.

'Dr Claybourn asks that you attend him in his study,' said Tabitha, appearing at the door.

Perhaps it escaped, back to the fields, Susan signed, and for a moment she felt envious of the little creature. She gave Mary a reassuring pat on her shoulder. *Go and eat.*

Dr Claybourn's study was on the first floor, adjacent to the family bedrooms.

'Ah, Miss Mottram. There you are, heh-heh. Come, come. Welcome to my little enclave of science!'

The study was a compact room that smelled strongly of vinegar. One wall was filled with shelved books, some lying across the tops of others for want of space. Behind the door hung a full-scale diagram of the male anatomy, so detailed that Susan blushed to look at it. Perched on an antique mahogany desk was the shrouded, child-like figure she had noticed in the infirmary. Next to it, a large glass jar held a fleshy pink object that resembled a savoy cabbage in size and shape.

'I have two reasons for asking you here,' he said. 'Firstly, I am concerned about your welfare. In recent days, you have seemed distracted and overwrought. And prone to making unfounded accusations—I have not forgot about the pendant. As a physician, this concerns me. These are classic symptoms of a developing neurasthenia. I fear you may be having a delayed reaction from your unfortunate exposure to Amelia and the others.'

'I am sure that is not the case,' said Susan, thinking that if she was distracted it was because of her feelings for Cassandra. She was uncertain what Dr Claybourn would say if she told him about those.

'Last night, you appeared particularly distressed. I wonder, did you see something, real or imagined, that troubled you?'

Susan decided it would be unwise to mention the creature in the yard. After all, she wasn't even certain herself it was real. And she didn't want to give Dr Claybourn the wrong impression.

'This is an interesting object,' she said, picking up the jar with the pink savoy cabbage. He retrieved it from her and set it back reverently on the table.

'That is my brain.'

Susan's eyes widened. If anyone was going mad, perhaps it was him. Seeing her expression, he chuckled.

'That is to say, it is not actually mine of course—I am happy to say that remains inside my skull, heh-heh. I meant only that I have possession of it.'

'You had another topic in mind, besides concern for my health?' Susan prompted. She desperately wanted to finish her letter to Cassandra before the post boy came for the collection.

'Indeed I did. I want to enlist your help.' He grabbed a corner of the shroud and pulled it away with a flourish, revealing a marble bust. The surface of the head was divided into small regions by dotted lines, labelled like countries on a map. Upon it rested an elaborate cage, secured in position with leather straps. Throughout the cage, long metal needles were arranged, pointing inwards with their sharp ends resting against the bust's head. Susan shuddered. It looked like some instrument of torture.

'Are you familiar with phrenology?' asked Dr Claybourn.

'Not at all.'

'I am sorry to hear it. I had believed you to be a young lady with an interest in natural sciences.' His face came alive as he expounded on his topic. 'Phrenology is the scientific study of the contours of the human skull. If one knows how to read them, the bumps and cavities can reveal the propensity for good or ill.'

With great care, he removed the cage from the bust's head and set it aside, then tapped his forefinger on a segment just above the right eye. 'Here, we have regions of intellect, such as language and reasoning. On the dome, we find the higher emotions like veneration and benevolence, and here...' he indicated a point just above the nape of the neck. '… at the furthest recesses, are the areas that control our, ahem, more animal instincts.'

'And this…?' Susan reached hesitantly towards the hideous contraption.

'Do not touch, I beg you!' he cried. Susan pulled back her hand. Dr Claybourn returned the contraption carefully to its perch atop the bust and gently replaced the shroud.

'It is my own invention. I call it the phrenomed. It directs surgical manipulations to precise areas of the brain.'

'You use that… that thing on your patients?' Susan asked uncertainly.

'It is gentler than current alternatives, which are crude at best. Lobotomy, for instance, as practised with great enthusiasm by my fellow alienists: it is like taking a sledgehammer to a walnut. I firmly believe my phrenomed will help mankind cure all manner of emotional and psychological diseases. Despite the occasional setback, it has showed great promise. It cured Helena of her fits. My greatest scientific achievement to date.'

'No wonder she has headaches!'

'Headaches?' he asked sharply. 'Who told you that?'

Susan bit her lip, recalling that Helena had sworn her to secrecy. She quickly turned the subject.

'I do not understand how you wish me to help.'

'My trip to Harrogate rekindled my enthusiasm for scientific discovery. I will no longer listen to fools crowing about trifling advances, when I have the means to make more significant leaps. Young Mary Martin would make a most interesting test case. I wish to measure her skull, and I hope you will persuade her to submit to it.'

'There is nothing the matter with Mary.' Susan was

determined to never let Dr Claybourn and his phrenomed anywhere near her pupil. 'She has plenty of intelligence and her
heart could not be more loving.'

'She is a damaged example of God's divine creation. I would
discover the cause.'

'She is only deaf. And that is no fault of hers.'

'Sadly, such defects are invariably linked to diseases of the mind.'

'That's not true,' Susan protested, thinking of Cassandra.

'I think I know more about the topic than an inexperienced
teacher, heh heh.'

'You are not infallible, sir. You were convinced that Mary
lacked sense, when she was only deaf. She is perfectly intelligent,
I assure you.'

He frowned.

'Has Mary communicated anything to you? Of things she
might have seen or, more likely, imagined?'

'Seen?' Susan echoed.

'Or imagined, yes. Anything that gives us insight into the
workings of her mind would be of extreme interest.'

She felt his eyes on her. There was something distinctly
unsettling about his eagerness. It reminded her of those zealots
who preached damnation from street corners.

'I do not recall anything,' she replied carefully. Mary had
always been afraid of Dr Claybourn. Why? Had she witnessed
something?

'It would help me greatly if you could persuade her to undertake some tests.'

'She would find it too distressing,' Susan insisted. 'It should
not be attempted.'

He placed his palms carefully on the desk and waited, as if

hoping she would change her mind. When it became clear she would not, he poured himself a large glass of brandy from a nearby decanter and took a long swallow. Susan was surprised to see him imbibing strong spirits at such an early hour. Her own father had never opened a bottle before dinner. She wondered if there had been some incident in the infirmary that had left Dr Claybourn requiring fortification.

'Very well. Although it pains me greatly, I will accept your assurances on the matter. You see, I do not force the issue. I am no monster, whatever wild accusations others may make. I hope you do not give them any credence. My wife and I insist on the complete loyalty of those in our employment.'

The sound of slamming doors and hushed whispers wafted up the stairs.

'I believe the girls are returning to their lessons,' Susan said, relieved to have an excuse to leave. In the corridor outside his office, the tabby cat slunk past, something small and grey in its mouth. With a sick feeling in her stomach, Susan realised it was Mary's mouse.

36

A Copybook Suffers a Grievous Injury

Susan paused at the bottom of the stairs to compose herself before returning to her class. Her conversation with Dr Claybourn had unsettled her. Although she believed him sincere in his desire to help his patients, she distrusted his intentions towards Mary. Was he really hoping to cure her, or attempting to silence a witness to something he wished to remain hidden? He had been angered by her refusal to help, she was sure of that. Although he had smiled at her as she left, there had been more than a hint of a threat in his parting words. She straightened her cuffs and smoothed down her skirts before opening the door to her classroom. The girls looked up, expectantly. Susan's eyes went immediately to the desk usually occupied by Mary. It was empty.

'Where is Mary?' She looked at Anne, who shook her head.

'I haven't seen her since luncheon, Miss.'

Susan felt a jolt of foreboding.

'Everybody remain here,' she commanded. She had barely reached the doorway when Richard barrelled in, dragging a pale-looking Mary by her arm.

'You have found her!' Susan cried with relief, as Mary shrugged off Richard's grip and threw herself at Susan.

'Oh, I found her all right. Trying to sneak into the madhouse.'

'I don't believe it! She's terrified of the place.' Susan looked down at her young charge, but Mary had buried her head in her skirts.

'Just wait 'til I tell Dr Claybourn.' Richard grinned wolfishly.

'Oh, I beg you would not!'

He laughed mockingly.

'You wish me to lie to my employers? And you always so keen to tell others about morality?'

'I ask only that you say nothing,' Susan said, concerned for Mary's fate if Dr Claybourn found out she had been sneaking about the infirmary.

'Ah, but I'm in his good books now, and intend to stay that way.'

He smoothed the lapels of his tattered frockcoat, before spinning on his heel and heading back into the corridor. Susan attempted to prise Mary from her skirts, so that she might discover what had happened. The little girl clung to her like a barnacle and it took Susan some time to free herself.

Mary, why were you in the infirmary?

Mary's lips trembled. Her fingers began to move, but then stopped, before they moved again.

To look. To see if miss… Mary froze, her eyes widening in terror as she looked beyond Susan's skirts. Susan turned to see Dr Claybourn burst into the room, a riding crop in one hand. His jaw was clenched and his ruby cheeks were mottled with tiny purple veins.

'Where is she?' he demanded. The buttons of his waistcoat strained and twisted as he breathed heavily. 'I shall horsewhip the hide off her!'

Mary scuttled beneath her desk.

'Dr Claybourn, pray calm yourself!' Susan moved into his path. Dr Claybourn pointed at the desk with the crop.

'That girl—who knows what distress she has caused my patients? What damage she has done? Let me by.'

His uncontrolled demeanour alarmed her. It was so unlike his normal self.

'I will not, sir, until your anger has cooled and you are more rational.'

Her response only inflamed him more. His chest swelled and he stepped towards her, a thick vein pushing out the skin at the side of his neck. There was nothing of the cheerful, affable Dr Claybourn in the enraged monster before her.

'Let me past, I say!'

Susan trembled before his rage, but her resolve did not waiver.

'These girls are under my protection.'

He raised the crop high above his head.

'Out of my way!' he cried. 'Or I will not be responsible for what happens.'

'We are each of us responsible for our own actions.' Susan spoke slowly, forcing the words through a throat that was suddenly dry as old yarn. She reached a trembling hand to the desk, bracing herself against its solidity and closed her eyes as the crop snapped down. Air brushed hotly against her cheek. The leather landed with a fearsome crack on Mary's copybook. The fragile paper split under the force of the blow. The vein in his neck pulsing, Dr Claybourn swung the crop again and again, thrashing the book until it was rent to shreds. Susan remained frozen, her body rigid with shock.

'Father!'

The cry from the doorway cracked like a gunshot. Marion loomed, ghostly pale, her mouth moving in unspoken words. Dr Claybourn turned and looked at her glassily. He blinked, then turned back to Susan and his eyes lost their glazed look. He placed his palm on his brow, threw down the crop as if it burned his hand and fled. Susan trembled as Marion approached.

'Miss Mottram—'

'Have the goodness to watch the girls,' Susan said tightly. 'I cannot remain here another moment.'

She ran from the room, along the corridor and burst out of the front door of the hall, desperate to breathe the fresh, unpolluted air of the open moor.

37

An Explanation is Given

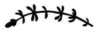

Susan's thoughts raced along with her galloping heart as she sank to the ground, just beyond the boundary walls of the hall. Where was the man she had trusted—the man she had sworn incapable of evil? After seeing him in the grip of passion, she could now believe Dr Claybourn capable of anything. Could he have attacked Miss Smythson, in such a rage? Poor Mary, no wonder she was terrified of him. She looked back at Matterdale Hall and her stomach curdled. The featureless grey walls mocked her. So bland and harmless it seemed, just like Dr Claybourn. Who knew what horrors had been committed behind its plain exterior? A door slammed and a figure strode across the yard, heading towards her. Susan grew breathless with fear before she realised it was Marion, not Dr Claybourn.

'Miss Mottram, I am relieved to find you. The nights draw in swiftly at this time of year.'

'I… the girls?'

'They are quite safe. My father's affliction, although severe, is always short-lived.'

'This has happened before?'

'Father strives to control this demon, but he has not always been successful.'

Susan remembered the look on Marion's face when she had beaten Isabella. So blank, as if she refused to let herself feel anything. Her hand went to her mouth.

'You suffered from it yourself?'

'I have unnatural feelings. If he has punished me, it is because I deserve it.'

'Surely, feelings come from nature? How then can they be unnatural?'

'After what you have just witnessed, you cannot believe that all emotions should be encouraged?'

Susan swallowed and was silent.

'My parents sent me to ask, or rather to beg, that you will give them a chance to make amends.'

'I must be assured of my safety. And that of the girls,' said Susan.

'Such assurances can only be given in person.'

'What really happened to Miss Smythson? Did your father...?'

'Speak with my parents. They will explain all.'

Susan clutched her elbows, hugging herself, her eyes darting from Marion to the infirmary and then to the main house. At length, her breathing began to slow and her heartbeat steadied.

'Very well,' she said, shaking out her arms. Although apprehensive about returning to that house, she owed it to her family to at least hear what the Claybourns had to say. She fell into step beside Marion, obliged to take two strides for every one of the taller woman's. Marion left her at the door to the parlour and returned to her own class. Susan hesitated in the dim corridor, summoning the courage to enter. From behind the closed door she heard voices.

'Henry, once again, you have put my school at risk.'

'Dearest, forgive me. I lost control of myself.'

'As if you do not cause me trouble enough, with your strange obsessions. Now you would stain our reputation just as Sir Peregrine Mandrake is about to send us his girls?'

'What can I do to make amends?'

'I will deal with Miss Mottram. I do not wish to lose another teacher—think how that would look.'

At the mention of her name, Susan roused herself and knocked on the door. Her mother had always told her that no good came of eavesdropping. Mrs Claybourn rose to greet her. Dr Claybourn sat with his head in his hands. Susan stiffened at the sight of him.

'My dear Miss Mottram. You have had a shock. Won't you take some tea?' Mrs Claybourn said.

Susan sank into a chair and accepted the proffered cup. Her hand trembled so much the china clattered, and tea spilled into the saucer. When she sipped the tea, it was lukewarm and sickly sweet.

'Sugar, to fortify your spirits,' Mrs Claybourn explained. She turned to the fire and poked it vigorously, that it might give more heat.

'A most unfortunate incident,' she began.

'Unforgivable,' cried Dr Claybourn. 'I cannot expect your pardon, Miss Mottram. My only consolation is that some good angel prevented me striking you.'

'I must know the truth.' Susan set her cup aside. 'Did you harm Miss Smythson in one of your rages?'

'You cannot think…' protested Mrs Claybourn. 'Miss Mottram, you have been reading too many sensational novels. You cannot believe my husband capable of such an outrage?'

'It is an unfortunate paranoia,' said her husband. 'I have been concerned about Miss Mottram's nerves for some days. Consider this, Miss Mottram, if you can yet be rational. What reason could I have to hurt Miss Smythson?'

'Reason was not at the forefront of your mind when you entered my classroom with a riding crop.'

Dr Claybourn snatched a bible from the table beside him. 'I swear, on this holy text, I did not harm Miss Smythson.'

'And the girls? Will they be safe?'

'I swear it.'

She knew him to be a devout man, and his protestation seemed genuine. She wished to believe him, but she was no longer quite so trusting of appearances.

'What do you know of what happened to Miss Smythson?' she asked. 'I must know the truth, if I am to remain here.'

Mrs Claybourn returned the poker to its stand.

'Miss Smythson left here with a man,' she said. 'I saw it myself. It was just before dawn. He came in a trap, and no doubt she hoped to sneak away unnoticed. However, I am a light sleeper and the horse's hooves, even though they had been muffled, disturbed me.'

'This information might have helped Mr Smythson in his search, as well as setting his mind at rest. Why did you not say something?'

Mrs Claybourn gave Susan a pinched look.

'An unmarried teacher, running off with a young man. Think what that would do for our reputation.'

'Surely her family has the right to know the truth?'

'After Miss Smythson's behaviour, I owe them no such consideration.'

'Miss Smythson was blackmailing you. What about?'

Dr Claybourn closed his eyes.

'There is a secret at Matterdale Hall,' he said softly, 'but it is not mine.'

'You know about Helena and Richard?' Susan asked, wondering what their daughter's secret engagement with Richard could have to do with Miss Smythson.

'There is no secret there,' Mrs Claybourn snapped. 'They are to be married. All is agreed.' She approached Susan and laid a hand on her shoulder. 'We spoke of this, Miss Mottram. Surely you have not forgot?'

Dr Claybourn examined her closely. 'A lapse of memory. Another worrying symptom.'

Susan looked at them in confusion. She had no recollection of any such communication. When had that happened? It had been only a few days since Mrs Claybourn had told Sir Peregrine how much she despised fortune hunters. Surely, the Claybourns would never agree to Richard marrying their daughter? Unless he had some kind of hold over them.

'What is this secret?' she demanded.

Dr Claybourn's brow furrowed.

'It is not mine, but Marion's. Must I reveal it to prove my innocence?'

Susan coloured. Delicacy made her shake her head. Whatever Marion's affliction, Susan would hear it from her own lips, or none.

'Miss Mottram, let us come to the heart of the matter,' said Mrs Claybourn. 'We hope you can be persuaded to remain here. Your courage prevented what could have been an unfortunate incident. I value such service.'

'Had I hurt any of the girls...' Dr Claybourn began. His wife spoke over him.

'I am prepared to raise your pay by twelve pounds per annum. However, if you should leave now, you would be obliged to forfeit most of your stipend for this quarter.'

Her face remained inscrutable. Had Mrs Claybourn somehow found out about her family's predicament? Did she know that Susan's mother and Florence would be cast out of their home without this quarter's earnings? Although Mrs Claybourn's offer was couched as a choice, it was not much of one. Susan was about to answer when Mrs Clegg knocked on the door with unusual urgency. A pale-looking Anne was hovering beside her.

'Forgive me, mum, but the little deaf girl has run away.'

38

A Child Goes Missing

'**M**ary was upset, Miss,' said Anne. 'She ran after you and nobody has seen her since.'

Susan's stomach pitched and rolled. She had been too taken up in her own emotions to consider how distressed Mary must have been, or to have noticed if the little girl had followed her out to the moors. She ran to the window. Only a sliver of the sun remained on the horizon, a rusty glow above the shadowy moors.

'We must find her!' she cried. She and Mrs Claybourn searched each room, but there was no sign of Mary. Her coat and hat were found to be missing and it was surmised that Mary had gone out onto the moors in search of Susan.

'We must get up a search party,' Susan insisted. 'There is not a moment to be lost.'

An awful image of Mary, alone and shivering in the darkness, choked off her ability to speak further.

'It is almost night,' said Mrs Claybourn. 'It would be impossible to conduct a proper search. Better to wait until morning.'

Susan could not countenance giving up.

'I will take a lamp. She may see it and come to us.'

'I will get Richard and Mr Clegg. We will spread out in every direction,' said Dr Claybourn. 'I will not rest easy until that poor child is found.'

Susan carried the lamp as high as she could, calling out Mary's name, before remembering that Mary could not hear her. The guttering light from the lamp did little to penetrate the gloom, and there was no sign of the little girl. Susan's path led east, towards the escarpment. It would provide the best viewpoint and she hurried forward, hoping to reach the top before the light disappeared completely. But the last of the light faded as she approached and it was only the rising ground beneath her feet that told her she had reached the outcrop. Casting about with her lamp, she located the path that led to the top of the cliff, a strong wind from behind assisting her upwards.

As she crested the ridge, a golden circle of light broke the darkness. Within it, like a gilded statue, stood Cassandra, an oil lamp at her feet, her long tresses swept back by the wind as she faced Matterdale Hall. Susan's heart plunged into an uneven rhythm of such thunderous notes that she felt even Cassandra must hear. And perhaps she did, for Cassandra turned, her lips parting in a silent gasp as their eyes met. Susan approached hesitantly, uncertain of her welcome, but Cassandra opened her arms and Susan surrendered to the offered embrace. Her cheeks grew wet with tears, her guilt and fears for Mary mixed with a sweeter emotion. Cassandra had not turned away—she did not hate her. Cassandra's chest rose and fell beneath Susan's damp cheek, and she felt Cassandra's heartbeat, strong and fast. She made to pull away, but Cassandra's arms tightened around her and Susan, feeling Cassandra's body heat even through their clothes, had no strength or will to resist.

Much later, like Persephone rising from the underworld, Susan pulled away. Cassandra took off her gloves and gently brushed away Susan's tears with her naked fingertips. Their eyes locked.

Tell me.

With stiffening fingers, Susan haltingly explained all that had happened. Mr Smythson's suspicions about his sister's disappearance and the Claybourns' denials. About Mary and the infirmary and Dr Claybourn's loss of temper.

Have you seen Mary? she asked, once all was explained.

Cassandra shook her head and Susan shivered for she had put on neither cloak nor bonnet in her haste. Cassandra removed the woollen shawl she was wearing and wrapped it round Susan's quivering shoulders. It carried its owner's warmth and Susan tugged it round her body gratefully.

How came you to be here? she asked.

Something called me out onto the moors. I cannot explain it. I knew that you needed me.

Susan longed to hold her again, to feel once more that comforting embrace, but it was an indulgence she could not permit herself. Not until Mary was found.

Perhaps she is at Heathersage. She might have come to see Eppy, Cassandra suggested.

Hope flared in Susan's breast. She took Cassandra's

outstretched hand, and they walked together through the darkness.

At Heathersage, they questioned the servants. There had been no visitors and nobody had seen any sign of Mary.

As soon as it is light, everyone here will search for her, Cassandra promised. *You will stay with us tonight?*

It was an invitation Susan longed to accept. But suppose Mary returned to Matterdale Hall and she was not there? Dr Claybourn might already have found her. Or Richard. She could not let Mary face them alone, knowing how much the little girl feared them.

I must go back.

Do not return to that place, I beg you! There is evil within, I can sense it. The light, shining from the windows—it looked like the devil's forge.

I must go. For Mary's sake, and for the other girls, signed Susan. Cassandra looked away, but then turned back, her eyes glistening with unshed tears.

Will you always choose duty over our friendship?

Cassandra clasped Susan's hands. Her grip was warm and comforting, and it cost Susan much to prise her own fingers away. With even greater reluctance, she offered to return Cassandra's shawl. It was still warm and its soft fibres exuded Cassandra's particular scent.

Keep it. Cassandra's signal was abrupt. *I will send for James. He will accompany you.* Susan observed that she had caused offence. If only there was some way she could mend it, without abandoning her duty. However, that seemed impossible without a complete explanation of her feelings.

They waited, silent and still, until the tall footman hurried down the corridor, tugging on his greatcoat. As he led Susan out into the courtyard, she felt a touch on her arm. She turned.

Be vigilant. Trust no-one. Cassandra's expression was anguished. Her slender figure was framed by the doorway, light streaming from behind her. The emotions swirling and buffeting within Susan broke free.

'I love you,' she whispered. Even though she knew her voice could not be heard, the words demanded to be spoken. She turned and followed James out into the night.

39

In Which Susan Suspects her Mind is Playing Tricks

It was very late by the time Susan arrived back at Matterdale Hall. It suddenly struck her how remote the school was. There was nobody nearby who could help her should she need assistance. She felt a strong desire to return to Heathersage, but she repressed it, telling herself she would stay only long enough to find Mary. The girls had been sent to bed, but the Claybourns were still up. They informed her that Mary had not been found but vowed to continue searching as soon as it was light.

Susan sent James back to Heathersage and retired to her chamber. Although exhausted by the events of the day, she was restless and slept only fitfully. She rose before dawn. Her head ached and she felt cold, even though there was no frost on her windows and the air felt warmer than it had been for days. She made for the kitchens, feeling her way in the darkness as she did not want to waste her precious candle stub. As she opened the kitchen door, a strong odour of decay made her gasp. Behind her, the floorboards of the corridor groaned under a heavy footstep.

'Who's there?' she cried, whirling around.

'If it ain't the little sparrer.'

There was the sound of a match striking and a candle sputtered into life. Richard leered at her through the flickering flame.

'Shouldn't you be tending your patients?' Susan asked.

'Missus wants me to go to Hustanton and put in a coal order.'

'At this hour?'

'Ain't it a liberty? But I'm happy to play the good son-in-law.'

'I thought you were helping search for Mary?'

'That little mute? She'll turn up when it's light.'

Mrs Clegg shuffled down the servants' stairs, her hair forming a golden halo in the light of her candle stub. 'Oh, is it you, Miss?' Mrs Clegg shuffled past her and into the kitchen. 'I suppose you'll be wanting your hot water.' She prised open the door of the stove and shook her head in despair.

'Quite empty.'

'I'll get the coal,' said Susan impatiently, seizing the scuttle and opening the hatch to the coal bunker. The rotten odour was stronger here, and she swallowed down bile.

'I think the rats are back.' She fanned the air in front of her face in an attempt to dispel the smell. The pile of coal was much diminished and too far beneath her to scoop any from the top.

'We used a lot of coal when Sir Peregrine visited,' said Mrs Clegg forlornly.

'Is there a way to get down?'

'There's steps through there.' Mrs Clegg nodded towards a low door beyond the hatch. 'But Mrs Claybourn has the keys.'

'You are not trusted with the keys to the coal bunker?'

'I never subject my servants to such temptation,' said Mrs Claybourn, appearing at the kitchen door in her usual ghostly manner. She pulled a ring of keys from deep within her skirts and reached for the scuttle.

'I'll take that.'

'You'll get coal dust on your skirts, mum,' said Mrs Clegg.

'Then you shall wash them.'

Mrs Claybourn unlocked the door and disappeared down steps that turned sharply halfway down. The noise of a bucket scraping against coal came up the stairs along with another burst of putrid scent.

'There's even less than I thought,' Mrs Claybourn said as she returned, hefting a full scuttle. She closed the door and locked it behind her. 'Richard, I see you lurking in the shadows. Did I not ask you to go to the coal merchant? Tell him I'll pay extra if he can deliver today.'

'Yessum.'

Richard departed swiftly.

'You will join us for breakfast, Miss Mottram,' said Mrs Claybourn as she headed for the parlour. 'We take it early, so we may begin the search for Mary as soon as it is light.'

'Well, I never,' Mrs Clegg said in a low voice. 'We're usually scrabbling in the dirt before the missus will open her purse for more coal. Last summer, we hadn't even enough to cook with. Lucky all the girls had gone, all except Isabella Brownloe and poor little Mary Martin. They didn't mind having cold pie, but

303

Miss Smythson took it bad when there was no hot water for her coffee.'

Susan's ears pricked up.

'Miss Smythson was still here in the summer? When did she leave?'

Mrs Clegg pondered the question while she painstakingly sifted oats into a large pot.

'Me and Jack went Liverpool to bury his sister. End of July it were. Miss Smythson had gone when we got back.'

'So you never saw her leave?'

'No, duck.'

'Was Dr Claybourn here?'

'Oh yes. All the family were at home. I hope you ain't believin' any of Mr Smythson's nonsense? That girl said she didn't mind she had been dismissed, for she would be rich soon. Reckon she'd snared some foolish gentleman into making a promise.'

That fitted with Mrs Claybourn's story of a young man picking up Miss Smythson in his trap. But if the man was rich, why the secrecy? Unless Miss Smythson had, without realising it, put herself in the power of a wicked man.

Shaken by that notion, Susan joined the family for breakfast in the parlour. Mrs Claybourn was very attentive, keeping Susan's teacup topped up and insisting she take as much bacon as she liked from the tray. Susan had little appetite, but the tea was hot and sweet, and she drank several cups.

'You look quite pale,' said Helena. 'You may borrow some of my rouge. A white face is most unbecoming. Just look at Marion.'

Susan did feel a little unwell. Her stomach churned with worry and her head was aching. Even so, she insisted on joining the search. By lunchtime, her head began to throb and rings of light clouded her vision. Dr Claybourn, who had paired himself with her, insisted she return to the hall.

'Not until we have found Mary.'

'These symptoms are most concerning,' he said. 'As is the lack of concern for your own health. You are overtaxed and must rest. Unless you wish to become one of my patients, heh-heh?'

'The infirmary!' cried Susan, pressing her palm against her heated forehead. 'Mary was looking for something. Suppose she went back?'

'Wait!' cried Dr Claybourn, but he was unable to keep up with her, as she lifted her skirts and ran back towards Matterdale Hall. All the snow had melted and thick, wet mud sucked at her boots and stuck to the hem of skirts, making them heavy, but Susan ploughed onwards. Dr Claybourn's cries receded as she lengthened the distance between them. Breathless, she burst through the iron gate and into the yard. The infirmary loomed ominously against the pale blue afternoon sky. She pounded on the locked door. Dr Claybourn joined her, blowing hard, just as Richard opened the door from the inside. A candle illuminated his crooked smile.

'You ain't allowed here—'

'Mary? Is she here?' Susan brushed past him.

'No. I scared her off, good and proper. Ain't nobody here but the mad 'uns.'

Susan hurried into the vaulted chamber. It was empty, save for the chair with its leather straps. She went through into the corridor. An old man, hairless and bent, sat in his cell, staring blankly at the wall. He did not respond to her pleas. Amelia appeared in the doorway of one of the chambers.

'I'm looking for one of my pupils. Mary. Have you seen her?' Susan pleaded.

'Mary!' Amelia broke into a smile and hope bloomed in Susan's breast.

'You've seen her?'

'We play together on Saturdays.'

Richard snorted. 'She's thinking of when she was a child. I tell you, there ain't nobody else here.'

Susan looked in every cell. Sarah was lying on her bed and could only shake her head in response to Susan's desperate enquiries. All the other chambers were empty. Susan pressed the heel of her hand to her forehead. This was all her fault.

'Miss Mottram, you must leave immediately,' insisted Dr Claybourn. 'Such extreme agitation will make you highly susceptible to contagion.' Dr Claybourn tried to lay his hand upon her arm, but Susan shrugged him off.

'I will be well, as soon as we find Mary.'

'As you can see, she is not here.'

Susan cast around for any signs of hope. The door at the farthest end of the corridor stood open.

'Maria!' she exclaimed. 'Perhaps she has seen something.' She rushed towards the padded cell, but it was empty. She turned to the others. 'Where is she?'

'Where is who?'

'Maria. The young woman who was here.'

'It is as I feared. Your nerves have been affected,' said Dr Claybourn, wiping his forehead with a bright yellow kerchief. 'There is no such person.'

'No such person,' added Richard. Dr Claybourn placed his hand on Susan's back, as if to guide her away from the cell.

'But I saw her,' Susan insisted, flinching away from Dr Claybourn's unwelcome touch. 'She was wearing a straitjacket. And a paisley dress.' Amelia had joined them and Susan turned to her in desperation.

'Amelia, you remember Maria? She was in this cell.' Amelia chewed the skin on her finger.

'I don't know anyone named Maria,' she said. 'And my kitty's gone.' She retreated to her chamber and closed the door.

Dr Claybourn took a firm hold of Susan's elbow and Richard took hold of the other.

'Miss Mottram, I must insist you leave.'

Susan could do nothing as she was half-led, half carried from the infirmary. Her head felt like an anvil being pounded with hot metal. Why would Dr Claybourn and Richard pretend that Maria did not exist? Did they conspire against her? But Amelia, too, had no recollection of the woman in the padded cell. Was it possible that Susan's mind had invented a memory that seemed so real, so definite? The strange creature in the yard was surely proof that the mind could play tricks. If she couldn't trust her own senses, then how was she to know what was true and what was false? Her blood went cold with dread. There could be nothing more terrifying than going mad. She felt dreadfully alone, longing for the presence of a trusted companion to reassure her of her sanity. If only Cassandra were here! How Susan longed for the comfort of her presence and the warmth of her embrace.

40

Cassandra Takes Charge

At first light, Cassandra insisted that her entire household search the moors around Heathersage for any sign of Mary. She forced Mrs Grainger into acting as her interpreter as she gave the orders. Her companion was reluctant at first, insisting the business of Matterdale Hall was none of their concern, until Cassandra reminded her that she had once been of great help to a deaf child around Mary's age, and now had a chance to save another. Mrs Grainger protested no further and began to organise the servants. She even donned her own coat and bonnet, ready to join the search.

Where shall we begin? Mrs Grainger asked.

Everyone was looking at her expectantly. Unused to taking charge, Cassandra swallowed nervously, even as a plan formed in her mind. Her need to help Susan and to find Mary overcame her reticence. She began, via Mrs Grainger, to give her orders. Searches were to be conducted in pairs, along all points of the compass. Each pair must take a white sheet, to use as a signal if... when... they found Mary.

Will you remain here? she signed to Mrs Grainger. *Watch from the tower. If the signal be given, raise our family standard. All will then know to return.*

I should go, and you should stay here. Suppose you encounter strangers?

I cannot bear to stay quietly here. I must do something.

With James as her companion, a white sheet rolled up under his arm, Cassandra donned her fur pelisse and headed out. Their designated route was to the southeast. A mile they went, and then another, with no sign of life except a few hardy thrushes. Every few minutes, she looked back hopefully towards Heathersage, the top of the spire poking out above their small parcel of woodland. No sign of the standard.

They reached a small coppice at the top of a gentle rise. It marked the limit of her previous travels in this direction. If she went beyond it, Heathersage would disappear from view. Cassandra had visited it often in spring or summer, when it was green and full of life. Now, it was empty and desolate, the tree branches bare. Crows flew up from the tree skeletons as they approached. She could tell by the way James was opening and closing his mouth, and the way his Adam's apple moved up and down, that he was shouting. He was wasting his time. Like her, Mary lived in a landscape without sound. They passed through the coppice, looking and hoping, but there was no sign of Mary among the mossy trunks and rotting leaves.

As they emerged from the coppice, Cassandra hesitated. Her heart began to thump as if it wanted to escape from her breast. She recognised her fear but was determined to go on. What if

Mary lay just beyond the next rise, freezing on the cold ground? She stepped forward, one step at a time, and her heartbeat began to ease. They came to a clump of dense gorse, its bright yellow flowers just coming into bud. Cassandra crouched down and saw a flash of calico among the closely packed branches. Her throat vibrated. She forced her way into the gorse, thorns snagging and tearing at her pelisse. She reached a small mound that moved beneath her gentle touch. From a face as white as paper, eyes opened sleepily. Mary! With infinite care, Cassandra drew the child from the gorse. Mary felt cold and light, as if her bones were made of paper. James attempted to take her burden from her, but Mary squirmed against Cassandra's breast as if she would bury herself within it if she could, and so Cassandra kept the girl in her arms. Once they came back out of the coppice, James made the signal with the sheet. Moments later, the gold and purple standard broke from the top of Heathersage Manor's spire.

Even with Mary being so slight, Cassandra's arms were burning by the time she deposited the little girl in front of the kitchen fire. Mary had not stirred during the journey.

You carried her all that way? Mrs Grainger asked, bringing blankets which they piled around the little girl. *I did not know you were so strong.*

Nor did I, Cassandra returned.

Mary's eyes were closed, her face grey and her lips purple. Cassandra rubbed her tiny hand between her palms. It felt like ice.

Her boots are soaked, Mrs Grainger observed. Together they unlaced them and peeled off stockings which were sodden with brackish water. The other servants returned and filled bottles with hot water, which Cassandra wrapped in linens so as not to burn Mary's skin, and slid them inside the pile of blankets. Once

311

Mary's forehead and hands began to feel warmer to the touch, Cassandra gestured James to carry the girl to her own bed-chamber, where a fire had been laid.

Should I call a physician? Cassandra asked Mrs Grainger anxiously.

Mrs Grainger rested her hand against Mary's head. *There is no fever. We should wait until she wakes.*

We must tell Susan. She will be so worried.

Mrs Grainger pursed her lips.

She should be ashamed. Allowing a pupil to wander off alone.

It was not Susan's fault.

I do not understand your friendship with that girl. She seeks only to entrap your poor father.

You have no reason to be jealous.

Mrs Grainger blinked rapidly, a flush spreading up her neck.

I would not presume, she protested, but Cassandra observed the subtle signs that betrayed her companion. She had long known Mrs Grainger's wishes regarding her father, just has she had known he could never return them.

It was late evening before Mary awoke, yawning and stretching. At first, as she looked around what must have been a strange chamber, her eyes widened in fear, but when she saw Cassandra, who had not left her side, she flung her arms around her, sobbing. Cassandra wordlessly soothed her. It was clear that any communication would have to wait until Mary was calmer. She ordered a hot supper to be brought up on a tray. Mary devoured two bowls of thick soup and four slices of bread, as if she had not eaten in days. Cassandra rang the bell and ordered more food be brought up. When Mary had eaten her fill, she began to gently question her.

What happened?

Mary looked at her, her eyes wide.

I was scared. I ran.

You were on the moors all night?

Mary sniffled and nodded. *I couldn't see. I found a bush. Hid beneath.*

Why didn't you return to your school?

Mary trembled and buried her head in her hands. Cassandra wondered what sort of place made a young girl so afraid she would rather risk dying of cold than return? Gently, she eased Mary's hands apart.

You are safe now. Tell me what you saw. What made you so afraid?

They took her to the place with no windows.

Who? Who did the taking, and who was taken?

My teacher. She never came back. They took her—the frog man and his wife.

44

Marion's Confession

D r Claybourn had insisted Susan return to her chamber and lie down. She was too confused and exhausted to protest. Mrs Claybourn brough her more tea, but it did little to settle her stomach. After another night of fitful sleep and disturbing visions, Susan woke to a knock at the door. It heralded Marion with a letter. The sky was pale and grey, and there was barely enough light from the window to see. Susan was so disorientated, she could not tell if it was just after dawn or just before evening. However, Marion's tall frame could not be mistaken.

'You have a letter, direct from Heathersage Manor. The servant waits below for a reply.'

Susan blinked and eased herself into a sitting position. Even that small movement made her stomach roil. The back of her eyes felt as if they were being used as pincushions.

'I will fetch my father,' said Marion. 'You are unwell.'

'I beg… do not trouble him,' Susan whispered hoarsely. 'Mary?'

'Still no news.'

She held out the letter with a stiff arm. Susan took it and pressed it to her lips. The handwriting was Cassandra's, and the paper was infused with the distinct scent of Heathersage, a mixture of woodsmoke and candlewax and exotic spices. To breathe it in made her spirits lift.

'Would that you ever looked that way at me!' Marion's throat writhed as though a nest of snakes lived within. Susan finally understood her fellow teacher's torment.

'Oh, Marion. All those gifts; the apples, the pendant, and the other things. They were from you?'

Marion examined the floor.

'I could not speak of what I felt.'

'Is this the evil of which you have spoken? For loving me, you condemn yourself?'

Marion bared her teeth.

'I tried not to. I did not speak to you when you first came. I tried to get my mother to send you away. But you would keep trying to make conversation.'

'It is a great failing of mine, I'm afraid,' Susan admitted.

'You have such a loving, generous heart,' said Marion, her voice low and trembling. 'Yet not even you could love me.'

She gave out a choking sob and departed the room. Susan could scarce believe what she had heard. How had she mistaken Marion's character so entirely? That poor woman, living in such torment, thinking herself a sinner merely for loving another. Susan wished to offer Marion what comfort she could, but her mind was too clouded at present to make any plan. No matter how she tried to gather them, her thoughts scattered like lost sheep. She pressed her hand to her burning forehead. Paper scraped against her delicate skin, a reminder that she was still clutching Cassandra's letter. She tore it open. Her headache was so severe the writing danced and swam before her eyes. It took several attempts to decipher the contents.

Dearest Susan,

You are in grave danger. Mary is found—she is safe with us and has a tale to tell. Your predecessor, Miss Smythson, Mary saw her being locked away. She describes a building with no windows—perhaps the asylum that my father so abhors? You are not safe as long as you remain in the Claybourns' power. I send James with this note so that he can escort you to us. Dearest Susan, come to me at once. Do not delay, I beg you!

Your own Cassandra

Susan uttered a sharp exclamation, and tried to rise, but her legs were so weak, she fell back onto her bed. Miss Smythson, locked away? Why would anyone do such a dreadful thing? Her brain was so fogged, the answer came but slowly. Miss Smythson had discovered a secret; she had said so in her letter to her mother. What secret could be so dreadful that the Claybourns would lock someone up for knowing it? Dr Claybourn had claimed to be protecting Marion, but this must surely be something far worse than Marion's tendencies. Susan tried to untangle the mass of confused thoughts that pounded against her temples. Mary's story made no sense, for there had been no sign of anyone in the infirmary that fitted the description of Miss Smythson.

'Oh!' she cried, the scales dropping from her eyes. Maria, whose shaven hair disguised its colour. She had thought it might have been auburn, but it could just as well have been red. And she had been wearing a paisley dress. 'Such bright colours', Helena had claimed, 'such pretty dresses'. She recalled the trunk in the attic, with the initials H.V. She had taken it for a family heirloom of the Claybourns. But Mr Smythson had said that his mother had been a Vasey. It must be his sister's trunk. Her throat closed off. No young woman would leave without her trunk, not even to elope. Its presence was proof that Miss Smythson had never left Matterdale Hall, or at least not of her own free will. No wonder Mrs Claybourn insisted the attic was not safe. She didn't want anyone finding the trunk. That could only mean that Mrs Claybourn must be in on it too—her tale of seeing Miss Smythson leave with a man a complete fabrication.

'What a gullible fool I have been,' she cried.

The door opened and Mrs Claybourn came in with a bowl of broth. Quickly Susan tucked the message from Cassandra into the top of her bodice. She did not know where to look, certain that her countenance would betray her suspicions. Although what was it that she suspected? So many questions remained unanswered. If Maria was Miss Smythson, why had she been unable to speak? Why had the Claybourns hidden her identity? Most importantly, where was she now?

Mrs Claybourn set down the tray, her keys clanging beneath her skirts.

'I brought it myself that you might have it hot,' she said with a smile that made Susan feel so nauseated she pushed the soup away.

'You must eat to keep up your strength. A weak body breeds a weak mind, so Henry tells me.'

Susan looked at the soup and wondered if her illness hadn't started very soon after Mrs Claybourn had started to ply her with sweet tea.

'My husband says you are afflicted with all sorts of strange fancies. We are both extremely concerned. I did warn you to stay away from the infirmary. You should have listened.'

Susan pressed her hand against her head. It was certainly feverish. Was this all in her mind? But then she felt the corners of Cassandra's letter against her breast. That was real. She had not imagined that.

'Marion informs me that you had a letter from Heathersage. You need not trouble yourself to reply. I sent the footman away. I have given orders you are not to be disturbed. You will not leave this room until you are better.'

'I, ah, thank you,' said Susan, realising that her only hope lay in convincing Mrs Claybourn that she suspected nothing. That she was the same gullible fool she had always been. 'I will do as you say,' she said. In any case, she felt too weak, at present, to leave her bed. 'I will rest. I am sorry if I have caused any distress.'

'That's a good girl. Now, won't you take some nourishment?'

Susan forced down a few spoonfuls, enough to satisfy Mrs Claybourn, who nodded and rose to leave.

'I will leave you to rest. When I return, I expect to find you have eaten every last drop.'

42

A Visit from the Constable

Cassandra had circled her curio-filled parlour so many times that her slippers, not intended for such hard wear, began to chafe the skin on her toes and heels. She stopped and perched on the edge of her favourite chair, but after only a few moments jumped up again and continued her pacing. Her stomach felt tender, as though she had eaten some bad meat. Her fears concerning Susan had only increased with the arrival of the new day, and every time she completed a lap of the room she chided herself on the weakness that prevented her ordering the coach to take her to Matterdale Hall and demanding the Claybourns let her see Susan. In her mind's eye, she pictured a bolder version of herself bursting into Susan's classroom and carrying her away to the safety of Heathersage. She flung herself into her chair. What was the use of such dreams? She could never act in such a way. If only her father were here. But he was long gone, and her aversion to strangers meant they had no friends to whom she might turn for help. The touch of a hand on her shoulder made her jump. It was Mrs Grainger, who must have come in when she was not looking.

Is James returned? Cassandra asked.

Mrs Grainger nodded.

Susan? He has brought her!

Mrs Grainger laid a hand on Cassandra's wrist to restrain her from darting into the hall to see for herself.

No. They said she was ill and not to be disturbed. He was sent away.

Susan, ill? What is wrong with her?

Mrs Grainger could not answer. Cassandra insisted on speaking to James himself, with Mrs Grainger interpreting. Had he seen Miss Mottram? No, only the lady of the house, who had taken the letter. He had waited for a reply, but Mrs Claybourn had insisted Miss Mottram was not well enough to receive visitors, and certainly not well enough to travel. Cassandra asked if he had attempted to gain admittance, to see Susan for himself? James said he had not. It was not his place to do so.

Cassandra, convinced that something was dreadfully wrong, insisted they send for the constable. Mr Jennings sent word that he was occupied all morning but promised to visit in the afternoon. When at last he arrived, he directed all his attention to Mrs Grainger, as though Cassandra was beneath his notice. After listening to what Mrs Grainger said, he insisted he would not interfere in matters that were of no concern to the law. Matterdale Hall had an excellent reputation, he said. They are soon to have the daughters of a baronet among their pupils.

And Dr Claybourn was a physician of the highest standing. Miss Sutcliffe was fortunate that Dr Claybourn was such an affable man, and unlikely to take proceedings against baseless slander.

Baseless? What about Mary—what she saw? Cassandra prompted.

Mr Jennings looked towards Mrs Grainger. After she had translated, Mr Jennings shook his head condescendingly and insisted there was no evidence of foul play. He had searched Matterdale Hall himself and could assure Mrs Grainger there was nothing amiss. Nobody was being held prisoner, and Miss Smythson had been witnessed running off with a young man. There really was nothing more to be done. He rose to depart. Unwilling to lose her only lifeline, Cassandra threw herself to her knees and clasped his hands in supplication. Mr Jennings' expression of condescension transformed into one of revulsion. He snatched his hands away. As he left, Cassandra saw him take a kerchief from his pocket and rub at his hands as if he had dirt on them. She suspected that he would burn the kerchief as soon as he could.

I did try to tell you. The briskness of Mrs Grainger's hand signals showed she had lost any last remnants of patience. *Your father will not thank me for letting you make a fool of yourself, based on the word of a confused child.*

I was once called confused. And worse. Mary did not invent her tale, I am certain. We must do something.

This excessive concern is not healthy. What hold does that young woman have on you?

Cassandra's fingers were unable to frame a reply. Her feelings for Susan were certainly powerful, but she refused to accept they were unhealthy. They had sprouted from a seed that had always been within her, requiring only light and nourishment to grow into something strong and wonderful. A feeling that had taken possession, root and branch, of her body and her soul. She felt a dreadful premonition, which grew stronger within her breast at every moment, that, without action, she might never feel the brightness of Susan's presence again.

43

A Discovery in the Coal Cellar

When Susan woke, all was dark. Her headache was no better, and her stomach felt as if someone had lit a fire inside it. The half-finished bowl of broth lay next to her. She shuddered and tipped the contents into her chamber-pot. Beyond her chamber, all was quiet. The girls must have gone to bed. She lay back to gather her thoughts, even as her head throbbed. She was certain now that something was dreadfully amiss at Matterdale Hall and Dr Claybourn and his wife were at the centre of it. But what exactly had they done? And how was she to find proof? No-one would believe the protestation of a naïve young teacher without evidence.

Her father had always taught her to think rationally. She set her mind to the problem. Miss Smythson had been in the infirmary, but now she was not. Therefore, the Claybourns must have moved her. Unless they had killed her and disposed of the body. A few months ago, she would have decried anyone who made such wild accusations, or chastised herself for reading too many gothic novels, but Cassandra's letter confirmed her own belief that something tainted Matterdale Hall. An evil even stronger than the smell of decay, a smell that had first become apparent a few days after Mr Smythson had been escorted from the premises. Had his threats to return prompted the Claybourns into desperate action? She recalled the creature in the snow-covered yard. It might have been a body, being dragged towards the kitchen by the shoulders. Why was Mrs Claybourn suddenly so concerned about filling the coal bunker? What might be revealed, if it were to be emptied? This half-formed idea was so horrifying that Susan almost fainted.

She swung her legs round and forced herself out of bed. She had to see what was in the coal cellar. Pulling on her dressing gown and slippers, she stepped silently across the landing and into the family corridor. She had stuffed her stub of candle into her pocket but dared not light it yet. Instead, she ran her fevered palm against the cool stone walls to guide her. Silver moonlight filtered in through the windows but only turned the corridor into a mass of lowering shadows. At the door of Mrs Claybourn's chamber she had to clamp her teeth together to prevent them chattering. For an instant, the temptation to return to the comfort of her bed tugged at her, but she thought of Mr Smythson, not knowing the fate of his sister. And the girls. If Dr Claybourn really was a murderer, she must prove it, or they would never be safe. She placed her damp palm against the doorknob and eased open the door. Its hinges squeaked, sounding to her heightened senses like a demonic shriek. Holding her breath, she slipped inside. A faint glow of coals in the hearth provided a cast of red light, outlining the back of a chair across which a garment had been draped. In the gloom, it looked like the hunched back of a crouching beast, throbbing and pulsing as if it were alive. She stopped in terror until realising the movement was only a product of her blurred vision. Reaching out, her trembling fingers met rough calico. Within its folds, her fingertips brushed against hard metal. Slowly she abstracted the keys, pressing them against her bosom to prevent them clinking, for her hands were shaking like those of an old woman. She backed towards the door. On reaching the safety of the corridor, she released a shuddering breath. A spell of dizziness swept over her and the corridor split into two, then four, identical oblongs of blackness. She closed her eyes, but the dark rectangles continued to dance on the back of her eyelids.

The putrid smell increased as she descended the servants' stairs and headed for the kitchen, planting her palms against the reassuring solidity of the wall to keep her balance. The keys scraped against the lock of the coal bunker door as she fumbled with each in turn. None seemed to fit. As she began again, a grating noise from above made her start. She stopped and listened, but the noise did not repeat itself. At last she found a key that unlocked the door. She stumbled into the dark maw of the narrow staircase. She dug her candle stub from her pocket, together with a box of matches. It took five strikes with her trembling fingers to get a flame. The candles flickered into life, all four of them, for her vision remained blurred and faulty. A shallow layer of coals glinted back at her. Susan stepped forward and began to scrabble blindly among the black nuggets. Her hands and forearms were soon stained black with the coal dust, but she cared not. Her fingers grasped something soft. She brought the candle close. A fragment of cloth. There was a hint of a pattern behind the coal dust that darkened its surface. A pattern of swirls and teardrops. She felt around some more and her fingers landed on something cold and clammy. She moved her trembling candle closer. Between her fingers was a woman's hand, grey and swollen and cold as wet clay. With a scream, she let go of the corrupted flesh and staggered backwards.

A scraping above her made her whirl round. The coal hatch had been opened. Above it, Mrs Claybourn's face was yellow, illuminated by an oil lamp.

'Well, Miss Mottram, you have found out our little secret,' she said.

44

In Which Cassandra Makes a Resolution

Cassandra breakfasted early. All that night, she had lain awake, shoring up her courage. She would visit Matterdale Hall and insist on seeing Susan. She was no servant and could not be turned away. In the morning, her resolution held, but she found that she was not brave enough to go alone. Mrs Grainger refused to countenance making a visit before noon. Morning visiting was not polite, she insisted. Cassandra chafed at the delay but no amount of pleading could persuade Mrs Grainger to change her mind. Eppy, sensing something was afoot, danced around her feet, tripping her up, until Cassandra took her on a walk round the lake to calm her spirits. The walk proved successful in settling Eppy but Cassandra's agitation only increased as her mind ran through all the ways her venture might end in disaster. What if her nerves got the better of her, as they so often did? Or suppose the Claybourns refused to even admit her?

On returning from her walk, she and Eppy went to find Mary, who had slept so late she was only now having breakfast. The puppy and the girl were delighted to be reunited, although Mary was still too weak to do more than pet her friend whilst sitting with a blanket around her shoulders. It was now almost noon and Cassandra put on her blackberry bonnet and coat with trembling hands. Mrs Grainger took an age making her preparations yet, when the moment came, it was Cassandra who hesitated by the carriage door. The last time she had set foot in it had been Christmas. The memory of all those faces, gawking at her outside the church, almost made her turn back. But she remembered Susan taking her hand, giving her the strength she had needed. She took a deep breath and stepped up into the carriage.

They went via Hustanton, where Mrs Grainger insisted on stopping at the milliners to place an order and then again at the post office. On each occasion, Cassandra shrank into the corner of the carriage so that she may not be seen. She wanted no-one to try and greet her, terrified that someone would peek in for a glimpse at Mr Sutcliffe's demon child. It seemed an age before her companion returned from the post office, holding a couple of letters.

Why must you stop everywhere? You are cruel to leave me here alone, Cassandra remonstrated.

I only stopped to ask the postmistress if there was any letter for you.

Cassandra reached eagerly for the letters, but her brief spark of hope was extinguished when she saw that both were addressed to her father and neither was in Susan's hand. She sank back into her seat, her heart fluttering with dread as Mrs Grainger signalled the coachman to make for Matterdale Hall.

The coach swayed and bumped along the rough track, limited to such a dawdling pace that Cassandra thought she might get out and walk faster. However, she did not. Despite her longing to see Susan, it was all she could do to sit upright. Her affliction was causing her heart to gallop like a runaway pony, and she felt as if a lump of iron had been sewn into her chest, forcing her to breathe in short, constrained gasps. The instant they pulled through the gates, Cassandra reached for the door, leaping out before the coach had come to a full halt. Yet the fresh air did nothing to ease her terror. Seeing Matterdale Hall up close for the first time, she was more convinced than ever that malevolence lay behind its bland exterior.

The short walk to the door was as painful and difficult as forcing her way through a tangle of gorse. Her weak knock produced no answer. Mrs Grainger's more energetic rapping was answered, after a long delay, by an elderly woman with a mop of straggly grey hair. The woman blinked at her expectantly, but Cassandra was frozen on the doorstep, incapable of action. Mrs Grainger exchanged words with the woman, their lips moving in that generally incomprehensible manner that Cassandra knew to be speech. The woman's hair wobbled in a flustered negative.

She says that Miss Mottram is not to be disturbed.

No, thought Cassandra, gritting her teeth against the urge to return to the blessed safety of home. I have not gone through this to be denied.

I will not leave until I see her, she signed, with emphasis.

Another exchange of speech followed. The Claybourns'

housekeeper shook her head again and began to close the door. Cassandra darted forward and held the door with the ball of her foot while she signed frantically at Mrs Grainger.

Tell her we have found Mary.

That was enough to grant them entry into a dim hallway. Cassandra felt her already fluttering heartbeat quicken to an alarming degree in response to the unfamiliar environment. If she was to find Susan, she must do so quickly, while she still had strength. She ran to the nearest door and burst in on a classroom full of older girls. More than two dozen heads turned towards her. Mouths gaped open, eyebrows shot upwards and fingers were pointed. A middle-aged woman wearing half-moon glasses turned towards her. Cassandra recognised her from church. Mrs Claybourn. Her glare could have iced over a cup of steaming coffee. Cassandra retreated and tried the next door along. It opened into an empty chapel. *Where was Susan?* She returned to the hallway, where Mrs Grainger begged her to wait to be properly received, but Cassandra hurried past her into another classroom, crammed full of younger girls. It was led by a tall, straight-backed woman. Amongst the sea of faces that turned towards her, there was one Cassandra recognised. Quiet, shy little Anne.

Miss Mottram—where is she? Cassandra signed desperately.

She is sick. She is in the... Anne's fingers stopped mid-sentence.

Where? Where have they taken her?

Anne hesitated, frowning, and then began to fingerspell.

I-n-f-i-r-m-a-r-y.

She ran to a window at the back of the room and pointed towards what looked like an old stable block. Its windows were bricked over. Cassandra turned to find her exit blocked by Mrs Claybourn, her lips opening and closing in a most vigorous fashion.

Mrs Grainger was also talking, looking apologetic. Cassandra was used to being talked over, but she refused to let it happen today. She snatched up a slate and chalk from the nearest desk and scribbled furiously, thrusting her words towards Mrs Claybourn.

I must see Susan.

Mrs Claybourn calmly held out her hand for the slate, but Cassandra could not bear to give up her only means of communication. Mrs Claybourn's mouth moved again. In response, the tall woman brought another slate and some chalk. With great deliberation, Mrs Claybourn wrote a response.

Calm yourself.

I will be calm when I have seen Susan.

Miss Mottram is very ill. Any disturbance may be fatal.

I insist. Cassandra's fingers trembled so much, her words were barely more than a scrawl.

You are making a spectacle of yourself.

Cassandra was suddenly aware that everyone was watching her. A sharp pain ran through her chest and her vision began to darken in a way she knew and feared above all else. She was about to faint. Mrs Claybourn, sensing her advantage, rubbed her slate clean and wrote another message.

You have Mary?

Cassandra could only flick her eyes helplessly at Mrs Grainger, whose lips moved incomprehensibly.

You will return her to us.

Cassandra shook her head as her breath shortened into hitching gasps. The tall woman was staring at her, her eyes filled with self-loathing. *She cannot help me. Nobody will help me.* Cassandra's slate slipped from her grasp and her vision narrowed to a pinprick. Mrs Grainger's face filled with alarm and her mouth opened and closed like a landed fish. Moments later, strong arms lifted her up and carried her from the room. She knew it was James by the scent of boot polish and beeswax that was always soaked into his clothes. Her head flopped against his broad chest as he carried her from that awful place.

45

A Cruel Letter

Susan awoke. Or, at least, she thought she was awake. She was reasonably certain her eyes were open, yet she could see nothing. The darkness was so complete that she feared for a moment she was dead. She cried out. Her voice faded away as if sucked into a void but it was enough to confirm she was alive. *But where?* Her stomach cramped and a noxious scent informed her she had been sick. She reached out blindly and felt a bed of some kind, but the thinness of the mattress told her it was not her own. Standing up, her slippered feet landed on something soft. Her stomach lurched and she retched violently, the bile burning the back of her throat. As she reached out to steady herself, her fingers brushed against leather that gave a little as she pushed. It smelled of horsehair. With an anguished sob, she understood where she was. She pounded at the horsehair, crying hoarsely for help, but she was weak, and the soft padding of the cell dampened the impact of her fists. No one would hear her.

She stopped her ineffective efforts to make herself heard and strived to compose herself. Hysteria would serve no purpose. How came she to be here? She remembered the coal bunker hatch opening. Mrs Claybourn, her face uplit by lamplight. After that, she recalled nothing. She must have fainted.

She cast around for any crumbs of hope. Mr Smythson might return. Unlike her, he had not been fooled by the Claybourns' explanations and assurances. What of Mr Jennings, the constable? Even his indolence might be stirred if another teacher went missing. Perhaps Cassandra would come to her aid. It was an encouraging thought until Susan recalled how much courage it took for Cassandra even to leave her house. Attempting a visit to Matterdale Hall would surely be impossible. It was too much to hope.

Sometime later, faint traces of light brightened the room. Peering up, Susan realised that there were narrow vents in the ceiling, through which light was slanting down. She yelled hoarsely, with fresh hope that someone might hear. A few seconds later, she heard the lock click and Mrs Claybourn entered with a lamp in one hand and a glass of water in the other. Beneath her arm was a sheaf of blank papers and a blotter.

'You waste your breath,' she said. 'No-one can hear you.'

Perhaps it was her sickness, still distorting her vision, or the knowledge of her employer's perfidy that caused Mrs Claybourn's features to take on a demonic twist, half lit by the lamplight. She held out the glass of water. Susan eyed it suspiciously.

'Clever girl,' Mrs Claybourn murmured drily, setting the glass aside. 'But your understanding comes too late to save you. Starving yourself to death will suit my purpose as well as poison.'

What a fool she had been! Defending Dr Claybourn as she

stumbled blindly round the truth. All the while, Mrs Claybourn had been pulling the strings.

'What purpose is that?' she asked, her voice as steady as she could make it, given the circumstances.

'Henry has prepared a diagnosis. A young woman with a brain fever brought on by melancholia after the death of her dear parent, coupled with the anxieties of a job for which she was quite unsuited. Committed to the infirmary for treatment but refused to eat.'

'Nobody will believe you!' Susan cried.

'Why not? Your behaviour has already been witnessed. By myself and my husband. And Richard.'

'Richard—he's in on it too?'

Even as she asked the question, she knew the answer. Why else would the Claybourns agree to let him marry Helena?

'You cannot keep me here.' Despite her protestation, icy fingers ran down Susan's spine.

'Physicians may confine any patient they deem clinically insane.'

'But I'm not mad! My family will come for me. And I have friends. They will not be deceived.'

'Your family will receive the tragic news too late, alas,' said Mrs Claybourn. 'As for friends, if you mean Miss Sutcliffe, you will dissuade her from ever coming here again.'

'Cassandra was here?' The words came out as barely more than a whisper, yet Susan's heart swelled at Cassandra's bravery.

'She caused a most unfortunate disturbance. It cannot be repeated.'

'I will do no such thing.' Susan's own courage rose, spurred by Cassandra's example.

'If you do not, the next time that half-breed creature enters Matterdale Hall, my husband will commit her. Put her in a straitjacket and all she can do is moan and groan. She will be the very picture of a lunatic.'

The mental image of Cassandra, her delicate, artistic hands restrained, unable to communicate, was so distressing that tears streamed down Susan's face.

'Her father will speak for her,' she protested feebly. 'And Mrs Grainger. They can prove she is an intelligent, feeling woman.'

'Their word will carry no weight against that of a physician. Besides, she is clearly hysterical. There is an excess of feeling inside that girl. However, strong emotions in one direction, if turned, will produce equally strong emotions in the other. You will make her hate you.'

Susan stared at her in dumb confusion.

'Do not play innocent. I have read your correspondence. Her unnatural affection for you is clear in every line. You will tell her that you find such feelings abhorrent.'

Unnatural affection? Was it possible that Cassandra loved Susan? If she hadn't been in such a desperate predicament, the possibility would have made her heart soar.

'I would rather drink any poison you care to bring than write such a letter.'

Mrs Claybourn set down the blotter and paper and retrieved a pen and ink pot from a pocket in her skirts. She dipped the pen in the ink and held it towards Susan.

'We must all make sacrifices. My husband is eager to study Miss Sutcliffe. He thinks she would make an ideal subject for his phrenomed. Let us disappoint him, shall we?'

As with all of Mrs Claybourn's ultimatums, there was no true choice. Defeated, Susan took the pen and wrote, as her employer dictated.

Dear Miss Sutcliffe,

I beg you will no longer force your presence where it is unwanted. You have mistaken my offer of friendship for something more than it is. Know that I could never truly be friends with someone such as yourself, whose swarthy skin should provide enough warning of the depravity beneath. I understand you are keeping one of our pupils a prisoner in your house. If you do not return Mary to Matterdale Hall at once, my employers will be forced to take out a warrant for you on a charge of kidnapping. That you would attempt to use a child as a tool to win my affections sickens me. I break off all acquaintance and return your letters. I beg you will destroy my own, for our brief acquaintance brings me nothing but shame.

Susan Mottram.

Mrs Claybourn examined the note that had given Susan so much pain to write and tore it up.

'Again,' she said, 'but without the tear stains.'

46

Cassandra is Convinced Something is Amiss

Cassandra was picking at her luncheon when she was interrupted by a servant carrying a sizeable packet, wrapped up with twine. Recognising Susan's hand, Cassandra tore it open. A bundle of her own letters fell out, wrapped in a piece of paper that contained just a few lines of writing. Cassandra read the short missive. Every word shredded her soul. Never had she felt such agony. For the letter confirmed her worst fears. Susan was a prisoner, locked up against her will. Her own dear Susan was incapable of such cruelty. She would never willingly write such hurtful words. It made Cassandra shudder to imagine what might have happened to compel Susan to pen such a dreadful letter.

What is wrong? asked Mary, who was with her.

Nothing, Cassandra returned, attempting a smile, even though her heart was breaking. That afternoon, as she watched Mary

341

playing with Eppy, she made a desperate resolution. Since nobody would help her, she must return to Matterdale Hall and rescue Susan herself. Her heart clenched. The idea of such an expedition terrified her. Suppose she had another fainting fit? She wrestled with her doubts and fears until nightfall. As daylight faded, Cassandra's resolve strengthened. Night was her friend. It would hide her from prying eyes. She would go.

Mrs Grainger made no protest when, after supper, Cassandra indicated that she was tired and would retire. The instant she was in her room, she changed into her stoutest walking boots and found out a shawl and rain-cloak. She left Mary curled around Eppy, both sleeping contentedly, and trod as lightly as she could down the stairs. No-one accosted her. A line of light beneath the parlour door told her Mrs Grainger was still within, and the servants were most likely taking their own supper below stairs. As she opened the door, the icy, grasping fingers of the wind swirled around her and she stopped. The darkness stretched out before her, filled with unknown terrors, and she felt a pressing urge to retreat back to the warmth and comfort of home. Yet something more profound called her from across the moors and would not be resisted. With a pounding heart, she stepped out into the night with only an oil lamp for company.

To Cassandra's imagination, even the elements seemed set against her. Perhaps it had always been so, for she recalled the heavy snowfall that had kept Susan from her. Now, rain lashed down from the sky, and the instant she left the gravel paths of their estate, her boots sank up to her ankles in squelching mud. The wind pressed against her chest, as if trying to push her back home, and the rain stung her eyes. She pressed her palm against the top of her bonnet to keep it on her head, and in her other the oil lamp swayed alarmingly. More than once, it flickered and almost died, and Cassandra realised, to her dismay, that she hadn't brought any matches. If the lamp went out, she was lost. Its pale yellow circle illuminated the ground in front of her feet. Cassandra stumbled forward, following the narrow gaps that weaved between the clumps of heather. At last she reached the top of the escarpment. The wind at this height was so strong it stole the warmth from her body. Tiny lights in the distance indicated the location of Matterdale Hall. She had never gone beyond this point alone. She waited for her heart to stop thumping against her ribs. It refused. She recalled the steep path down the other side, and knew that any false step would take her over the cliff edge. *You are stronger than you know,* she told herself. *Did you not carry Mary all that way? Susan needs that strength, now.* She began to inch forward, holding the lamp as high as she could, until she at last found the beginning of the narrow path. Fear choked her breath and held her captive. Cassandra clenched her fists, summoning her courage. Across the moors, the woman she loved more than anything in the world was in terrible danger, and only Cassandra could help her. With a shuddering gasp, she stepped onto the path and began her descent.

I'm coming, Susan. I'm coming, my beloved.

47

The Phrenomed is Employed

D r Claybourn closed the cell door behind him. He carried the phrenology head in the crook of his arm and a carafe of water in the same hand.

'Miss Mottram… Susan, if I may address you so?'

'You have taken my liberty and my health. Why should I mind a little presumption?' Susan returned bitterly.

'I have brought water.'

Susan's nose wrinkled.

'I give you my word it is not poisoned.'

'As you swore you did not harm Miss Smythson?'

Dr Claybourn approached the bed. Susan tried to inch away but the cell was small and there was nowhere to go.

'I told you the truth. I am no murderer, heh-heh.' His nervous chuckle grated against her already strained nerves.

'You do not deny she is dead?'

'You have observed Mrs Claybourn. You know that I cannot command her.'

'Why? Why would she do such a dreadful thing?' Susan asked.

He reached for her hand and seemed put out when Susan snatched it away.

'Susan, I have come to admire your spirit and intelligence.'

'From such a wicked, deceitful person, that is no compliment.'

He started back, his cheeks ruddier than ever.

'This is most unfair! All this misfortune arose from the purest of intentions. My phrenomed has the potential to cure every disease of the mind.'

'How many people must suffer for your ambition?'

'No scientific advances of importance are made without set-backs,' he said with a smile so patronising Susan wanted to hurl something at him. Unfortunately, unless she removed one of her slippers, there was nothing to hand, and she decided it would be a waste of a slipper.

'After the harm your instrument did to Helena, you cannot think it a success?'

He examined her as if she had said something quite stupid.

'What can you mean? Helena is my greatest achievement.'

'Crippling headaches and addicted to laudanum. A great achievement indeed,' Susan said bitterly.

'That cannot be true!'

'I assure you it is. It is a poor physician that cannot see such obvious symptoms. Your ambition clearly exceeds your abilities.'

He stared at her.

'Impossible! Why did she not tell me? If I had known there were such side-effects, I would have been more careful in my treatment of those two little girls. That was the start of all this.'

'What girls?' Was there yet more wickedness to discover?

'Two of Miss Smythson's pupils were extremely disruptive. I measured their skulls and each showed a significant enlargement of the same area.' He tapped the phrenology head at a point just behind its left ear. 'I hypothesised a small reduction in brain tissue would improve their behaviour.'

Susan almost choked with horror.

'I believed it would cure them. Unfortunately, the juvenile skull is more fragile than I had anticipated.'

'This is the secret that Miss Smythson discovered!' Susan gasped.

'Her father was an apothecary. She knew the girls hadn't died of typhus, as I tried to make everyone believe. She threatened to have Mr Jennings exhume the bodies unless we gave her a thousand pounds. My wife proposed a less costly solution, but I persuaded her to let me try my phrenomed before taking such a permanent step. I saved Miss Smythson's life, for a while at least. As I would save yours.'

Susan recalled poor Miss Smythson, in the padded cell, unable to speak. He had used his instrument to steal her words from her, yet he was so utterly convinced that he had done nothing wrong, Susan began to see how he had fooled her. Why should anyone suspect Dr Claybourn of evil when he himself was unaware of it? He twisted the phrenology head so that it sat upright on his lap.

'Leading phrenologists believe that memories are lodged just above the right ear. The results with Miss Smythson, although not entirely as I would have wished, were consistent with that hypothesis. With a slight adjustment, I believe I can remove your memories. There would be no reason for you to die and my hypothesis would be proven. It would be a great step forward.'

His expression was so earnest and enthusiastic that Susan felt quite ill. He was utterly convinced he was offering her something of value.

'I would lose everything that makes me who I am,' she said slowly. 'The knowledge of who I love, and those who love me. My dear father would be lost to me forever.' *And Cassandra would be nothing but a stranger.*

'You refuse then?'

'Absolutely.'

His expression soured.

'Then I must choose for you, for who but the insane would choose death over living?'

Cassandra approached Matterdale Hall. The lights had long since disappeared and the building loomed darkly out of the ground, its sharp edges silhouetted against the silver glow of moonlit clouds. She located the asylum, a smaller block of darkness near the perimeter. She reached the border wall and halted, looking for signs that anybody was about. Seeing no movement, she used her hands to feel her way along the damp wall until she reached an iron gate. As she went through, a strong hand clamped her arm. Cassandra's throat vibrated and another hand covered her mouth, choking off her breath. She pulled back with all her strength, swinging her lamp wildly to see who had accosted her. A tall figure, deathly pale, pressed a forefinger to her lips. Cassandra stopped the vibration in her throat. She recognised Marion from her earlier visit. Marion's lips moved and Cassandra's fingers fluttered, but neither could understand each other. It was a moment of uncommunicable agony. Yet Cassandra knew she was in no danger. Marion had tried to silence her to prevent her giving the alarm. She meant to help. Cassandra scanned the ground for an object solid enough to make an impression on the soft ground. She found a stick and scraped a single word into the mud.

Susan?

Marion jerked her head toward the asylum, confirming what Cassandra already knew. Cassandra took a step towards it, but Marion held her back and seized the stick.

Too dangerous.

Cassandra wrenched back the stick.

If you love her, help me save her. It was a guess, yet she was almost certain she understood Marion's feelings. A tear ran down Marion's cheek. After a moment of painful hesitation, she entwined rough fingers about Cassandra's and pulled her into the shadow of the infirmary. Cassandra let herself be led forward until they reached a doorway. As Marion put her hand on the handle, her nostrils flared and she clutched the back of her head. A thin sliver of light streamed out from beneath the door. Cassandra looked to Marion, but the woman was frozen to the spot, her face a rictus of terror. Cassandra grasped the door handle and plunged inside before her own fear could bind her also.

She found herself within a vast chamber. Dr Claybourn had his back to her, his arms crooked like bird wings as he fiddled with something. Cassandra circled until she could see what he was doing. Her legs almost gave way beneath her. In the chair was Susan, her skin sallow and her lips dry and cracked. An awful instrument made of metal screws and clamps had been placed on her head, and it was this that Dr Claybourn was adjusting. Susan's terrified expression turned to dismay as her eyes met Cassandra's. Her wrists were secured to the arms of the chair with leather straps but her hands began to move. Cassandra realised she was making a sign, but with her hands separated it was hard to understand what it was. Susan repeated the same movements, again and again. Her left hand lay flat to the ground, her right forefinger was pointing towards the corner of the room. Putting them together Cassandra understood the meaning.

Flee!

But she could never leave Susan to such a fate. Thoughtless for her own safety, she pushed past Dr Claybourn and tore the contraption from Susan's head. She flung it aside and reached tenderly for Susan, whose bruised and sunken eyes were fixed on a point beyond her shoulder. Cassandra turned. Dr Claybourn had retrieved the metal and leather contraption and was examining it, his jaw clenched and his temples wormy with raised veins. He advanced towards her, his garish waistcoat overpowering her senses. She could see from the way his mouth twisted, spittle flying from it, that he was yelling. Confronted by such palpable rage, Cassandra could only stagger backwards, her throat vibrating. Dr Claybourn seized her by her wrists and dragged her firmly down a narrow corridor. Cassandra tugged ineffectually, but her captor was too strong. He flung her into a padded cell and slammed the door in her face. As the door closed, it took the light with it, and she was plunged into darkness. How had she been so foolish as to think she could save Susan? She couldn't even save herself.

48

Susan Attempts a Deception

'Please don't leave us without light,' begged Susan, as Dr Claybourn thrust her into the padded cell alongside Cassandra. He paused in the doorway, his back towards them, clenching and unclenching his empty fist. Without turning, he set the lantern on the floor.

'It is fortunate I have a kind heart. The Lord knows what damage that... that young woman has done to my delicate instrument.'

The door clanged heavily behind him and Susan heard the key turn in the lock. She looked at Cassandra, tenderness mingling with disbelief. She had thought she would never see her again, or not recognise her if she did.

Are you truly here?

Perhaps she was, after all, in the grip of a delusion. Cassandra took Susan's hands and pressed her lips against Susan's fingertips. A sweet vibration shivered through her veins.

I am truly here.

Susan's trembling fingers stumbled over the words.

What courage that must have taken. I do not deserve…

I fear nothing more than losing you. What was that contraption?

Susan swayed as she recalled the tips of the phrenomed spikes pressing against her skull. If Cassandra had not arrived when she had… She felt Cassandra's arm snake round her waist and guide her to the bed.

You saved me from something worse than death, Susan signed.

I fear I have only delayed your fate.

I have been such a naïve, trusting fool. I did not imagine there could be such darkness in the world.

Cassandra gently brushed a strand of hair from Susan's forehead.

Do not blame yourself. To see good in people is no sin.

Susan rose to her feet.

We must escape. Before he returns.

However, the abrupt movement made her head spin and only Cassandra's embrace stopped her falling. She was eased, once more, back onto the narrow bed.

Do not despair. Mrs Grainger will look for me. Or my father.

But Susan remembered Mrs Claybourn's words. Cassandra's family could not save them. If they were to escape, they must rely on their own cunning. Unfortunately, as the past few months had taught her, she had about as much cunning as a somnolent sheep. She needed to think of a plan, but the threat of having holes drilled into her brain seemed to have stifled her ability to think. Perhaps if she rested her eyes for a moment…

Some hours later, Susan awoke. Cassandra was asleep beside her, breathing softly, and Susan was overcome with protectiveness.

'No!' she cried, leaping to her feet. 'I will not let them have you. I will lie, cheat or even kill if it comes to it. They shall not hurt you.'

Despite her resolution, fear plucked at her heart and throat. Their lamp had almost burned down, but still gave off just enough light for her to be able to examine their prison. Aside from the bed, which was bolted down, there was only a slopping out bucket inside a metal cage, also bolted to the floor. The Claybourns had left nothing that might serve as a weapon, or with which she could attempt to force the door. She pushed against the walls of the cell, but it was clear they were thick and sturdy. A giant could not have broken them down, let alone an undersized young woman already weak from poison. She sank back onto the bed, close to despair.

Later, daylight slanted in through the slits in the ceiling and the door opened. Richard entered with a tray balanced on one forearm and the key to the door in the other. On the tray were two bowls of porridge. He set it down on the floor and placed the key carefully in the hip-pocket of his green frock coat.

'You!' Susan exclaimed bitterly. 'You knew about Miss Smythson, all this time. Why did you not say something?'

'I was biding my time, until the Claybourns were in so deep they could not refuse me Helena's hand.'

He looked at Cassandra, who was blinking sleepily. 'Who's this lovely creature?'

His admiration was so obvious that Susan's mind began to churn. A plea for mercy would be a waste of time. Richard had no more compassion than a starving wolf. But suppose she could convince him that releasing Cassandra would be to his advantage? She made a sign behind her back. *Smile at him.* Cassandra frowned.

At this cock-of-the-walk? Why?

I have an idea. Can you pretend to admire him?

'What is she saying?' Richard asked. 'Ain't she Mr Sutcliffe's girl?'

Susan sighed heavily. 'I fear her mind is disordered, else she would not say such ridiculous things.'

Cassandra's expression was one of friendly interest. Richard stood taller and straightened his coat.

'Come, Miss Sparrer. What did she say? And the truth now. We both know you ain't capable of lying.'

'She says you are a fine-looking man,' Susan said stiffly. 'I told her not to be deceived by appearances.'

'Fine looking, eh?' Richard lifted his chin. 'She has a discerning eye.' He offered Cassandra one of the bowls with a bow. She took it with a shy smile worthy of a young girl being asked for her first dance. Richard wetted his fingertips on his tongue and used them to flatten his hair.

'She's a rare beauty, ain't she? That skin—so smooth and dusky. And them lips—they look as ripe as—'

Susan's composure fractured.

'Don't you dare!' she cried. Richard chuckled.

'Save your protests for when old puff-guts fixes that precious device of his.'

Susan's anger quickly turned to fear. 'He means to try again?'

'You shouldn't have broke it, Miss. I reckon he loves that thing more than his own daughters.'

'Richard, won't you help us?' Susan begged, her plan abandoned in her panic.

'No use pleading with me, Miss. I know where my bread is buttered.' He bowed towards Cassandra and mouthed the word 'charmed'.

At last we are rid of him! Cassandra signed with relief as he backed toward the door. Richard raised his eyebrow questioningly towards Susan, who closed her eyes and gathered herself. Her barely thought-out scheme might be their only chance.

'She says she hopes you will soon return,' she said, as if the admission came painfully.

Richard bowed again, before leaving them alone in the near darkness. The padded walls seemed to throb and pulse at the edge of the shadows, an ominous, formless presence, like the monster in a child's dreams. Susan and Cassandra clung to each other, their mutual terror requiring no communication.

The Claybourns made no appearance that day. For an awful moment, Susan wondered if they would be left in the cell to die, but she dismissed that thought as unhelpful. It was more likely that Dr Claybourn was repairing his phrenomed, and Mrs Claybourn must be busy keeping up appearances in the school. To distract herself from her fears, she explained her plan to Cassandra. It was difficult to read signs in the gloom, but, eventually, by a combination of touch and using the faint light provided by the air vents, Susan outlined her idea. Cassandra was doubtful it would work but agreed to play along. It wasn't as if they had any other options. They must hope that Richard would return. That she must pray for the appearance of such a despicable man was sickeningly ironic.

'Good evening, ladies!' Richard entered the room smartly, the tails of his tattered coat flaring behind him. From somewhere, he had acquired a grey cravat, which was wrapped inexpertly around his neck. Susan stifled a cry of relief as lamplight burst into the room and forced the oppressive walls into a temporary retreat. On his tray were two plates of bread and cheese and a single glass of port wine. Cassandra started up eagerly.

The strutting cock has returned.

'What's she say?'

'I will not tell you,' Susan said primly. 'You are already too full of your own self-importance.'

'She likes what she sees, I can tell that.'

Monstrous conceit! Cassandra signed, yet she continued to smile at him with the appearance of great interest. Richard offered her the glass of wine. She brushed her fingers against his as she took it, and Richard's Adam's apple bobbed up and down.

'Tell me what she says and I'll get you a glass of the same.'

'She cannot believe such a fine-looking man is subordinate to Dr Claybourn,' said Susan, although the idea of drinking anything, let alone wine, made her queasy. 'She thought you must be his master. I have assured her of her mistake.'

'Maybe she ain't so wrong. How come she's here?'

'She tried to rescue me. The unfortunate creature has no other friend but me.'

Without thinking, Susan signed her words as well as speaking.

That is true, at least, Cassandra returned.

'Friendless, is she?' asked Richard. 'Why's that then? I thought they was rich, them Sutcliffes.'

'Oh, they are. Terribly rich. But Cassie is deaf and, alas, rather dim-witted.'

Dim-witted!

'Her father longs to be rid of her, but who would take such an unfortunate creature for a wife?'

You slander my dear papa!

Richard smoothed down his whiskers.

'He wants rid of her, you say?'

'He told me he would gladly settle two thousand pounds on any man who would take her.'

Cassandra almost choked.

Two thousand pounds! Papa would not give a penny to this monster!

'She does not seem to agree with you,' Richard said suspiciously.

'Four thousand pounds,' Susan said, as if Cassandra had corrected her. She leaned confidentially towards Richard. 'But who would take her, even for that much?'

She had to turn away then, lest her face betray her.

'Four thousand pounds, eh? Don't matter if she ain't a talker. Why, that might be an advantage,' Richard muttered beneath his breath. 'Does this generous offer only apply to gentlefolk, like everything else in the world?'

Susan pressed her lips together, as if she was holding back some great secret.

'What!' cried Richard. 'You know something, I can see it. Tell me!'

'No, I won't. I refuse to tell you! In any case, you are already engaged to Helena.'

'Engaged ain't married. Come now, Miss. Your fate is sealed, but perhaps I can help your pretty friend here.'

Susan made a show of considering his words.

'Mr Sutcliffe has often said he has no time for gentleman landowners,' she admitted after a long pause. 'He is a man of trade himself.'

'Then he might be glad to have a working chap like me for a son-in-law?'

Cassandra had started to look a little sick.

Courage! Susan signed and Cassandra rose to her feet and approached Richard. Susan flung herself dramatically across her path.

'No, Cassandra!' She injected her voice with extreme distress. 'You cannot trust him. He wants only your father's money.'

But Cassandra, seemingly in thrall, pushed past Susan to run her fingers up Richard's upper arm.

It is torture to touch such a man.

'What did she say?'

'She observes what a fine figure you have.' Susan grimaced, as if the admission was being forced from her. Richard swiftly shrugged off his frock coat and folded it neatly on the end of the bed. He crooked his arm and clenched his fist, so that Cassandra might see more clearly the bulge of his muscles.

Cassandra let her mouth open a fraction and ran her tongue over her lower lip. Richard was transfixed. Cassandra placed her hands on Richard's shoulders and gave Susan, who was standing behind him, equally enthralled, a pointed look. Startled into action, Susan rifled through the pockets of Richard's discarded coat while Cassandra fixed his attention. Her fingers closed round a key just as Richard leaned towards Cassandra to kiss her. Cassandra's poise shattered and she jerked back with a cry of disgust. Susan flung the coat over Richard's head, tying the arms around his neck so it formed a hood and spun him round.

Cassandra ducked under his flailing arms and they darted towards the door.

'What the—' cried Richard, his voice muffled by the coat. He was disorientated just long enough for Susan and Cassandra to shoot through the door and force it shut behind them. A bellow of rage was followed by something heavy slamming against the door, but Susan had already turned the key. She grabbed Cassandra by her wrist and they ran down the corridor and across the large chamber where Susan had so nearly become another of Dr Claybourn's victims. The outer door, and freedom, was just beyond. Alas, the door was shut fast! Susan turned and twisted the doorknob in all directions, but the door was locked and there was no sign of a key. Richard must still have it, but the idea of returning to the padded cell was too horrific to contemplate. Susan felt her strength ebbing away.

Is there no other way out? Cassandra asked. Susan roused herself. She would not give up, not until Cassandra was free. There was somebody who had escaped from the infirmary. She hurried to Amelia's chamber. The old woman was lying on her bed, sleeping. A gentle shake of her shoulder roused her.

'Who are you?' she asked, yawning.

'Susan. Don't you remember me?'

Amelia shook her head. She was surrounded by dolls and reached for one made from knitted wool with stitches for eyes, drawing it close to her chest.

'Is that Bessie?' Susan asked, smiling at the doll. 'Do you remember—you invited me to tea.'

'You've come for tea?' She brightened and began to assemble miniature cups and saucers on a tea tray.

'I need to ask you something,' Susan began desperately, but Amelia would not be distracted from her preparations.

'Tea first and then talk. That's how ladies do it.'

She held up the tiny teapot and looked at them expectantly. Susan reluctantly took a little cup and Cassandra did the same. Once they had accepted their imaginary tea, Susan tried again.

'Amelia, remember when we met on the moors? You were looking for your cat.'

'I was looking for Kitty. She's gone now. The devil and his wife took her.'

With a jolt, Susan realised she was talking about Miss Smythson. That she had always been talking about Miss Smythson.

'How did you get out? Isn't the door always locked?'

'Oh yes,' Amelia agreed amiably. 'It isn't safe for us to go out.'

'So—how did you escape?' Susan prompted.

'What's that?' Amelia jumped as Richard began to pound furiously against the door of the padded cell.

'Nothing,' Susan said quickly. Amelia's eyes narrowed.

'Who are you? You don't belong here.'

'I quite agree,' Susan said. 'We would very much like to leave. Won't you tell us how?'

But Amelia was muttering to Bessie about liars and deceivers and her attention could not be regained.

Let us try the door again, Cassandra suggested, supporting Susan as they returned to the large chamber, for Susan's efforts with Amelia had taken the very last of her strength. Through heavy eyelids, she saw Cassandra tug and twist at the door handle. With a stifled cry, Cassandra released the doorknob as if it burned her hands. They watched in terror as the handle began to rotate. Someone was turning it from the outside. Cassandra let out a moan of dismay. Susan looked around for a weapon—anything with which she might defend them. Her eyes lit on a broom. Her only previous experience with such an implement was to nudge mice out of the vicarage pantry. Which end should she direct towards her attackers to have most effect? Never had she imagined she would be required to hold off villains with only a broomstick. Beside her, Cassandra squared her shoulders. Susan took strength from her courage. Whatever happened, they would face it together. Susan's fingers tightened round the broom handle as the door opened. The tall figure framed in the fading evening light was neither Dr Claybourn nor his wife. The broom slipped from Susan's hand and clattered to the ground.

'Marion?'

Cassandra turned to Susan, her eyes shining. *Do not be afraid. This woman has a good heart. She will help us.*

49

In Which our Heroines Converse on a Topic of Some Interest

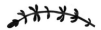

Susan had some recollection of stumbling across the moors, but she experienced it as if it were a strange dream. She felt rain, spotting against her dry lips and her parched tongue, gloriously fresh, painfully stinting. Marion's long shadow flicked in and out of focus and Cassandra was there too, supporting her, her expressive eyes giving light and hope and strength.

Then they were in a dim chamber, and she was enclosed in something soft and heavy. Someone was feeding her tepid soup. A cool cloth was placed against her forehead. There was more soup, and water, held against her dry lips. Servants attended her, their faces blurred and indistinct as they whirled around her in a fervour of activity. Only Cassandra was still and steadfast. She was always there, by Susan's side.

At last, Susan came to her senses. She was in a four-poster bed within a cosy chamber whose curtains were drawn. A fire crackled cheerfully in the grate. An armchair had been pulled up next to the bed and there Cassandra slept, her face tilted to one side exposing her long, slender neck. Susan watched. Cassandra's lashes fluttered gently as she dreamt. Her lips were slightly parted, and Susan thought she had never looked more beautiful. She yearned to reach out and touch her. As if sensing Susan's gaze, she woke, her eyes turning immediately to her patient.

You are awake!

Where am I? asked Susan.

At Heathersage. Safe.

I do not recall—how did we escape?

Marion stole the key to the infirmary and came to find you.

Marion? Why would she do that?

You must know that she is in love with you.

Susan coloured. *She confessed it a few days ago. I had no idea. I was blind to that, like everything else.*

Cassandra gazed at her affectionately.

You should not be so surprised. Those who know you cannot help but love you.

Susan's colour deepened. *Not everyone. Not the Claybourns. Or Richard. Oh, those lies I told him!*

You called me dim-witted! Cassie prodded Susan playfully in her ribs.

I did not mean it, Susan protested.

I did not think you could be so deceitful.

No, Susan had surprised both of them in that regard.

You were just as convincing. I really thought you were going to kiss him.

Cassandra arched an eyebrow. *You were jealous?*

Susan did not think her face could get any warmer without bursting into flame.

I did have an irrational urge to throw something at him.

Perfectly rational.

It was less difficult than I thought to fool him.

A man so full of himself is easily tricked. Pity me—I almost had to kiss him!

Despite her protestations, Susan suspected Cassandra was quite proud of herself. And with good cause.

I still cannot believe you came to rescue me. After that horrid letter. Susan shuddered at the memory. Mrs Claybourn had dealt in all manner of poisons. Being forced to write such cruel words had been more traumatic even than being tied to Dr Claybourn's chair.

Cassandra assured Susan that she had known her to be incapable of willingly writing such a letter.

And it wasn't the most effective rescue. A poor act of heroism, getting myself locked up as well.

Susan shook her head.

I disagree. Your coming was the most heroic act I've ever witnessed.

I was very afraid, Cassandra admitted. *But I felt alive—more than I ever have before. I hope we will have many adventures together.*

Susan demurred.

Perhaps, but none so perilous, I hope?

Cassandra smiled, so tenderly and so earnestly that Susan could hardly bear it. She must know if Cassandra wished for only friendship, or something more. She eased herself into a more upright position. *There is something I must tell you. A confession.*

At that moment, Mary came in with Eppy in her arms. Seeing Susan was awake, she dropped Eppy and rushed over to hug her teacher.

Careful! Cassandra signed. *Miss Mottram must be treated gently.*

Mary jumped back in alarm and then gave Susan such a delicate, hesitant peck on her cheek that both Susan and Cassandra burst into laughter. Having seen for herself that Susan was safe and well, Mary's attention soon returned to Eppy, who was running around the room. Cassandra leaned forward and took Susan's hand. The heat from Susan's face raced downwards, deep into the pit of her stomach. Cassandra's fingers began to form new words. *My own, dear Susan! There are three words my beloved father has addressed to me so often that I know the shapes they make. I saw them on your lips the night you returned to that awful place. If you would let me, I would return them back to you again and again and never stop.* She pressed her lips against Susan's, leaving nothing more to ask and nothing more to say.

50

Epilogue

Richard, seeing the game was up, turned evidence against the Claybourns. He explained that Miss Smythson's body had been hidden in the coal bunker because the day Mrs Claybourn had poisoned her, the ground had been too frost-hardened for them to bury the body. The little girls who had supposedly died of typhus were exhumed and the evidence of their skulls was enough to ensure the public demanded no lesser sentence than the gallows for Dr Claybourn and his wife. After legal costs, nothing remained of their fortune. Matterdale Hall was sold to pay their remaining debts, and the infirmary torn down, its bricks sold for ready money. Their daughters, who had been ignorant of their parents' crimes, were left penniless, and Helena's hopes of Richard were dashed, for, without the promise of money, his interest in her vanished. The pupils all returned home. Some were sent to other schools but most parents were wary of sending their daughters away again, once the awful history of the establishment to which they had been entrusted was known. Anne and Isabella's families lived not far from each other, and through a series of hints and manoeuvrings the girls induced their parents into an acquaintance. Their friendship grew strong, for where parental affection is lacking, other sources of regard must be highly valued.

It took some time for Mrs Claybourn's poison to be purged from Susan's body. Mr Sutcliffe returned from his travels and Cassandra, who could not withhold any confidence from so beloved a father, told him everything, including her love for Susan. It took him some months to reconcile himself to so unusual a situation, especially one that society frowned upon, but his partiality for Susan, which returned once all had been explained, and his remembrance of falling in love with a person that society frowned upon brought him to accept their relationship, and eventually welcome something that made his daughter so happy. Mrs Grainger, who had never been fond of Susan, was less accommodating, and Mr Sutcliffe was forced to suggest a separation. Mrs Grainger, realising her long-cherished hopes had been in vain, accepted his offer of a generous annuity and settled in a distant county where she might pursue any rich widowers she chose.

When she had recovered, Susan wrote to her mother, extending an invitation from Mr Sutcliffe to visit Heathersage with Florence. She said little about what had happened, fearful that if her mother knew the full truth, her poor opinion of the natives of Yorkshire would be so far confirmed that she would refuse to set foot in such an iniquitous place. However, once they were happily settled in the guest quarters, Susan confided all to her sister, who saw only that Cassandra was lovely and her sister was happy. Her delight was complete when Mr Sutcliffe extended to Mrs Mottram and her daughters a permanent invitation to live at Heathersage Manor. Such a fine characterful house, surrounded by beautiful moorland, and a generous allowance was something that Florence had thought would never again be hers, and she was as contented as any young girl on the cusp of womanhood could be. Susan's mother, while happy in her new accommodations, was not ready to understand the truth and, despite various attempts on Susan's part to explain her relationship with Cassandra, they were rebuffed. Her mother would turn the subject, preferring to remain ignorant, at least in theory, if not in practice. If she ever wondered why, in such a large house, her daughter shared a room with Cassandra, she never mentioned it.

Cassandra had assured Marion that she, too, would be welcome at Heathersage, but Marion declined the invitation.

'I cannot stay here like some spectre at the feast,' she told Susan, with her customary stiffness. 'You have lifted a great burden by showing me that feelings such as mine can be accepted and even bring joy, but I cannot acquit myself of jealousy. I wish you and Miss Sutcliffe well and by leaving I do what little is in my power to make it so. Besides, I have my sister to take care of. We haven't always been good friends, but it is my duty to care for her now.'

Susan went up on tiptoe and kissed her on the cheek. Marion's face and neck came out in pink blotches.

'Stop hating yourself and you will find someone to love you. Know that you will always have a friend here at Heathersage.'

Two friends, added Cassandra, for whom Susan had been signing every word she spoke. *I shall never forget how brave it was of*

Marion to come and find us, despite her fear of that awful place.

'Why were you so afraid?' Susan asked Marion.

Marion pressed her fingers against the back of her neck and bent towards them. A raised scar marred the skin at the nape of her neck.

'My father believed he could cure me with that cursed instrument. When I was fifteen, I became fond of one of the girls. Well, you will understand, it went beyond fondness. Father hoped to rid me of such infatuations. He was wrong.'

With her grimacing smile, she took her leave. A few days later, she secured a position in a public school near London, and she and Helena set out to begin the next phase of their lives.

Once Susan returned to health, she was keen to be active. She very much wished to continue in the profession of teaching. It felt right and proper to put her talents to some useful activity, instead of pursuing only amusement like so many other young ladies. Now that she was wiser and more experienced, she felt she might acquit herself with some credit. After much discussion on the topic, she and Cassandra opened a school for the deaf in an unused chapel in the grounds of Heathersage Manor. Cassandra took courage from Susan's presence and gentle persuasion to teach their pupils art and sign language, whilst Susan focused on reading, writing and mathematics. Mary Martin was their first pupil. More followed and all prospered under the tender and thoughtful care of Miss Sutcliffe and Miss Mottram. Backed by Mr Sutcliffe's fortune, they charged no more than their pupils' parents could afford, and many were admitted *gratis*. The reputation of their school soon spread, and they began to receive applications from every corner of the country. Yet, as contented and grateful as their pupils were, their happiness was nought compared with that of Susan and Cassandra when, at the end of every day, they could each return home and feel blessed by the company of the person dearest to their heart.

THE END

Acknowledgements

Many people have provided help and encouragement along my writing journey. I would particularly like to thank Wendy Tomlinson and Michele Hutchison for being my first readers and constant cheerleaders, giving up their time to critique my work and providing so much sound advice along the way. For the *Secret of Matterdale Hall*, I am grateful to Nicky Lovick for editorial comments on an early draft and to our sensitivity readers, Anita Midha and Liam O'Dell. Huge thanks to Alice and Lisa at Bellows Press for having the faith to make Matterdale Hall their first project. Your passion and commitment to the Bellows Press mission is truly inspiring. Last, but far from least, I am immensely grateful for the support of my parents, Richard and Sylvia Ratcliffe, and my amazing wife, Sharon, to whom this book is dedicated.

About the Author

Marianne Ratcliffe grew up in Lincolnshire. A biochemist by training, she has always found creating new worlds and interesting characters every bit as rewarding as discoveries at a laboratory bench. She has had short stories published in literary magazines and was runner up in the Guildford Book Festival short story competition in 2010. In 2017, redundancy spurred her to focus on creative writing; the result being *The Secret of Matterdale Hall*. Marianne lives in Cheshire with her wife and two dogs.